"I DIDN'T KNOW
you demanded to se⟨
yourself over for d

assume you'd claim the guest room, too." Which was also Jean's old room.

He stepped around the table and entered my personal space, but I refused to back down. His six-foot-plus height didn't intimidate me. Neither did that devious twinkle in his irises. Or the half grin gracing his full lips. Or the scent of leather and man that seemed to surround me as he moved even closer. Or the way his pupils dilated as they dropped to my mouth.

My pulse skipped a beat because Jamie sat so close by. It had nothing at all to do with this man or the solid body bumping up against my folded arms.

"I think we both know I'd be staying in your room, Avery," Wyatt murmured, his mouth scant inches from mine. "But feel free to deny it all you want. It'll only intrigue me more." Those last words were a breath against my cheek, seconds before he pressed a warm kiss to my too-hot skin.

The wine sent my hormones into a tizzy while my sanity searched for reason.

I'm not attracted to him.

Liar.

Butterflies danced in my lower belly as he pulled back just enough to check my expression. Whatever he saw there caused his dimples to appear again.

"Mmm. That's what I thought," he murmured. "See you in the morning, Miss Perry."

Electricity hummed through my veins, disengaging my ability to form a proper comeback.

Nothing coherent formed in my mind. Just a bunch of gibberish about his masculine scent, how much I disliked him, and what it would be like to kiss him. Because a man like Wyatt Mershano would know how to handle a woman... and well.

Wrong.

But so right.

MERSHANO EMPIRE SERIES

The Prince's Game

The Charmer's Gambit

The Rebel's Redemption

The Devil's Denial

The Rebel's Redemption

USA Today Bestselling Author

LEXI C. FOSS

The Rebel's Redemption

Content & Line Editing by: Twitching Pen Editing

Line Editing by: Love2ReadRomance

Proofreading By: Outthink Editing, LLC

Cover Photography: Wander Aguiar Photography

Cover Model: Nick C.

Cover Design: Black Widow Designs

Published by: Ninja Newt Publishing, LLC

Print Edition

ISBN: 978-1-950694-05-1

*To Melissa, for always having my back and being an amazing friend.
I hereby gift Wyatt Mershano to you for always. <3*

The Rebel's Redemption

PROLOGUE
AVERY

"Avery Perry?" The slender male in my doorway flashed a badge, as did the woman beside him.

Officers Bradley and Mahoney.

Considering the late hour, I doubted they were here with positive news. "Yes, that's me. Is everything all right?"

"May we come in?" Officer Mahoney asked, her gray eyes emanating sympathy.

The lack of a commotion in the neighborhood confirmed nothing was wrong nearby, leaving only one real possibility for their visit. "This is about my sister, isn't it?"

Jean left three days ago without giving an explanation of her intended destination or an anticipated return date. Typical behavior. She expected me to handle everything for her, as per usual. As far as roommates went, she was great, since she never stayed long. But as my only living nuclear-family member, she caused a heck of a lot of trouble.

"What did she do now?" I asked when they didn't

confirm or deny my statement.

The last time she ended up in trouble, she called me for bail money, which I provided because that was what sisters did for each other. Or at least, that was what *I* did. Jean rarely did anything for me, and when she did, it was always half-assed. Hell, she couldn't even take care of her own son.

Officer Bradley scratched the red hairs dotting his chin, his mouth twisting into a grimace. "We would really rather do this inside, Miss Perry."

"Please." Officer Mahoney implored me with her eyes, leaving me little choice but to comply.

"That bad, huh?" Great. I opened the door and gestured for them to enter. "Jamie's asleep." I closed the door softly. "Jean's son," I added, in case they required the clarification.

Not that she claimed the role of mother in any shape or form. I raised Jamie, fed him, and loved him as my own. Meanwhile, my sister worked odd jobs and disappeared every other day. She rarely contributed to the mortgage on this place, let alone the other household and childcare bills.

Mahoney shared a look with her partner before saying, "Miss Perry, we have some troubling news. Jamie should probably be present for this, and anyone else who is home."

I didn't like the sound of that.

"There's no one else here." My parents died a decade ago. Jamie and Jean were all I had. I swallowed and cleared my throat. "Look, whatever you need to say, tell me first." Because I sensed where this conversation was going. Needing all the family present to deliver news? That could really only mean one thing.

Bradley cleared his throat and glanced sideways at Mahoney. She pinched her lips to the side, her expression clearly calling him out for being a coward, before pinning me with her gaze.

"Miss Perry—Avery—would you like to sit down?"

A shiver rocked my spine at the coaxing note in her tone. *She's hurt.*

Or worse.

Dead.

"I—I'd rather stand." The words scratched my dry throat. I couldn't say anything more. Their matching looks of pity already confirmed my worst thought.

She's gone.

"Avery." Mahoney's voice was pitched so low I barely heard it over the blood rushing in my ears. "We're sorry to have to tell you this, but your sister, Jean Perry, was found this evening in a nightclub bathroom. We regret to inform you that, despite the medic's best efforts to revive her, she was too far gone. She's dead."

1

AVERY

I ran my palms over my blouse and black dress pants for the thousandth time.

When Scott Mackenzie called me to request this meeting, I suspected something was wrong with the paperwork. And the frown marring his broad brow confirmed it.

"Scott," I greeted him, shaking his hand.

"Miss Perry." His brisk tone did not bode well. "Follow me." He turned on his heel, his bald head gleaming from the overhead lights.

Okay.

Not a good start.

The jovial man usually welcomed me with a wide grin and sparkling hazel eyes.

Well, damn.

I had combed through all the documents a hundred times, signed all the places he requested, and submitted every detail of my life. What more needed to be done to adopt a four-year-old with no other next of kin?

Scott continued past several glass office doors before stopping at the conference room where we first met. Also a negative sign, since all our previous meetings were held in his office.

Two men waited inside, one clad in an expensive designer suit and the other in a leather jacket wearing a cocky smirk. I studied them both as I entered and tried to put on a placative expression.

"Hello," I said with an awkward glance at Scott.

He shut the door and pulled out a chair for me before taking one for himself.

"Miss Perry, this is Mister Mershano and his legal representation."

"Garrett Wilkinson," the suit added, his stature exuding confidence and superiority. "I'd say it's a pleasure, but clearly, it's not."

My pulse skipped a beat at the decidedly hostile tone. "I beg your pardon?" I focused on Scott. "What the hell is going on?"

"Oh, that's cute." Garrett's striking blue eyes ran over me in disgust while he spoke. "Continue to play dumb, Miss Perry. See where it gets you."

"Mister Wilkinson," Scott growled. "Please refrain from badgering my client. She's not aware of your purpose here, since I only learned of it this morning myself."

"Purpose for what?" I demanded. "Why am I here?"

"My son." The deep voice came from the man across from me—the one with the cocky smile who appeared to be merely amused now. He relaxed into his chair, legs sprawled in a distinctly masculine manner, and spread out his hands in a *your move* sort of gesture.

"Your son?" The words left my mouth before they registered. Then ice drizzled down my spine. "You can't mean…?" I couldn't finish. As much as I tried to say the name, it refused to leave my heart.

"Jamie Mershano." Garrett passed over a document and

cocked a brow. "You must be aware that birth fathers have full custody rights to their children, unless otherwise determined in a court of law. And I can guarantee you that no judge is going to side against my client."

I gaped at the birth certificate lying before me. It matched the one Jean once gave me, save two major details.

This version included the father's name.

And it referred to Jamie as Jamie Mershano, not Jamie Perry.

Everything Jean kept on Jamie left the paternity line blank. The one time I had asked her about it, she'd stated it was a one-night stand and claimed not to remember the father's name, or even what he looked like.

But the official hospital seal and signatures proved that to be a lie.

As did the striking similarities between Jamie and the man before me.

Jesus. I should have noticed the likeness the moment I entered.

The male's dark chocolate irises, thick brown hair, strong jawline, and chin dimple—Jamie possessed all those traits. The only Perry gene he exuded was our trademark Irish skin—not our ash-blonde-colored hair or greenish-blue eyes. He hardly looked like me or Jean, but he bore a strong resemblance to the tanner man across from me.

"I… I had no idea," I admitted, looking between the two men and Scott. "I've never seen this man before in my life. Jean told me…" I swallowed, trying to finish, but I couldn't think over the words rattling around in my brain.

If he's the father… Jamie…
But he can't.
I've… He's mine.
I raised him as mine.

"He's four years old," I said, cutting off whatever the men in the room were saying. "*Four. Years. Old.* Where the hell have you been?" I locked gazes with the *father* threatening *my* child. "Do you even know anything about

6

him? His favorite story? Favorite words? His allergies? How many times he fell trying to learn how to walk?" A hysterical laugh bubbled out of me of its own accord. "Are you serious?"

"Miss Perry, I'm going to need you to calm down." The suit-clad lawyer sounded so imperious and self-assured that I wanted to introduce my fist to his too-handsome face.

"Calm down," I repeated. "Seven weeks of unending paperwork, resolving my sister's death and trying to do right by Jamie. Then you waltz in here and say this man"—I stabbed a finger at the joker across from me—"has full custody of my nephew? He's never even met him!"

"That's not true." The would-be father didn't move from his lazy sprawl but cocked his head to the side. "I met Jamie briefly during the paternity test that Garrett arranged four years ago."

Tears prickled my eyes as I laughed. "Oh, that's fantastic. You didn't even believe he was yours, but now you want to play dad. Yeah, okay."

Jesus Christ.

No.

I refused.

Jamie was *my* responsibility, my only living blood relative. No way would I give him up to a man who didn't even want him to begin with!

"Can I have a moment alone with my client?" Scott requested softly.

So much for hiring an attorney with a backbone. Not that I knew I needed one until right now.

"Of course." Garrett closed his portfolio and pushed away from the table. His client sat for a moment longer, his dark eyes assessing me in a lazy manner that bespoke of uncanny confidence. Then he stood and followed his lawyer from the room.

I stared after them in shock.

No words.

Nothing.

"Do you have any idea who that is?" Scott asked, his voice holding an awe I did not understand or return.

"No! I already said I've never seen him before in my life. Surely there has to be a law against this. Something that doesn't allow some deadbeat father to walk back into the life of his son and take him back? I've raised him, Scott. Jamie is *my* son. Perhaps not by birth, but I've been the one—"

"Avery." His sharp tone silenced my rant, but the tears continued to gather in my eyes.

"He can't…" God, I was losing it. In the middle of my lawyer's damn conference room. "I need a minute."

I moved to the windows and wrapped my arms around myself. Midtown Atlanta glimmered back at me in the midday sun, reminding me of the long drive back to Acworth I had ahead of me.

Damn it.

"This can't be happening," I muttered and pinched the bridge of my nose. "This really can't be happening."

Scott cleared his throat and joined me by the floor-to-ceiling windows. "Avery, I'm sorry, but there is truly nothing I can do. The system grants him full custody automatically. I mean, he is the child's father. The birth certificate and paternity test prove it, and his name… No judge in the country would ever side against his family."

I blinked, confused. "What? Why should his name matter?"

"Mershano?" he prompted. At my blank stare, he added, "Mershano Suites."

"The hotel chain?" What the hell did that…? *Ohhhh.* "As in, he's related to the family?"

"He *is* the family, Avery. Wyatt Mershano is the youngest son. His older brother manages the company—which explains all the documentation his lawyer showed up with today. It seems Jean was very much aware of his paternity to her son, despite the lack of documentation on her side. When doing our due diligence in confirming the

8

birth records, we discovered a discrepancy. And Mister Mershano reacted to our database inquiry accordingly."

That explained the timing. I returned all the paperwork for Jamie's adoption five days ago. Between the funeral arrangements, caring for Jamie, working full-time, and sorting through the lack of documentation left by Jean, it'd taken nearly two months to put the affairs in order. I acquired temporary guardianship right after my sister's death, but adopting him had required a lot more due diligence. And I'd still missed a rather substantial detail.

"What about my version of the birth certificate? The one that shows no father?" Was it even legal to create such a document? One that hid the father's name?

Scott shrugged. "Money is power, Avery. And it seems Wyatt Mershano struck a deal with your sister to help protect Jamie's identity. But when my office filed through the appropriate channels, his attorney was notified. Hence…"

Their abrupt appearance, I thought, finishing his sentence.

"He didn't even know Jean was dead." Which showed how often he checked up on Jamie.

"No one knew to notify him," Scott replied.

Because no one knew he existed. Least of all, me.

"Jamie has a father," I mumbled. Obviously, he did, but I never in my wildest dreams expected him to show up and protest my legal right to adopt Jamie. "There's nothing I can do?"

"I'm really sorry, Avery. Unless you can prove him to be an unfit father, it's out of our hands."

"Meaning, the fact that he was absent for the last four years of Jamie's life doesn't qualify as 'unfit'?" I would have fallen over in laughter if I wasn't trying so hard not to cry. "There has to be something…" I bit my lip to keep it from wobbling and closed my eyes. "He's *my* son." The words came from the depths of my heart. Birthrights be damned. I loved him unconditionally.

"You could request visitation rights," Scott suggested.

"It's ultimately up to the father, but he might be willing to grant them. You'll need to be very apologetic and understanding, though. And it might require some begging, considering *who* we are dealing with here."

He kept talking, but I stopped listening.

All my energy went into trying to remain standing under the onslaught of emotions weighing on my shoulders.

How could everything go so wrong so quickly?

My biggest worry three months ago was guaranteeing that Jean would show up to Jamie's fourth birthday party.

Now, losing Jamie indefinitely loomed over my head. And I'd done nothing wrong, aside from fall in love with a little boy who never actually belonged to me. But I made him mine in every sense of the word, put all my time and devotion into nurturing him, caring for him, and cherishing him.

I swallowed the lump in my throat.

Crying fixed nothing.

Screaming would scare everyone.

I needed a calm, collected approach, not an emotional one. Even if it felt as if my chest had been cracked open for the world to see.

Pull it together, Avery.
You can do this.

My quivering soul said otherwise. However, I had no choice but to face this head-on and see what damage control could be done.

I turned, resolved, and found Jamie's father leaning against the wall just inside the room with his hands tucked into the pockets of his jacket. Curiosity mingled with some discreet emotion in his eyes as he studied me. I couldn't quite read it, nor was I sure I wanted to.

"Mister Mershano," Scott said, startled. "We didn't—"

"I want to see him." His abrupt words held a note of authority that sent a chill across my skin. "Where is my son?"

I steadied my breathing and straightened my spine.

"Preschool." Something he would know if he had anything to do with Jamie's life prior to today.

"Where?"

"In Acworth." Another thing he should already know. "Where he lives."

"Lived," he corrected me. "Take me to him. Now."

"Excuse me?"

"He's my son. I want to see him. You'll take me." He pushed off the wall with an expectant look. "Our lawyers can chat afterward."

Garrett walked in at that moment and tucked his phone into his pocket. "What did I say about staying in the hallway?"

Wickedness lurked in Wyatt's expression as he faced his lawyer. "You should know by now that I never follow your advice, G."

"Clearly." Those piercing blue eyes traveled to me, then back to his client. "What did I miss?"

"Avery just offered to take me to my son. Isn't that right, sweetheart?" Delight danced in his gaze as he grinned at me.

Pompous prick. My fists curled as several retorts lined up on my tongue.

"She did," Scott said before I could voice a far more accurate response.

"Excellent." Garrett grinned. "Then we're in agreement already?"

"Not quite." Wyatt's intense stare captured and held mine. "I want to see my son first. Then we'll continue our discussion."

My heart skipped a beat. What did he mean by that? Was the decision not set in stone? He never wanted Jamie before; why would that change now?

Scott mentioned the possibility of visitation rights, stating they were at the discretion of the father. Did Wyatt want to discuss them?

Garrett gripped his client by the arm and yanked him into the hallway with a "We'll just be a minute." The glass door slammed behind them, silencing their conversation as the two men squared off against each other.

"That… was unexpected. But potentially a good sign, Avery. He might be willing to work with you." Scott's words barely registered.

All of my attention fell to Jamie's father as he raised one dark brow at his lawyer. Wyatt seemed both amused and bored—a contradictory reaction. Perhaps his expression just defaulted to haughty arrogance.

His full lips moved lazily as he responded to Garrett, almost as if trained to only give smart-ass replies.

My sister sure knew how to pick them.

I rolled my eyes upward, chastising her in my head, when the door opened.

"Ready when you are, sweetheart." Wyatt's deep voice grated on my already tired nerves.

"Avery," I corrected him in as polite a voice as I could manage. "Or Miss Perry, if that's easier to say."

The edges of his mouth twitched. "Okay, Miss Perry. Let's go."

"We'll reconvene first thing in the morning, Scott." Garrett pulled his phone out again and took off at a brisk pace down the hallway without a backward glance.

Scott shuffled on his feet. "Uh, yeah. I'll clear my schedule tomorrow, then."

It seemed I would be doing the same. Family always came before work, something my boss thankfully understood. Still, he wouldn't be pleased by me rescheduling all my project calls.

Anything to keep Jamie.

Wyatt cocked an impatient brow. "Miss Perry."

"Mister Mershano," I returned. "Sorry, did I offer to drive you as well?" I couldn't help the sarcastic note.

"Indeed, you did." He sounded so sure of himself. So overconfident. And not at all like a dad.

My brain flickered to life as I recalled Scott's words from minutes ago.

Unless you can prove him to be an unfit father…

Could I accomplish that? What would it take?

I'd have to ask Scott for clarification.

But first, I'd take Wyatt to his son and see how they interacted. Something told me Mister Mershano didn't have a whole lot of experience with four-year-olds.

"All right. I'll take you." Not that I had a choice in the matter, but if I played along, I could observe them together and perhaps stumble onto something I could use against him.

Because I refused to go down without a fight.

Wyatt's last name might intimidate Scott, but it didn't scare me.

And if my coward of a lawyer wasn't up for it, then I would find someone to help me win.

I vowed to protect Jamie with my life the moment I met him. No way would I let this overconfident prick break that promise on my behalf.

2

AVERY

Wyatt's presence overwhelmed my SUV. His minty aftershave taunted my senses, as did the subtle leather aroma coming from his jacket. Being stuck on I-75 in midafternoon traffic did not help matters.

He fiddled with his phone beside me, smirking at whatever message had dinged seconds ago. His long fingers typed something back while I fought to focus on the road.

Not that there was much to look at. Just the rear end of a car stopped in front of me.

Days like this made me miss rural Pennsylvania. Sure, nothing existed out there aside from farm fields and trees, but at least I could drive the speed limit.

I tapped the steering wheel and blew out an irritated breath. This was why I refrained from going downtown during weekdays, but I couldn't avoid this afternoon's meeting. Had I known the outcome, however, I may have tried.

This can't be real.

I refused to accept it.

Introducing Wyatt to Jamie was one thing, but if he tried to take him tonight… My grip tightened. *Not going to happen. Ever.*

"Are you always this uptight?" Wyatt asked as he pocketed his phone.

I cut him a sideways glance. "It hasn't exactly been a great day, Mister Mershano." Or a great few months, for that matter.

He remained quiet for a moment as I inched the car forward. "You're like an older version of Jean."

I snorted. "She was my younger sister by five years, so I should look older. But thank you for commenting on my elderly appearance."

"Someone is touchy about her age," he teased softly. "I didn't mean it as an insult. I just meant that you look very much like her, only more mature."

I almost replied that Jean would resemble me in a few more years but caught myself before the words could escape. Because they weren't true. She would never catch up to me in age. *She's dead.*

My nails bit into the leather of the steering wheel as I forced the tears to back off.

Crying fixed nothing—a phrase I repeated numerous times over the last few months. I had to be strong for Jamie.

"You might look like her, but you're clearly nothing alike." Wyatt sounded far too amused, which only irritated me more.

"Oh? And what makes you say that?" I regretted the words the second they came out, but I couldn't take them back fast enough.

"Well, for one, she'd have offered to suck my cock by now. And secondly, you're far more high-strung than she ever was."

My mouth parted on a response that didn't exist. How did one reply to that? The cock-sucking comment? Uh, no. I so did not want to even think about what—

My eyes went to his crotch of their own accord. I quickly forced my stare back to the road ahead. *No.* And as to the other statement, well…

"Jean lived a carefree existence. Meanwhile, I grew up and handled everything. Including raising *your* son since neither of you could bother to be there for him." My voice came out softer than I intended, but talking about my sister hurt.

We had our differences, but I still loved her. And although I knew logically there was nothing I could have done to save her, blame sat heavily on my shoulders.

Maybe if I'd tried just a little harder, she wouldn't have overdosed.

Maybe if I had forced her into rehab, she wouldn't have died.

I swallowed the lump in my throat and tried not to ram into the bumper of the guy in front of me as traffic started to move again.

The stages of grief sucked.

I spent so much time being angry and frustrated with Jean and not nearly enough time helping her. But Jamie had been my primary concern. Such an innocent life—he didn't deserve to be pulled down because of his parents' lack of involvement.

I chose between them…

"Raising my son," Wyatt repeated, a touch of curiosity lining his voice. "While Jean did what?"

"Great question." Because I didn't know half the time, and if I'd paid more attention, then—

"No, I meant that. What was Jean doing if she wasn't raising Jamie?" The hint of authority in his tone said so much about him. Wyatt Mershano led a privileged life where everyone conceded to his every demand.

And given our situation, I fell right into the same category.

If I wanted any chance of keeping Jamie, I had to play nice. Even if it rankled my nerves.

"Jean, when she came home, typically only stayed a few hours, maybe a night. She worked odd jobs, which I thought was part of her bizarre schedule. But her death showed me a whole new side of her that I didn't know existed." The party world she resided in that she never mentioned. The one that addicted her to opioids.

I flinched as I always did when I considered her secret life.

How could I have been so blind?

She'd always been erratic and unpredictable, but I should have seen the signs. Instead, I chalked up her behavior to her being typical old Jean. She favored danger at a young age, frequently accepting dares first or coming up with a few dangerous challenges of her own. My parents called her the *wild child*, while I was the straight-A student with a big future.

Until Jamie.

I would never regret my decision to leave graduate school for him. Ever.

"Odd jobs." Wyatt didn't appear to approve of the term. "She worked?"

"She had to help pay for Jamie somehow," I pointed out. Which piqued a few inquiries of my own. "You clearly come from means, Mister Mershano. Why didn't you help her financially? Give her a place to stay? Or, I don't know, take care of your *son*? Why now?" I bit my lip to keep from throwing additional words at him because the more I thought about it, the angrier I became.

Would Jean's life have been different if he'd stepped up and taken care of her and Jamie?

And why did he decide to show up now?

"Very interesting questions that have me wondering if you know anything at all" was his reply. "Tell me, what preschool have you enrolled Jamie in?"

I growled the name at him and added, "Something you would know if you bothered to be involved before today."

His amusement radiated through the SUV. "Very different from your sister, indeed."

I rolled my eyes and maneuvered toward our exit. The back roads would still be littered with cars but not nearly as bad as the highway.

"What do you do for a living, Avery?"

"What do you do for a living, Wyatt?" I countered.

"My family owns a multibillion-dollar hotel chain. What do you think I do?"

"Impregnate women and disappear on them?" I suggested, unable to help myself.

He snorted. "You can do better than that, sweetheart. And Jean would be the only one I've ever made that mistake with."

I bristled at his word choice. *Mistake.* And yet, here he was, trying to claim that *mistake* as his own. Unbelievable.

And you're driving him to meet Jamie.

God, how was I going to introduce them? *Jamie, here's the father who abandoned you and wants you back now that Momma Jean is dead?*

Fuck. I ran my hand over my face as I waited for the red light to change.

I missed the days when being late to pick up Jamie was my biggest concern.

I missed wine.

I missed being able to breathe.

My chest ached as I turned right. Hot and cold lined my veins, sending spasms of panic down my limbs. But I had to remain calm. For Jamie.

Everything I did was for that little boy.

"Where will you take him?" I whispered, my voice heavy with emotions I couldn't hide. "I don't even know where you live."

"We'll discuss it after I see him."

"That's not good enough for me."

"Well, it'll have to be." His tone brooked no argument and further sliced my heart open. I pulled the car off into a random parking lot, killed the engine, and stared blankly out the window.

"*No.*" One word. A single syllable. Flat. And yet underlined in pain. *My* pain.

I took a steadying breath and turned to face him. Smoldering brown eyes captured mine, set in the face of a handsome man used to controlling everyone around him. The confidence practically radiated from him, as did the underlying hint of wickedness.

He liked to play.

I'd met men like him dozens of times, perhaps not as well-off but just as cocky and otherwise devious.

My sister's type of man.

Not mine.

My backbone settled, strengthening the words I needed to say, as I threw all sense of caution to the wind. Because when it came to Jamie, reason no longer mattered.

"I don't care who you are, or how much money you have, or who you think you are to Jamie; I will not take you to him until you tell me your plans for him. At least for tonight. Because I have to be the one to explain to him why, after four years of loving and protecting him from every hurt in the world, I have to release him to a complete stranger. You can at least give me this after demanding I give up the most treasured being in my life to you."

His dark irises dropped to my lips, lower, then returned to my face and flared with obvious irritation. "At no point did I demand you give him up. I merely requested you take me to see him, after which we will continue the discussion."

"Your lawyer said—"

"Garrett does not speak for me, Miss Perry," he interjected coolly. "I own all of my decisions, this one included, and I cannot arrive at a proper course of action until I have seen Jamie. But I can assure you, I have no intention of taking him anywhere tonight. I merely wish to see him, which the law clearly grants me the right to do."

The intensity in his features had me sitting back in my seat, stunned. Gone was the arrogance, and in its place, determination and conviction.

But it was his words that shocked me most of all.

I have no intention of taking him anywhere tonight.

He could never know how those words relieved me. Temporary, yes, but part of me feared he intended to rip Jamie from my arms the moment we arrived and leave without a backward glance. Not that he had a car to drive off in, but the nightmare remained.

I lowered my forehead to the steering wheel and battled for control.

Funeral planning took so much out of me, mostly because I kept having to explain to Jamie over and over that Jean would not be coming home. So many mornings, he asked me when she would be done playing with the angels and return to him. And every time, I had to explain *again* that death was permanent.

All the unending paperwork, the long meetings with the lawyer, making up work through all hours of the night... I was exhausted. With no family to help, it all fell on me, and I couldn't show any weakness around Jamie. He needed me to smile, to foster his childhood, and to hide all the darkness.

But I couldn't hide this. Not the very real possibility that he could be taken away from me.

Even if Wyatt said it wouldn't happen immediately, the word *eventually* hung between us. Unless I could prove him to be an unfit father. Surely four years of not providing any assistance for Jamie qualified? Especially when he clearly had the means.

Too much, my heart cried. *Too much.*

But I couldn't break.

Not here.

Not with this stranger, this man who threatened everything.

I had to keep going and find a way to fix this.

There had to be a way to fight him.

I couldn't give up.

For Jamie.

3
WYATT

I refused to console Avery or say another word.

She's another version of Jean. Just a more attractive, slightly older version.

But the motives had to be the same.

Fuck my life.

I never wished anyone dead, but I wouldn't mourn Jean, either.

All the lies and deceit… and the endless blackmail. I wouldn't miss it or her.

Avery straightened beside me, her expression one of resolve. She'd avoided my question about her job because she probably didn't have one. And without permanent guardianship of my son, she couldn't force a dime out of me. Which was no doubt the purpose of going behind my back to claim legal custody. Then she could require child support. Too bad for her, she stood no chance of accomplishing that.

Still, she put on quite the emotional show. I almost

believed she knew nothing about my financial arrangement with Jean. This SUV certainly added to her charade. With the amount of money I sent her sister every quarter, they both could have afforded much better cars than this outdated model.

"Okay," Avery whispered. She cleared her throat. "Okay, I'll take you to see him. But let me introduce you."

"Sure." Why not? He was four. How difficult could it be?

Except I knew all too well how much a four-year-old could remember.

No. This was different. *Avery isn't his mom.*

She restarted the car and pulled off onto a side street that led into a residential area. I observed in silence, confused by our direction. When she pulled into a driveway, I glanced at her. "This is Jamie's preschool?"

"No, this is Katrina's house." She unbuckled her seat belt, but I grabbed her hand before she could exit.

"You said he was at preschool."

"Yes, earlier. It's after four, which means Katrina has already picked him up and brought him here." Her alluring blue-green eyes finally lifted to mine. "I sometimes work until six, so she watches him for me after preschool."

I blinked. So she did have a job? Why not answer me before? And… "Why not hire a nanny?" I paid more than enough money for one.

She gaped at me before throwing her blonde head back on a laugh. "Are you serious? I'm lucky Katrina lets me pay her as little as I do." She wiggled her hand out from beneath mine. "You're welcome to wait outside, but—"

A squeal from outside the car cut her off, and she immediately opened the door to hop out.

"Auntie A!" a high-pitched boyish voice yelled before a boy with a mop of dark hair tackle-hugged her legs a few feet from the driver's seat. Avery laughed at the excited welcome and fell to his level. "I missed you. So much. Guess what we made today? It's sooooooo a'sum. Lemme show you." He tugged on her hand, and she disappeared with him into the house.

Okay, so the boy obviously liked her. But that meant nothing. This could all still be a ruse, and kids were easily manipulatable.

I tapped out a message to Garrett letting him know I'd set eyes on Jamie and he appeared to be healthy. Happy, even.

Avery appeared in the doorway a few minutes later with a short brunette who glowered daggers at me in the passenger seat. I grinned back at her. She flushed in response, as most women did.

Except Avery, who showed no interest whatsoever.

That was part of the reason I had deviated from Garrett's plan. The woman intrigued me, mostly because I wanted to figure out her game. Jean had played me better than anyone ever had, and a twisted part of me craved the opportunity to pay her sister back in kind. Cruel, yes. But life wasn't fair.

Avery lifted a backpack from just inside the house and looped it over her shoulder while Jamie held tight to her other hand. He waved goodbye rather enthusiastically to the brunette and almost skipped alongside Avery.

"…and then nap time, which is soooo boow-ring. But after that, we played a game of duck, duck, moose."

Avery's smile reached her eyes as she replied, "A moose instead of a goose, huh?"

"Yup." He sounded quite pleased. "I won free times."

"Three," she corrected him as they approached her still-open door. Her smile fell as she caught sight of me waiting for them, almost as if she'd forgotten about me until now. Her tongue peeked out to lick her lips. "Jamie, I, uh. Well, there's someone who wants to meet you."

"An angel?" he loud-whispered at her, and the grimace in her features had me frowning.

"No, not an angel."

"So no Momma Jean."

"No, Jamie. I told you, Momma Jean won't be coming back."

His shoulders fell as they rounded her door, and he pouted up at her. "It's 'cause of me?"

"No, Jamie. Not you. Never you." She went to her knees again to be on his level just as his brown eyes—the same dark shade as my own—landed on me in the passenger seat.

Jamie's pupils widened as he ducked behind Avery. "Auntie A." The kid really needed to work on his whispering skills. "Who's th-that?"

She cleared her throat, and although I couldn't see her, I *felt* her hesitation.

I expected this to be entertaining, watching her struggle to say my name, but it wasn't amusing in the slightest. And the audible hitch in her breath broke any and all of my resolve to see this part of our game through.

"It's, uh, well—"

"I'm Wyatt." I opened the door to walk around the back of the car and paused when Jamie ducked even further behind Avery. He clung to her in a way I recognized immediately.

It was the same way I used to cling to my birth mother on the days Jonah came to pick me up after my monthly weekend with her.

My feet cemented to the ground, unable to take another step.

Protection and love radiated off Avery in a way I knew all too well.

That can't be an act…

Mothers had a look to them that very few could replicate, and everything about Avery in that moment felt very real. As did the warning in her gaze to back off immediately.

I lifted my hands and squatted to their level in a sign of acquiescence. I wouldn't push this.

"I knew your Momma Jean," I explained softly, using the phrase I overheard from their conversation. "An old friend." Those three words hurt to say. She was a friend. Once. Until she betrayed me.

"Friend of Momma Jean? An angel?" That last part was directed at Avery.

"Definitely not an angel," she replied as her eyes ran over me. "More like a rebel."

I narrowed my gaze at the choice of nickname. It served as the first sign she knew exactly who I was despite her earlier claims not to have a clue of my existence. Unless she chose *rebel* by coincidence, which I severely doubted.

"R-rebel," Jamie repeated. "What's *rebel* mean?"

"Someone who likes to cause trouble," she replied, holding my gaze while saying it.

Jamie gasped. "Trouble bad."

"Yes, trouble is bad," she agreed. "But some rebels like to cause trouble to be funny."

Jamie's brow pinched. "Funny good?"

"Funny is good," she said, mirth dancing in her eyes.

"Okay, he a rebel friend."

Avery grinned. "Yes, he's a rebel friend."

Jamie nodded, pleased with himself. "Rebel friend Wyatt."

"Apparently, that's my name." I did not share their amusement since *rebel* was the nickname the media had given me nearly a decade ago. But I forced myself to play along for Jamie's sake. "And you are?"

"Jamie," he said, still half hiding behind Avery. "I'm four." He held up four fingers while Avery smiled.

"Good job," she praised him. "But you're supposed to wait until he asks your age."

"Oh." His lips pinched, then he shrugged. "I'm four."

"That's good to know," I replied, grinning. "I'm twenty-nine."

Jamie's eyes went wide as he studied his fingers, his lips moving as he counted. When he reached ten, he looked to Avery for help.

She smiled indulgently. "We'll learn later. Remember

how we counted to twenty-eight for me on my last birthday?"

His eyebrows drew down, then he nodded. "Yep. With the candles."

"So if we did that for Wyatt, he would have one more candle," she explained.

"Making me positively ancient, at least according to your aunt." I couldn't help the jibe. She'd completely overreacted in the car when I mentioned her looking different from Jean. I'd meant it as a compliment, and she inferred it as me calling her old. Most women didn't even need the praise from me, just a glance, but this one proved challenging.

"Very old," she agreed as she stood. "We should probably get out of Katrina's driveway."

I glanced over them to see the brunette standing in the doorway with her hand against her heart. Well, at least someone found me endearing. I grinned at her as I stood to my full six-foot-two height and adjusted my jacket for show.

Avery cleared her throat and raised a brow, then glanced at the car beside me. Jamie clung to her leg but peered up at me with obvious interest.

I stepped back with an *after you* gesture and observed as she settled Jamie into his forward-facing car seat. She reached around him to secure the belts in place before bending to pick up the backpack she'd let drop to the ground.

Her long legs and shapely hips would look so much better in a skirt, but her three-inch heels were nice. And the blouse really did nothing for the figure beneath, yet I found the whole outfit sexy, in a mature way. Very different from the nightclub girls who tried to seduce me with their barely-there skirts and see-through tank tops.

It seemed like a lifetime ago when I found that look attractive. Lately, it'd been women like Avery who caught my eye. Sophisticated, well dressed, and now glowering right at me.

Oh, that look added to the whole package.

I smirked, not ashamed at all to have been caught in the act of checking her out. "Yes, Avery?"

Her lips flattened, but a faint pink touched her cheeks. "Nothing."

She stepped forward, presumably to close the door, and ran into my chest. Because I'd purposely not moved. When she tried to shift backward, I grabbed her hip with one hand and used the other to gently nudge the door behind her. The snick told me it'd secured itself just fine.

"A rebel?" I asked, my gaze dropping to her mouth. "Shall I redefine the word for you?" Why I chose now to punish her for the wounding nickname, I couldn't say. But she felt quite nice beneath my hand. My fingers itched to explore more.

"I—I didn't mean anything by it." She cleared her throat and pitched her voice low. "Jamie can see us."

"Mmm," I murmured. "Yes. Maybe later, then."

I let her go, though it took more effort than I cared to admit. To her credit, she held her ground and didn't stumble away from me. But the faint blush decorating her pretty face suggested she wanted to either scold me or do something more adultlike.

Not as immune to me now, are you, sweetheart?

I winked at her and sauntered over to the passenger side. After settling in my seat, a little voice from the back piped up with a loud "Seat belt."

"Very good, Jamie," Avery said as she buckled herself into the driver's side.

I followed suit because who was I to argue with the wise four-year-old?

"Is tonight pizza night, Auntie A?" Jamie asked as she reversed out of the driveway.

She waved to Katrina, who still stood in the doorway, before responding, "No. Pizza night is Friday, and today is Wednesday."

"Hmm, 'kay." Jamie didn't seem all that bothered, but a glance back at him showed he was thinking very hard about

27

something.

"What is for dinner?" I wondered out loud.

She licked her lips. "Are you joining us?"

"Are you driving me back to Garrett?" I countered. I doubted she was eager to return to the five o'clock traffic crowd.

"Uh, we didn't actually talk about that, did we?"

"No." I already had a plan, not that I intended to share it yet. "But I'll join you for dinner."

"Oh?" she asked, a note of defiance in her tone. "Did I invite you?"

"I don't believe I require an invitation, *Aunt* Avery." It was a dick thing to say, but true nonetheless. If I wanted to take Jamie from her right now, I could. But I didn't want to until I knew more about their relationship.

If the loving-mother charade turned out to be real, I would have to reconsider my intentions.

Jean deceived you once, my memory reminded. *And you're still paying for it.*

Too true.

No.

I couldn't go easy on Avery. Not like I did with her sister.

I refused to be tricked by a Perry again.

This woman tried to obtain custody of my son behind my back. She claimed not to know about me, but how could she not? I paid for everything. Obviously. And it wasn't like Jean conceived Jamie magically.

"I guess we're having pizza, then," Avery muttered, her hands going white on the steering wheel. "Since I didn't grocery shop for a party of three."

"Pizza?" Jamie repeated. "It's pizza night?"

Avery sighed. "Yes, Jamie, it's pizza night."

"Yaaaay!" His resulting squeal had me cracking a smile even as I winced. The kid had a pair of lungs on him.

"And wine," Avery grumbled. "So much wine."

4
AVERY

I glanced at the well-used movie case Jamie shoved at me and asked, "Again?"

"Yep!" He hopped up and down for emphasis and started parroting one of the songs. Despite having watched the same movie over and over for the last two weeks straight, he still didn't sing all the right words. He made up his own version of the lyrics and went from there.

Wyatt observed from the dining room table. He'd remained mostly quiet, allowing his eyes to do all the speaking for him as he studied every corner of my three-bedroom home.

Disapproval radiated from him.

Well, screw him. This was the best I could afford on my salary, and a huge part of my paycheck went to childcare. Maybe if he'd helped Jean financially, we could have invested in a bigger place more to his liking.

Or, more likely, I would have put it all away for Jamie's future. We didn't need a mini-mansion—only each other.

I smiled as Jamie settled into his favorite chair. It dwarfed him adorably, but he still managed to command the air around him like a king.

"Okay, dude." I ruffled his mop of hair on my way to the television. "We'll watch this until bedtime, but no dillydallying tonight, got it?"

"Got it." The angelic smile he flashed me did not fool me in the slightest. I knew devilish horns lurked beneath it, just waiting to come out at seven thirty on the dot.

But I let him think I believed him.

"Good." I turned on the film and handed Jamie a blanket before joining Wyatt in the dining area. His leather jacket hung over the chair, leaving him clad in a black shirt that clung to his biceps as he moved his elbows to the table.

"You're really great with him." His low voice soothed some of my nerves but not all of them. He'd been so quiet and judgmental throughout dinner that I didn't know how to proceed.

I took the chair across from him with a murmured "Thanks." Sometimes I felt like the worst mom in the world, but then Jamie would give me this look that made me feel like supermom. Those were my favorite days.

"So what is it you do for a living?" Wyatt asked, gesturing to my mess of an office just off the living area.

I grimaced at how that must look to him—all the papers, notebooks, and computer monitors sprawled out all over the small space.

"Uh, yeah, I'm an IT project manager, and my work sort of comes home with me a lot. Especially lately." I picked up my glass and finished the last of my wine. Wyatt retrieved the bottle before I could and held it out to give me a refill. I accepted with a soft "Thank you."

"I suppose you need it after today."

"Understatement." I couldn't help the sarcastic snort that accompanied that single word. "I thought losing my sister was the biggest shock of my life. Until today." I swallowed two healthy gulps before setting down the crystal stem a little harsher than I meant to. "Sorry. Yes, my day sucked. Tomorrow will probably be worse."

I scrubbed my hand over my face as the weight of everything settled over me again. Would I ever be granted a break from the reality of my life? No. Probably not.

"Avery." My name on his tongue should not sound nearly as erotic as it did, but somehow, he managed to twirl the syllables in a way that drew me right to him.

With a face like his, I doubted he begged much for bed partners. The man practically oozed sex, something Katrina had noticed immediately. She'd swooned over him without even meeting him. And yeah, I could see the appeal, minus the fact that he fathered my sister's child and was now trying to take him from me.

"Yes?" I prompted, more irritated with myself than with him. Because no way could I find this man attractive. Ever. It was wrong on so many levels.

"I have a few questions." He picked up his water and swirled the contents, his gaze thoughtful. He'd refused my wine earlier, likely because it didn't suit his tastes. Too cheap. "Why do you live here?"

I blinked at him. "In Acworth? Georgia? This house?" He'd have to be more specific.

"This home."

"Because I like it." The defensive note in my tone couldn't be helped. His obvious disapproval unsettled me. "Not all of us are rich, Mister Mershano. I work very hard to provide for myself and Jamie, and this was the best I could afford."

"Jean didn't help?"

A laugh tickled my throat but didn't quite reach the surface. "She tried, in her own way. Most months, she helped with a third of the mortgage, but as she rarely lived here, her contribution wasn't reliable."

I plied myself with more wine to avoid rubbing my chest. Hearing the words from my own mouth further proved how blind I'd been. Rather than demand an explanation from

Jean, I just accepted her behavior and learned to deal with it. All of my energy went to caring for the center of my world—Jamie.

He cocked his head to the side. "I see. And the money, it came from the odd jobs you mentioned earlier, right?"

I nodded.

"What were those odd jobs?" he pressed when I said nothing else.

A defensive retort prickled my tongue, but I didn't voice it. I wanted to blame him for not being involved in Jean's life enough to know the answer to that, but I didn't know, either. Which was the real issue.

"I honestly don't know," I whispered and hid my shame behind my wine glass. Jean never elaborated much on her life, and whenever I did pry, it always ended in a fight. So I'd given up. "My sister and I weren't very close, Mister Mershano. I didn't even know you were the father until today."

Those dark eyes flared with something I couldn't interpret, but I felt judged on some level. And whatever judgment he'd arrived at did not appear to be positive.

Distrust. An emotion I recognized and understood all too well.

But in this, I had proof.

I set my glass down and pushed away from the table to find the file on Jamie in my office.

Wyatt didn't move or say anything when I returned. He just kept observing me in that cocky manner. Wealth and privilege emanated from him. It was woven into his designer clothes, the artful style of his purposely messy hair, and the overall way he carried himself. Casual, lazy, arrogant. As if he had no worries in the world and knew it.

"Here." I placed the papers on the table as I reclaimed my seat. "This is everything my sister kept on Jamie. I gave copies of these to my lawyer for custody purposes. Nowhere does it list you as a father."

"It wouldn't," he said without looking at the file.

"Because Jean and I agreed to keep my involvement a secret. The original birth certificate, the one Garrett showed you today, is the official copy, while your sister maintained a secondary one drawn up in accordance with our agreement."

He flipped open the folder and found the document in question. "This was to be used for identity purposes until his eighteenth birthday. That's what we decided."

I gaped at him. "Why?"

"Why?" Jamie asked, hearing my raised voice and repeating the word. "Why, why, why?" he sing-songed, using the tune from his cartoon movie.

"I told your aunt she can't have any more wine," Wyatt replied without missing a beat. "She's not taking it well."

"Ohhhhhh, Auntie A, no more wine for Auntie A." Jamie waggled his finger in an interpretation of me scolding him. "No, no, no."

"Cute kid," Wyatt murmured, amused.

"Go back to your movie." I didn't share the amusement—even though Jamie giggled—but thankfully, he listened. I gave it a minute before I shifted my attention to the still-smirking man across from me. "Why would you both decide that?"

His grin settled into a flat line. "You act as though you have no idea."

"Because I don't, genius. Or did you miss the part about my having no idea you were the father until today?"

His pupils flared as he held my gaze. "I almost believe you, sweetheart. But you're related to Jean, and I know all too well how gifted she was at lying to me."

My brow furrowed. "I… I don't know how to reply to that."

He grinned. "Impressive indeed." He stood and stretched his arms over his head, revealing a sliver of tan skin beneath his shirt. Definitely pure muscle. Not that I was looking. "My ride is here, but we'll pick this up in the morning."

His ride? "You're leaving?"

Two dimples peeked at me as his grin morphed into a smile. "Asking me to stay the night? Now you're acting like Jean."

"That's not what I meant." My cheeks burned with the insinuation in his tone and doubled with annoyance at the knowing gleam in his eyes as I stood. "I didn't know what to expect after you demanded to see Jamie today and then invited yourself over for dinner. It wasn't a stretch to assume you'd claim the guest room, too." Which was also Jean's old room.

He stepped around the table and entered my personal space, but I refused to back down. His six-foot-plus height didn't intimidate me. Neither did that devious twinkle in his irises. Or the half grin gracing his full lips. Or the scent of leather and man that seemed to surround me as he moved even closer. Or the way his pupils dilated as they dropped to my mouth.

My pulse skipped a beat because Jamie sat so close by. It had nothing at all to do with this man or the solid body bumping up against my folded arms.

"I think we both know I'd be staying in your room, Avery," Wyatt murmured, his mouth scant inches from mine. "But feel free to deny it all you want. It'll only intrigue me more." Those last words were a breath against my cheek, seconds before he pressed a warm kiss to my too-hot skin.

The wine sent my hormones into a tizzy while my sanity searched for reason.

I'm not attracted to him.

Liar.

Butterflies danced in my lower belly as he pulled back just enough to check my expression. Whatever he saw there caused his dimples to appear again.

"Mmm. That's what I thought," he murmured. "See you in the morning, Miss Perry."

Electricity hummed through my veins, disengaging my ability to form a proper comeback.

Nothing coherent formed in my mind. Just a bunch of gibberish about his masculine scent, how much I disliked him, and what it would be like to kiss him. Because a man like Wyatt Mershano would know how to handle a woman... and well.

Wrong.

But so right.

5

AVERY

Wyatt left me confused and cold beside the table as he pulled on his jacket. "Oh, and don't worry about bringing Jamie with you. No need to disrupt his schedule." He winked before loudly adding, "It was good to meet you, Jamie."

"Rebel friend leaving?" Jamie asked, hopping up on the chair in a manner he knew was forbidden.

"Yep, but I'll be back soon. Maybe tomorrow."

My chest ached at the blossoming smile on Jamie's face. "To play?"

"Sure," Wyatt replied. "Whatever you want."

"Race cars?" Jamie sounded so hopeful I wanted to cry. Despite Wyatt's silent act through dinner, Jamie had taken to him, almost as if he sensed their bond.

Wyatt's eyes crinkled at the sides as a sense of awe infiltrated his features. "I loved race cars growing up and still do. You're on, little man."

"Yesss!" Jamie did a little jig that only broadened the joy

radiating from Wyatt and further cracked my heart.

The physical similarities between them were uncanny. And although they'd just met, there seemed to be a mutual understanding between them I couldn't define.

This can't be happening.

But it is…

God, I would never want to take both parents from Jamie, but I promised to protect him. And I had no way of knowing whether or not Wyatt was a suitable role model or father figure. The way he looked at him now felt right, but he was a virtual stranger to us both.

I'd have to research him.

Scour the internet for anything and everything I could find. Tonight. Because we were meeting again in the morning.

Surely there had to be some information available about him as a member of the Mershano family, right? Some of those hotel heirs were practically celebrities. Maybe he had a following as well that I could read about, some news articles, anything to give me more insight into him.

Aside from the obvious womanizing tendencies, sexy grins, and heated glances.

"Good night, Avery." He started toward my foyer—unescorted. Manners forced me to follow. Jamie had settled back into his movie, easily distracted by his favorite song playing.

"What should I expect tomorrow?" I asked, unable to help myself.

Wyatt paused at the door to glance over his shoulder at me. "An ultimatum, I imagine. Garrett doesn't care much for Atlanta, and he'll be wanting to return to Texas."

"An ultimatum that says…?" It hurt to ask, hurt to show any vulnerability, but my heart couldn't remain quiet. "I've spent the last four years raising him, Wyatt, and I've done the best job that I could, given the circumstances. If you're going to shatter my world and take him away from me, I deserve to know."

"Do you?" He tilted his head to the side. "And if I said yes, that I plan to take him with me, what would you do?"

A punch to the abdomen would have hurt less than those casual words, spoken in such a nonchalant way, as if musing about my pending destruction. The tears rushing my eyes refused to obey my commands to leave, and the lump forming in my throat clogged my ability to respond. I pressed a palm to my stomach and tried to force the emotions back under control, but the room spun around me.

His callous confirmation of what tomorrow held...

God.

How would I tell Jamie?

How would I explain it?

And where would Wyatt take him?

"Will I be able to see him?" The words sounded loud in my ears, but I knew they'd come out softly. Probably incoherently as well. I wanted desperately to try again, to utter them clearly, but I couldn't focus enough to speak.

Jean's death had hurt. I'd mourned her, hated her, and missed her.

But Jamie...

My knees wobbled with the effort to remain standing, and I touched the wall for support. It felt hotter than it should, probably because my body had gone cold.

I closed my water-filled eyes and strove for reason. He'd confirmed my fears, just as I asked. But I hated him for it. For being here and for threatening my world and my purpose for being.

"Four years," I mumbled. "You didn't care. Why now? What did I ever do to you?"

I needed to lie down before I fell. But my legs refused to move, and the wall seemed to be holding me upright. It'd grown arms...

"Auntie A?" Jamie's concerned voice pierced the dark clouds hovering over me, and my body performed on autopilot.

"Yeah, Jamie?" I turned to find him standing in the hallway with a little frown that blurred in my vision.

"Auntie A is sad?" He looked over my shoulder. "What'd you do?"

I opened my mouth to reply, but the wall behind me spoke over me.

"I said something mean," Wyatt replied, surprising me. "I accidentally hurt your aunt's feelings."

"Bad, rebel friend," Jamie chastised, his voice far too stern for a four-year-old. "Say you're sorry."

Any other moment, I may have laughed at hearing him parrot my own words at someone else. But my heart ached too much to allow humor.

I'll miss you so much…

"I'm sorry, Avery." Wyatt sounded so contrite that I was almost impressed. But I knew he didn't mean it. "Can I have an adult minute with your aunt, Jamie? I promise I won't say anything else mean to her."

Jamie's lips pinched to the side. "Promise? What's that?"

"A promise happens when you tell someone you're going to do something, and then you do it, no matter what." Wyatt's definition shocked me almost as much as the hands he placed on my hips to hold me in front of him. "So I promise you that I won't say anything else mean to her."

Jamie's brow crinkled as he looked between us. "No more sad?"

"No more sad," Wyatt said, speaking for me again.

Jamie nodded. "Okay. No more sad." He skipped back to the living area, leaving me alone with my heart in my throat.

The hands on my waist forced me to turn. I was too tired to resist and too emotionally done to fight.

"Sorry. I didn't… I wasn't as prepared as I thought. I'll…" I coughed to dislodge the raspy quality from my voice. "I'll try to pack some of his things after he goes…" I closed my eyes, unable to finish.

Had it only been a few hours since the meeting with our

lawyers? It felt like a lifetime ago. Tomorrow, everything would change. Again.

And according to my lawyer, there was nothing I could do to stop it.

Unless I could prove Wyatt to be an unfit father. Given his financial resources, family name, and the brief interactions I'd observed between him and Jamie, that would be close to impossible.

"I didn't mean to upset you," he murmured, one of his palms sliding to my lower back. "Actually, that's a lie. I wanted to see how you'd react. And either you're an amazing actress or I really fucked that up."

I glowered up at him. "Actress? You think all of this is an act?" My voice finally rose above a whisper toward the end, but it still held a raspy quality to it that I loathed. It left me feeling and sounding far weaker than I'd ever been, and I hated him for it. "Is this all a game to you?"

"I prefer the term *test*, but we can call it a game, if you like that more." He held me in place as I tried futilely to shove him away. "Don't make me break my promise to Jamie, Avery. I told him I wouldn't say anything mean."

"Too late," I growled as I squirmed in his grip.

"The truth may be cruel, but it's not intentionally mean." He wrapped both arms around my back and used his strength against me. "Listen to me. Jamie's not going anywhere until I can figure all this out, okay? I don't want to trust you any more than you want to trust me, but the circumstances require it. For Jamie."

I stopped moving and replayed his words in my head. "You're not taking him tomorrow?"

"Not unless you give me a great reason to," he replied. "And so far, you've given me every reason to trust his care in your custody." His grip loosened slightly as he sighed. "Look, it's been a long day for us both. Just try to get some sleep, and we'll continue our conversation in the morning, okay?"

His eyes almost appeared remorseful as he studied me,

but I couldn't allow myself to believe it. Because then I would start to hope, and that was the most dangerous emotion of all. It would be so easy for him to placate me with words tonight, just to take Jamie tomorrow. Especially now that I knew he could whenever he liked.

I don't want to trust you any more than you want to trust me, but the circumstances require it. For Jamie.

I couldn't refute that logic.

Everything I did was for Jamie.

"Avery, I can't leave until I know you're... okay." The conflict in his tone confused me.

"Why would you care?" It seemed contrary to everything he'd done and said today. Why would he suddenly be concerned with my well-being? He clearly hadn't cared earlier, or even five minutes ago.

"It's complicated," he replied and pressed his lips to my temple. "For what it's worth, I meant my apology. I am sorry."

My lungs burned with the need to breathe—apparently, I'd stopped when his mouth met my skin. Or maybe even before that.

This tender side of him bewildered me. How had he gone from jackass to almost sweet in the span of a few minutes? It had to be a trick, but I didn't know why he bothered.

Another game? Or a "test," as he called it?

How did I pass?

"Are you okay?" he asked as he pulled back to study my face.

No. "I'll be fine." Also true. I always found a way to survive.

"Then we'll talk more in the morning. I think we both have a lot to learn about each other." He brushed his lips over my forehead and stepped back. "Good night."

I tried to respond, but my voice failed me. Again. Yet, rather than smirk at me as he seemed to enjoy doing, he just nodded. And quietly left.

A blonde woman met him in the driveway, her tight dress showcasing her curves and long legs. She twirled something in the air that he took from her, followed by a kiss against her cheek before he slid into the driver's seat. It all unfolded like a movie through the window, including the part where she settled into the passenger side of the sporty two-seater.

What insane world did Wyatt Mershano live in where a girlfriend waited outside another woman's house, for God only knew how long, to merely come out without much of a hello and take control of the car?

And would that sort of behavior change when he took Jamie? Or would it continue?

I had been on exactly five dates in the last four years. Raising a child required a certain amount of responsibility and planning.

Why not hire a nanny? he had asked earlier.

Was that what he would do? Hire a nanny while he took blondes out on dates in expensive cars?

I frowned. *Not on my watch.*

Wyatt Mershano wanted to play a game with me? Fine. But I'd win. Because I had no other choice.

6
WYATT

"He's a womanizer!" Avery's proclamation slapped me across the face as I paused on the threshold of the conference room.

Both she and her lawyer were facing away from the door, engaged in some sort of a heated debate.

I had no doubt it was about me.

I rested my hip against the metal jamb, folded my arms, and settled in for the show.

"That's hardly cause for calling him an unfit parent." Her lawyer sounded exasperated, indicating they'd been at this for at least a few minutes. Maybe longer. "He's a billionaire, Avery. And yes, he has a bit of a reputation—"

"A bit?" she repeated. "A bit?! Are you kidding? Google his name. He's all over the tabloids, Scott. And not in a good way."

"I'm well aware of his, uh, aptitude for partying, but no judge is going to care when he proves he's more than capable of providing adequate care for his son. Most celebrities have personal caretakers for their children, and my guess is, he'll follow suit."

"Okay, what about the fact that he hasn't bothered to financially care for his kid these last four years? I mean, that has to qualify for something. He was too busy getting drunk and partying with hookers to properly care for his own child. Who's to say he won't repeat that behavior? Scott, I saw him get picked up by an escort last night at my house. What if Jamie had seen him?"

My frown deepened with every word. There were so many misunderstandings in that rant that I didn't even know where to start.

Drunk? I hadn't touched alcohol since the day after Jean had told me about Jamie.

Hookers? Fuck no.

Escort? Esther would love that and probably kick my ass for not immediately correcting it.

But it was Avery's comment about the finances that floored me most. She had no reason to lie to her lawyer about what she knew, which implied she truly had no idea I'd contributed to Jamie's well-being.

How was that even possible?

"You should know better than to believe the gossip columns, Avery," her lawyer muttered. "Photos can be manipulated, and all celebrities are subject to rumors—most of which are untrue."

"Some of those photos have to be real," she replied. "And what I saw last night was very real."

"A woman picking him up in a sports car—something that is likely part of a service he requested for transportation."

"Or something else," she pointed out.

"You think I need to hire someone for sex?" I couldn't help it. I had to comment. "Would you like a preview of how inaccurate that assessment is? Because your lawyer's receptionist has been eye-fucking me since I walked into the building yesterday."

I glanced over my shoulder toward the young redhead's desk to find her gaping at me with a guilt-ridden expression. My responding smile didn't appear nearly as easily as it should have, mostly due to Avery sputtering in the conference room a few feet away.

I returned my attention to her and raised an eyebrow.

"Well? Do you require a demonstration on my ability to seduce a woman without paying her?" Because I'd gladly provide a personal demonstration in Avery's bedroom later. Appropriate or not, the woman appealed to my basic needs.

I'd actually been looking forward to seeing her today and apologizing again for my behavior last night. Now, I just wanted to rile her up more and see how far that beautiful blush went. She'd worn another blouse but paired it with a skirt this time. One that revealed a pair of gorgeously toned legs that would look fantastic around my hips.

"Wyatt," Garrett greeted me as he met me in the doorway. "Have I missed anything?"

"Only Miss Perry trying to convince her lawyer that I'm an unfit father due to my alcoholism and obsession with hookers." I gave her the sweetest smile I could muster. "Does that summarize it, sweetheart?"

Garrett snorted beside me. "Maybe if you stopped flirting with the tabloids, your reputation would improve."

Ah, an age-old conversation in the Mershano family. "And what would be the fun in that, G?"

"I don't know about fun, but it would appease your brother immensely."

I snorted. "Not a good reason. You know how much I love living up to my rebel nickname." I gazed pointedly at Avery and enjoyed her grimace.

"I—I didn't know… yesterday, I mean. Until I read—"

"A likely story," I said, cutting her off.

"Didn't know what?" Garrett asked, looking between us.

"She told Jamie I'm a rebel, and he now refers to me as *rebel friend Wyatt.*" I didn't feel nearly as irritated by that as I should have, mostly because of the abject horror in Avery's gaze.

Yesterday, I would have applauded her acting abilities. Today, I viewed her through a new filter, one that allowed for the possibility that she told the truth.

I'd expressed that possibility to Garrett last night, something he had ruthlessly refuted, but in the end, he agreed to call an acquaintance who specialized in investigations. Some guy named Kincaid who supposedly worked quickly and efficiently.

I'd have all the details I needed on Avery Perry's life within the next week or two, if not sooner. Then we would see just how much of her act was real. I also tasked the investigator with tracking the funds I had sent to Jean because, from what I'd observed last night, they were not being spent as expected.

Apparently, I should have kept a more watchful eye on the mother of my child. However, after the hell she'd put me through, I'd stayed as far away from her as possible and sent money as needed in exchange for updates on Jamie.

Updates that I now suspected were fabricated.

"You're lucky my client has tough skin, Miss Perry," Garrett said as he unfastened his suit jacket button and sat with his usual regal flair. I didn't care much for my brother's best friend, but I couldn't deny his usefulness. Particularly in these situations.

I remained standing since we wouldn't be here long. Garrett knew exactly what I wanted him to say, despite his advisement against it. But as I told Avery, I managed my own decisions. And this one was nonnegotiable after last night.

"I assume her accusations haven't changed your mind?" he asked without looking at me.

"Nope, but I'm looking forward to correcting some of her allegations." Specifically, the one that implied I needed to pay for sex.

Her beautiful blue-green eyes peeked up at me through a cluster of blonde lashes, and she visibly swallowed.

You should be afraid, I told her with my gaze. *Because I'm not known for holding back, even when I should.*

Avery being decidedly off-limits only intrigued me more. I didn't have to trust a woman to fuck her. Sometimes that allowed for more freedom in the bedroom.

Except, with this particular woman, I might be able to like her as well. She had a fire in her I admired, and her motherly love for Jamie endeared her to me all the more.

And the way she glared at me right now with equal parts interest and hate fascinated the hell out of me. How would that translate to a night in bed?

"Right." Garrett set his portfolio on the table and steepled his fingers over the expensive leather. "Against my advisement, Wyatt has a proposition for Miss Perry."

His tone indicated how he felt about my plans, but my devilish attorney should know by now that I rarely followed legal advice. A lifetime of being reminded I was just the bastard son of a billionaire had framed my rules in a rather unconventional manner, something Garrett and my older brother knew all too well.

"We're listening," Scott Mackenzie said from across the table. The chubby, second-rate attorney would never be able to hold his own against Garrett Wilkinson, a conclusion I drew before Avery arrived yesterday. Her only option here was to agree to my terms, and I couldn't wait to watch her squirm.

"Jamie may remain with Miss Perry for the next two months, so long as Miss Perry agrees to allow Wyatt to stay with them at her home in Acworth. We feel this will soften the transition for Jamie and give him time to acquaint himself with Wyatt prior to any future living arrangements."

And grant me time to ascertain her motives—motives that remained unclear after observing her last night. Jean had wanted my money and name, while Avery seemed more preoccupied with protecting Jamie than asking me for a dime.

"Wyatt mentioned that Miss Perry offered him a guest

room last night, so I assume this arrangement won't be an issue?" Garrett could be so amusing when he wanted to be, and I approved wholeheartedly. Especially since it resulted in a glower from Avery.

"'Offered' is a bit of a stretch," she muttered.

"Does that mean you disagree with the terms?" Garrett's haughty tone drained the color from Avery's face. He truly was an asshole, and he knew it, too. But I couldn't deny that his methods worked.

"No, I just meant that I, uh…" She trailed off as the eyebrow of my jackass lawyer arched her way. I'd asked him to tone down the intimidation factor today, but it seemed ingrained in his code of ethics.

"Are there additional terms?" her lawyer asked in a poor attempt to regain control of the situation.

I leaned against the wall, hands in my pockets, and held Avery's gaze. So much emotion resided in those dilated pupils—fury, hope, lust. I accepted them all with a tilt of my lips, which resulted in a furious blush painting her gorgeous face.

Oh, this would be fun.

Garrett pulled out the contract he'd whipped up last night after our conversation and slid it across the table. "There are several; however, the primary stipulation is that Wyatt wishes to reside with Avery and Jamie."

Scott studied the document while Avery demanded, "What else?"

Garrett grinned but not in a friendly manner. It was his devil-may-care expression, the one he used when he knew no one stood a chance against him. He always won, no matter what it took.

"Wyatt can void the agreement at will should he decide the arrangement is no longer suitable, and he maintains full custody of his son. You, Miss Perry, are in no way considered the primary caregiver by law, meaning Wyatt can remove Jamie at any time."

Avery swallowed visibly. "Okay. Anything else?"

"This arrangement is purely at the discretion of my client, and it's only being offered in the best interest of his son. If you object to any of the provisions, our deal is forfeit, and Wyatt leaves with his son. Today."

Harsh but accurate. When her attention shifted to me, I merely lifted a shoulder. He'd given her the overview. I had nothing to add. For now, anyway.

"We'll give you and your lawyer a moment to review the contract. Be advised, there will be no amendments or additional offers on the subject." Garrett stood and refastened his suit jacket. "The offer expires at five this afternoon because I have a flight to catch, and I will not be staying in Atlanta any longer than necessary."

He grabbed his portfolio and met me at the door.

"Because Houston is so much better?" I asked, delighted by his obvious discomfort.

He did not share my enjoyment and started toward the receptionist desk. "I miss my bed."

"You miss the women who occupy it," I corrected him and winked at the blushing redhead as we passed her.

Garrett pressed the elevator button and attempted to intimidate me with a glower. "I have no idea why I put up with you."

I grinned. "I pay you very well."

"You mean your brother does."

I shrugged. It was true. "And how is my big brother? It's been a minute since I last saw him."

Garrett winced. "Very engaged."

I smirked and followed him into the elevator. "I'd ask if you were missing him as a wingman, but we both know your proclivities vary from my big brother's."

Garrett preferred to dabble in the darkness, while Evan enjoyed short-term monogamous relationships. I'd observed them both while growing up and considered Garrett a god among women. The man rarely took the same one to bed twice and sometimes went through a few a night. Definitely not the type to ever settle down, and he showed no signs of stopping now. Thirty-six and clearly loving life.

"His fiancée does not care for me."

"I can't imagine why. You're positively charming, G." The sarcasm in my voice earned a snort from my lawyer as the doors opened to the lobby.

"Are you planning to meet Sarah prior to the wedding?" he asked, leading the way to what I presumed would be an early lunch.

"You assume I'm going." The invitation arrived last week and mentioned something about fourteen days in Hawaii. *Pass.*

Garrett shot me a look over his shoulder. "You're attending."

My eyebrow inched upward. "Oh? Am I your date?"

He snorted. "You wish. But you're in the wedding party and, therefore, will be there, even if I have to drag your ass through the Pacific myself."

Yeah, there was that minor detail. Evan called me a few months ago to ask me to be one of his groomsmen. It was all a ploy our father likely required, which didn't make the idea of attending very appealing to me. All the Mershanos treated me as if I were a child incapable of running my own life.

"Looking forward to it," I lied. It wasn't Evan or the wedding I dreaded but seeing Ellen and Jonah Mershano, otherwise known as my legal parents.

"Seriously, with Will and Evan both tied down, I'll need someone sane to keep me company." Garrett opened the door to a coffee shop a few doors down from the building we'd just exited.

"You'll be too busy fucking the bridesmaids to even notice my presence."

The petite barista's hazel eyes went wide at my not-so-quiet response.

I grinned at her. "Morning, sweetheart." She wasn't my type at all—not blonde or curvy—but her blush reminded me a bit of Avery. "I'll take a large dark roast, no cream or sugar. The devil beside me would like one of those frozen chocolate mocha drinks with extra whipped cream."

"Ignore him; he's an infant. I'll take a large dark roast as well with a single cream and a scone." He handed over his card to pay, and I knew he'd bill me for two or three times the amount later just to be an ass. "And that's a *no* to the bridesmaids. One is Will's fiancée, the other is Sarah's identical twin, who I have no interest in entertaining, and the final is your little sister."

"Mia." I smiled with the name. Now, she is someone I would go to Hawaii to see. "Have you seen her since she moved back?"

Garrett's shoulders stiffened as he shook his head. "No. We're not friends, nor will we ever be friends."

"She's not that bad, G."

"She's a brat," he growled. "And obnoxious."

I shook my head and smiled. "She's energetic and young." Only two years younger than me but so full of life. She loved everyone unconditionally, a trait that helped me survive my childhood. I'd never speak ill of her.

"Sure." He took the cup and scone from the counter after the barista passed it over with a bemused expression. The darling girl had no idea how to handle us, not that someone as green as her ever could. My desires didn't run as dark as Garrett's, but I wasn't vanilla, either. One bite and she'd run for the hills. Poor thing.

Garrett checked his watch and sighed. "My presence here wouldn't be needed if you'd just use your damn Harvard law degree."

"Oh, save me the lecture, G. You know what I'm going to say."

"That you only chose to pursue a law degree because it cost your father a small fortune." The irritation in his tone amused me. "Yet you graduated with high marks and had your pick of opportunities."

"That I turned down," I reminded him as I accepted my cup from the still-gaping barista. "I would enjoy entertaining you further, sweetheart. Alas, we have a meeting room to return to." And a woman I very much wanted to *entertain*, in every aspect of the word.

Her mouth opened, closed, and opened again, still silent. Hmm. No, definitely not my type at all.

"And what do you plan to do with your life, Wyatt?" Garrett pressed, ignoring my exchange with the barista. "Other than live off the family's wealth and continue to flirt with every female you meet?"

"You make it sound like an unfulfilling life, G."

He held open the door and nailed me with his knowing gaze. "You loathe it. Otherwise, we wouldn't have drafted that offer for Miss Perry."

"Yeah?" I moved past him with a chuckle. "You have me all figured out, do you?"

"Yes." He sounded so certain. "You're tired of the rebel charade, which is why you asked for my help. Yes, we're guarding the family's fortune, but with Jean out of the picture, you finally have an opportunity to know your son." He leaned in while we walked, his voice lowering. "That doesn't sound very rebellious to me, Wyatt. It sounds rather honorable. But don't worry; your secret's safe with me. Attorney-client privilege."

"You're a dick."

"I'm astute," he corrected me. "But can I make a recommendation?"

"You're going to anyway," I pointed out, feigning a boredom I didn't feel. He was right about Jamie. I did want to know him, but I hadn't been able to with Jean in the picture.

Damn. I'd been an idiot to agree to our arrangement—proof that good intentions didn't always lead to the best decisions.

"Don't fuck Miss Perry," Garrett advised as we returned to the building. "It'll only complicate matters."

I grinned. "Oh, but, G, you know how I like complications."

He shook his head, unamused. "Well, when this all blows up in your face, remember that I tried to warn you."

"Sure," I replied. "I'll remember how hard you tried, G." Which would be not at all because he knew better. I made the rules for my life. Always and forever. And I wouldn't change that, not even for a woman as beautiful as Avery Perry.

7
AVERY

I regretted my decision already, and we'd only made it to the parking lot.

"No," I repeated, arms folded, foot tapping. "Absolutely not."

Wyatt glanced at his sporty death trap and back at me. "I fail to see the problem. Jamie likes cars, right?"

"Yes, as toys. You will not be picking him up from preschool in that."

"Why not?"

"He's four." I thought that was answer enough, but his cocked brow told me he needed more. "He needs a car seat."

"So let me borrow yours. Or I'll stop at the store and pick one up. Problem solved."

"They go in the backseat, Wyatt. Not the front."

"Seriously, you live, like, five minutes from the preschool. I think he'll be fine for two fucking miles."

"Most accidents happen within a few minutes of home."

Or so I had heard, anyway. "And my answer is still no. Give the death trap back to your girlfriend and have her drop you off at the house. I'll meet you there."

He grinned. "Upgraded from escort to girlfriend, huh? Esther will be thrilled."

I narrowed my eyes.

Clearly, we needed to establish some ground rules.

"Look, there will be no girlfriends or escorts in my house. I've agreed to allow you to stay in Jean's old room, which I imagine won't be too awkward for you since you're clearly familiar with her bed. But that does not mean you can bring random women into *my* home for whatever it is that you do." I waved a hand over him in an attempt to dispel the heat rushing over my skin. I did not want to think about what he did in any bed, especially my sister's.

Wyatt stepped forward, forcing me to move backward into the side of my SUV. Both of his palms flattened against the metal on either side of my head as he caged me between himself and my car.

"First of all, Esther is the Southeast Regional Manager for Mershano Suites and did me a favor by helping me procure the 'death trap' so I didn't have to rely on you to chauffeur me around."

He shifted closer, the smell of coffee and leather overwhelming my senses.

"Second, I am not at all familiar with Jean's bed and, in fact, have no recollection of ever being in it in the first place. Nor do I ever want to be in a space claimed by her. I will have furniture delivered by the end of the day as a result."

I opened my lips to protest that last bit, but he pressed a finger to my mouth, silencing me.

"And finally, should you ever be interested in learning what I do in the bedroom, let me know, and I'll happily provide an intimate demonstration." He traced my lower lip with his thumb, his eyes following the movement. "Any other questions or concerns, Miss Perry?"

Um…

I swallowed.

There was something I wanted to say or protest, but his smoldering gaze hypnotized me into silence.

His presence overwhelmed reason, causing my mind to blank on whatever I needed to say. Something about a bed. Which only painted a picture in my mind of how he would look in one.

Heat radiated from him through the fitted black shirt he wore beneath his jacket. I suspected solid muscle existed beneath those clothes.

"Avery." His murmur solicited my gaze upward to his brown eyes. Amusement teased his lips while a dark emotion dilated his pupils. "I will work on finding a more suitable ride and meet you and Jamie at the house later. That should give you an opportunity to inform him that his 'rebel friend' is going to be staying for a while."

I winced at the reminder of his nickname. "I really didn't—"

His thumb halted my explanation. "It's fine. Perhaps Jamie will teach me to like the nickname." He pushed away from my personal space and started toward his sporty car. "See you in a few hours, Avery. My number is in the contract should you need me between now and then."

"I…" *I what?* My tongue dampened my lips as I strove for a coherent thought. "Okay."

Yes, very good, Avery.

"Okay," he replied as he opened the driver's side door. "I'll follow you out." He gestured to my SUV. "Get in. Go get Jamie. We'll talk later about renovating."

I blinked. "Renovating?"

"Yes. If I'm going to live with you, there are a few things we'll need to upgrade. Starting with the kitchen."

Bedroom! That was what I wanted to talk about. "You can't just replace all of Jean's things." Not that any of them were truly hers to begin with. Her room was more of a vapid closet with minimal decor and barely used sheets.

He folded his arms on the hood of his car. "Any items

of sentimental value can be kept, but I will not be touching anything that belonged to that woman."

A laugh tickled my throat, then halted as his words from a few minutes ago came roaring back.

I am not at all familiar with Jean's bed and, in fact, have no recollection of ever being in it in the first place.

What did that mean exactly? That he didn't remember sleeping with her? But it obviously happened; Jamie was proof of that.

Had he been drunk? Jean, too?

His reputation online painted him as a party-boy rebel who fucked everything that walked. And he had the money in his account to do and live any way he preferred.

Yet, twenty-four hours of knowing him and I saw not one sign of that being true. The cockiness, yes, but the other tendencies, no. He had refused my wine last night in favor of water, something I thought might be meant as an insult, but his online persona suggested he didn't usually care about the brand.

"If it means that much to you, I'll rent a storage unit for her things," he said, drawing me back to our conversation. "But either you let me order my own furniture or I'm staying in your room. Your choice, sweetheart."

"That isn't going to happen." Ever. "And it'll be fine. It's more of a guest room since she didn't really live with us." I fought the urge to rub my chest at the thought of erasing her presence, but it was true. She rarely stayed in that room, and all the furniture was a cheap brand that would probably repel his rich blood.

Besides, if I granted him this concession, he would be more comfortable, and Scott suggested I do everything in my power to help Wyatt feel as welcome as possible. If I kept him happy, he might be more amenable to future negotiations.

As it was, my lawyer couldn't believe Wyatt had agreed to this arrangement. It offered me the opportunity to learn more about him and also granted me more time with Jamie.

And maybe, if I played my cards right, Wyatt would agree to share custody in some capacity.

It was a long shot but my only option. If living with a man—a practical stranger—helped me keep Jamie, I would do it.

I would do anything.

"Are you sure?" Wyatt asked.

I blinked. "Uh, am I sure about what?" How far I would go for Jamie? Had I said that out loud?

"Not needing a storage area for Jean's belongings," he prompted.

Oh, right. "Um, yeah. I don't…" I closed my eyes and swallowed the lump in my throat. "There isn't much. Just a few drawers of clothes and some bedding I bought. She really didn't have a lot because she stayed elsewhere." I thought for work or maybe with friends. Whenever I pried, she'd tell me to mind my own business. I shouldn't have listened, but I did.

And now she's dead.

We're not doing this here. Or anywhere, for that matter. I had to be strong.

"Avery." The concerned voice startled me into opening my eyes. Wyatt stood in front of me again, his brow furrowed. "If it means that much to you, I can stay in her room. As is."

I stared at him. "You'd do that?"

"Yes."

No elaboration.

Not even a blink.

"I… I don't know what to say…"

"You don't need to say anything." He tucked a strand of my hair behind my ear and cupped my cheek briefly before letting his hand fall to his side. "But if I am going to purchase a more suitable car today, then I need to head to the dealership now."

I nodded, and he started toward his admittedly sexy ride. "You know, he'll appreciate that more when he's older."

Wyatt turned with a cocked brow. "He'll appreciate what?"

I tilted my chin at his hot rod. "That."

He grinned. "I'll keep it in mind for when he's out of the car seat."

I returned the smile. "He's tall for his age, so I'd say in about five to six years, you might be able to entertain him with it."

"Good to know," he murmured as he reopened the driver's side door. "I'll see you in a few hours."

"Okay." I started to climb into the SUV when I thought better of it again. "It's an old bed."

He paused on his way into his own car. "What?"

"The one in the guest room. It's old. You're welcome to replace it. And there's only one dresser, so you might want to replace that as well with a larger one, depending on how much you're bringing with you." I pictured the rest of the items in my head. "There's not much else, other than a lamp, some curtains, and a few knickknacks. I'll box those up with her clothes." It needed to be done anyway. I'd put it off because there hadn't been an immediate need, but Wyatt changed that.

"You're sure?"

I swallowed at the intense way he studied me, as if he wanted to peer into my head. Probably because I wasn't being all that forthright or decisive. "Yes, it'll be fine."

"Fine," he mused. "That's a dangerous word from a woman."

"Maybe, but I mean it. You're welcome to order furniture." I couldn't believe those words had just come out of my mouth, but saying them actually felt right.

Clearly, all the stress is causing me to lose my mind.

"I'll, uh, see you later, then," I said in an effort to avoid thinking about what I'd just agreed to. "And I hope you like lasagna." Because that was what I planned to make for dinner.

At *my* house.

For him and Jamie.
Yeah, that wouldn't be surreal at all.
Or weird.
Perfectly normal.
Right.

8

WYATT

"How did you manage to accomplish all of this in less than eight hours?"

Avery's voice came from the doorway of my newly furnished bedroom. I finished signing the last of the documents—the ones regarding the storage unit I had purchased for Jean's old belongings—and handed the clipboard to the mover.

"Thank you, Mister Mershano," he replied. "You'll need this." He handed me a key. "We'll leave the other with the unit owners."

I nodded. "Sounds good, Larry. Thank you."

"Anytime, sir." He grinned as he passed Avery in the doorway. "Have a good evening, ma'am."

"You, too…" She blinked at him before glancing around the bedroom again. "Seriously, how is this possible?"

"Money." A blunt reply, but true. "I contacted a handful of Mershano Suites vendors and requested a few favors." Pretty straightforward.

I'd called Avery a few hours ago to request dimensions—my way of giving her another chance to deny my request to refurnish the room—and she'd readily given me the information I needed. I took that as a sign she was truly okay with my moving forward, but I still secured the storage area, just in case.

Her reaction in the parking garage earlier concerned me, but I suspected it had more to do with Jean and less to do with the physical property. After surveying the removal of items, it seemed Avery's comment regarding the lack of belongings was accurate.

Jean clearly had not used this space often, which begged the question: Where did she live?

"I should go lock up," Avery said as she started after Larry down the stairs.

Jamie had been in bed already when the movers arrived. Apparently, my son could sleep through anything, because his door across the hall remained closed. I wasn't sure how he would feel about my presence in the house, nor did I know what Avery told him about me being there, but she didn't seem very concerned.

Would he mind that I took his mother's old room?

The morning events would reveal that answer.

I followed her downstairs and detoured to the kitchen for a drink. My stomach rumbled, reminding me that I'd missed dinner in my effort to secure a bedroom and a new car, all in a handful of hours.

"The rest of the lasagna is in the oven." Avery joined me and grabbed a pair of mitts from a drawer. "Here, I'll get it." She removed the contents while I finished filling my glass. "It's nothing fancy, just a frozen dinner. You'll probably hate it. Sorry."

I observed her with a grin as she grabbed a plate from the cupboard and silverware from the drawer.

"Uh, there's salad, too." She turned toward the fridge, but I hooked an arm around her waist to stop her from continuing.

"Avery." I set my cup on the counter and pressed my chest against her back. "Relax. You don't need to play hostess with me."

"O-okay." She didn't try to move away, even when I dropped my hold and leaned over her to open the fridge.

"Do you need a drink?" I asked against her ear. Her responding tremble caused my lips to curl. For someone who had been completely averse to me twenty-four hours ago, she seemed to be coming around now.

"Wine," she whispered, grabbing the bottle.

"Good choice," I murmured before slowly moving away to fix myself a plate. I met her at the table, where she'd already finished a glass of wine and was pouring herself a refill. "Do I make you uncomfortable, Avery?"

She hid her lips behind her drink and mumbled, "No." Her throat worked as she imbibed more.

Liar. Her flushed cheeks, dilated pupils, and rapid breaths told me exactly how her body felt about being so close to mine. But if she wanted to hide behind her alcohol, I wouldn't press it.

I took a bite of the mediocre lasagna and shrugged. "Not bad."

"You mean it's horrible." She spoke into her glass. "I prefer homemade, but that requires time."

I had no response to that so I continued eating while she watched. Questions floated in her gaze, and I waited for the wine to provide her with the courage to voice them. With every sip, I sensed the walls of her resolve crumbling.

She nibbled her lower lip while pouring her third glass. "Okay, I need to know something."

Obviously. "Yes?" I prompted, unwilling to commit to a response.

"Earlier, you mentioned Jean, uh, her bed, and not remembering it."

I finished my final bite of food and set my fork down. "And?" None of that required clarification, as far as I could tell. It all seemed pretty straightforward to me.

Her brow furrowed, and she shook her head. "Never mind. It's not my business."

"I'll decide that." Since it was up to me whether or not I would elaborate. "Tell me what you want to know, Avery."

She swirled her wine and pinched her lips to the side as a fresh shade of red decorated her otherwise pale cheeks. I folded my arms on the table while I waited for her to spit it out. The alcohol would loosen her tongue eventually; all I had to do was remain impassive and patient. Two emotions I excelled at exuding.

"There were exactly two times I asked Jean about Jamie's father." She didn't meet my gaze while she spoke but instead focused on her drink. "The first time was when she told me about the pregnancy. The second time occurred about six months ago when I needed her to sign some documents." Her eyes lifted with a thousand questions that I knew were about to fill the air like rapid fire.

"She told me it was a one-night stand and that she didn't remember the father's name. Clearly, that wasn't true. But if neither of you remembered it... How and when did she contact you? Wait, you had a paternity test. So you've known about Jamie since the beginning. But why didn't you try to see him at all after that? And why did no one tell me? If you have all this money, why not help Jamie? I've done fine on my own, but you could obviously do better for him. So where have you been?" She slammed her mouth shut as if realizing she'd just thrown up a whole hell of a lot of words at once. But her eyes begged me for an explanation.

"You really don't know." A statement more than a question because the desperation spilling from her couldn't be an act. Well, it could be a well-played scheme, but confusion and hurt radiated from her.

I would know her intentions soon enough, thanks to Garrett's private investigator. But in the interim, a few answers couldn't hurt anything. Especially if Avery already knew the truth.

All I had to do was not fall victim to her ploy, assuming

she even had one.

Easy.

"To make a long story short, your sister drugged me, fucked me, and contacted me about four months into her pregnancy." My blunt summarization of the events caused Avery's mouth to fall open. Not the expression of someone already familiar with the story, or perhaps a reaction to my straightforward analysis.

"I didn't believe her since I maintained no recollection of that night, but a thorough investigation into her claims revealed the truth. Video footage doesn't lie, something your sister took into account. The paternity test after Jamie's birth provided the final nail in the coffin, and our negotiations began. The rest, as they say, is history."

Avery's lips moved, but no sound escaped.

"Either you're very skilled or Jean told you nothing about any of this," I mused. "So let me ask you, how has my money been spent over the last four years? Because—and I don't mean this to sound rude—you clearly haven't spent a dime of it on this house."

The home was decent for a middle-income family, but I provided more than enough funds to place Jamie and several of his relatives in an upper-class mini-mansion. Not a three bedroom, two-story home with a laminate countertop kitchen and faux wood floors.

"I… You've…" She shook her head on a strangled noise. "Jean knew the entire time you were the father."

It wasn't a question, but I answered her anyway. "Yes."

"And you've been paying for Jamie?"

"Yes."

She openly gaped at me. "For four years?"

"Yes."

Another odd sound erupted from her throat, forcing her to finish the rest of her wine. "Un-fucking-believable." She slapped a hand over her mouth and sputtered a laugh. Tears graced her eyes as she continued to giggle. "I'm s-sorry." She put her head down as her shoulders shook—from laughter, I thought, until I heard the telltale hitch in her breath.

Oh, shit.

Crying females were not my thing. Particularly, hysterical ones.

I didn't know whether to excuse myself politely, offer her a hug, or find a box of tissues.

Or run.

That final option sounded best, but the idea of leaving her like this... *Fuck*.

She appeared so frail and broken, her body shaking as she cried silently. Her hands fisted while she pulled them over her head, as if trying to fight and hide at the same time.

Rather than seek comfort as most women would, she relied on herself to fix it. That was what she did in the parking garage earlier when I mentioned wanting to refurnish Jean's bedroom. Avery clearly hadn't approved, yet she'd rallied herself in the end to give permission.

Or maybe it wasn't so much my taking over the room that had upset her as it was thoughts of her sister.

Her breathing slowed as she pulled her emotions under control, right before my eyes, without me having to do a thing.

And it made me feel like an ass for watching her. An intruder for joining her in such an intimate moment without lifting a finger to help her.

How fucked up was that? I owed this woman nothing.

Except, perhaps, gratitude for taking care of my son.

I frowned. Maybe she deserved a little more than gratitude.

Damn. I was supposed to hate her, not commiserate with her. But what if none of this had been her fault? What if everything she said was the truth?

No, I couldn't afford to consider that. Not until I knew for sure her intentions weren't malicious. Because if she was anything like Jean, then I couldn't trust a word she said.

"Excuse me," Avery mumbled before she pushed away

from the table and ran off in the direction of the stairs.

And like an asshole, I stayed put.

All of this felt wrong. Allowing her to cry, not offering support, being callous and blunt.

"Shit." I ran my palm over my face and blew out a breath. Even if I followed her, it could be construed as invading her privacy.

You moved yourself into her house uninvited.

Not to be an overbearing dick but to help foster the transition for Jamie and to learn more about Avery. The last thing I wanted to do was rip my son away from a woman who truly cared about him.

Which was exactly how I fell into Jean's trap.

I'm making all the same mistakes, just in a different way.

I blew out another breath and stood. Avery might be harmless. Hell, she could even be a victim in all of this, but until I had more information, I couldn't offer her an ounce of sympathy.

If I found out any of this was a ruse, Jamie would be on the first flight out of Atlanta with me by his side. Because no way in hell would I allow this game to continue. Even if it meant breaking his heart.

He would heal.

And he'd forget all about her over time.

I'd make sure of it.

9
AVERY

By the time I returned to the kitchen last night, Wyatt had already cleaned up all the dishes and disappeared to his room.

The coward in me refused to go after him to apologize or ask additional questions.

That same coward kept me in my home office when I heard him venture into the kitchen for breakfast and again for lunch. It helped that I had two days' worth of work to make up for today and back-to-back conference calls. Wyatt stayed out of my way until just after three when he softly knocked on the already open glass door.

I silenced my phone and forced myself to meet his gaze. "Yeah?"

"Do you need me to pick up Jamie?"

I shook my head. "They won't allow it. I'll need to introduce you to everyone so they know you have permission to pick him up."

His brow furrowed. "What last name did you give him?"

"The one on his birth certificate. Perry." Even as I said it, I realized the issue. "My version of the certificate has him listed as Jamie Perry."

"I see." He turned and left without another word. I would have trailed after him, but I had to wrap up my call first.

Once I finished, I stood and found him sprawled out on the couch with a remote in his hand.

"I'm upgrading your cable to satellite" was all he said.

"Uh, okay. Why?"

"That you even have to ask says so much." He turned off the television and hopped to his feet. "Time to pick up Jamie?"

"Yes. Do you want to come with me?"

"Yes."

"Let me grab my purse, and we'll go."

Wyatt had purchased a new SUV, but he didn't know the location of the preschool. Or maybe he did. But I wanted to drive. His expensive ride could be used another day.

He met me by the garage door, hands in the pockets of his leather jacket and shades in place. If "bad boy" had a look, Wyatt Mershano embodied it all the way down to the cocky smile gracing his full lips.

Sexy.

Unattainable.

Bad news.

He opened the door with an *after you* gesture and followed me into the garage.

"I'll have to clear out some space for your car," I realized, eyeing the gardening tool mess.

"I can work on it tonight or tomorrow, if you're okay with me rearranging a few things."

I stared at him over the hood of my SUV. "You want to organize my garage?"

He shrugged. "My new Porsche Cayenne would appreciate the shelter." He opened the door and slid into the passenger seat while I settled into the driver's side.

"What all did you tell Jamie about my staying with you?"

"I told him you needed a place to stay and would be living with us for a while." I reversed out of the garage carefully. His sexy black SUV looked too expensive for me to risk hitting in the driveway.

"He didn't ask questions?"

"He's four." And very inquisitive. "He wanted to know why, if you were bringing toys, how long you would be here, and where you would sleep." Jamie repeated several of those questions, but I had answered them all the same each time. "I didn't tell him you're his father, if that's what you're wondering."

"I wasn't," he murmured. "Just wondered how he felt about me sleeping in Jean's room."

I pinched my mouth to the side as I considered how to answer that. "His relationship with my sister wasn't... I don't know how to word it. They weren't very close? Jamie misses her, but he's not as distraught as one would expect. I've taken him to see a counselor, as that's the expected action in these cases, but Jamie doesn't seem to understand the gravity of the situation. He has moments of sadness, especially when I remind him that Jean isn't coming back, but he was so used to not seeing her that he doesn't really react."

"Do you think my being in her room will inspire a reaction?"

I shrugged. "It's possible. Death isn't a concept that children easily grasp. He'll get it at some point, but he's not all that bothered right now."

"How did he act at the funeral?"

"He cried, but I suspect it was because he saw me crying." I'd tried to stop it, but seeing my sister lying there in that coffin had momentarily shattered my walls. One glance at Jamie, though, had forced me to pull myself back together. I couldn't show weakness around him, not when he needed me to be strong. "He's too young to truly grasp that he'll never see his mother again. You staying in her room might confirm it, or he may not react at all."

Wyatt remained quiet, his focus on the passing buildings.

I cleared my throat as I strove for the strength to address my reaction last night. Confirming Jean knew about his paternity hadn't bothered me nearly as much as his comment about sending money for Jamie's care. For the last four years.

Part of me wanted to call him a liar, while the other part acknowledged Jean had more reason to lie about it. I always wondered where she stayed at night, assuming she spent it with friends, but with Wyatt sending her money, who the hell knew where she'd been. Or what she'd done.

It infuriated me. She'd taken complete advantage of both of us at Jamie's expense. If she were still alive, I'd throttle her.

For months, I blamed myself for not seeing the signs that she was in trouble, but I'd been too busy raising my sister's son to notice much else.

As much as it pained me to admit, I wouldn't change my choices. Jamie deserved care and devotion. And my sister, well, she should have known better.

I chewed my cheek while thinking of how to word what I needed to say. We were approaching the school, so I needed to speak now or wait until after Jamie went to bed again. That would leave this cloud hanging over us all evening, and I really didn't have the energy to withstand it much longer.

"About last night," I started, pausing to lick my dry lips. *Rip the Band-Aid off.* "I, uh, well, your information surprised me. Jean never mentioned receiving money from you, let alone your name. She barely helped with my mortgage and never spent time with Jamie because of her supposed jobs. And, um, to learn that you'd been assisting her, well, it shocked me. Sorry if my reaction made you uncomfortable."

He shifted in the passenger seat, and I felt his eyes on me. Even with sunglasses on, the man somehow managed to smolder. "No apology needed. I think we're both learning a lot this week."

I turned into the parking lot and found a spot near the front, then killed the engine. We were about twenty minutes early, which left us time to fill out the requisite forms to add Wyatt to the visitor's list. There was, however, one minor detail to discuss.

"Uh, how do you want to be introduced to the preschool director? As Jamie's dad, or…?" I had no other real suggestion beyond that. Legally, and ethically, he should be noted as the father. But how would we explain that to Jamie?

"Can we trust them?"

I unbuckled my seat belt. "To not tell Jamie?"

"That, yes, and to not tell anyone else."

My brow furrowed. "Like who?"

His lips quirked. "Do you think it's a coincidence that the tabloids have no idea about my relation to Jamie?"

I blinked. He was right. In all the articles I found about him, none of them mentioned his son. "Does your family know about him?"

"Of course. My father—if you can call him that—was positively thrilled to have something to hold over Evan's head. It's how he forced him onto that ridiculous show."

"I…" *Show?* "Okay. Not sure what you mean, but I think you're implying that you're worried someone might leak your paternity to the press. Right?"

He removed his sunglasses to meet my gaze. "You really know nothing about my family?"

"Uh, I know they own a massive hotel chain. But I focused primarily on you the other night when researching." I grimaced with the memory. "Not a lot of flattering information."

His chuckle warmed me in a way it shouldn't. "Be careful what you believe, Miss Perry. Most of it is bullshit."

"So you didn't climb onto a table in a New York City nightclub and put on a striptease for a bachelorette party?"

I raised a brow, knowing full well he did. There was proof online in video form. Not that I had watched it beyond him losing his shirt. "And you didn't get into a fistfight with what's-his-name outside that gentleman's club in Stockholm last year?"

Amusement radiated from him. "The fistfight was staged with a buddy to help him out of a predicament, and the striptease happened during my law school years." He leaned into my personal space, pressing his lips to my ear. "My skills have improved since, if you're interested in a private showing."

His hot breath on my neck scattered goose bumps up and down my exposed arms. *Not at all where I expected this conversation to go.*

I swallowed a variety of responses, none of them sounding right in my head. They varied between eager acceptance and crude denial.

This man…

"Mmm, I'll take your silence as a potential yes." His lips brushed my neck before he pulled away to open his door. "We can tell them who I am as long as you trust them not to run to the tabloids. I don't mind the world knowing Jamie is mine, but I'd prefer to announce it myself and avoid having a horde of entertainment magazines harassing you." He unbuckled himself and climbed out.

I'd barely found the handle on my side when the door moved for me and a very amused Wyatt stood waiting. "You're cute when you're flustered, Avery."

"I'm not." I cleared the raspiness from my throat and managed to plant my feet on the ground. "Uh, thanks."

"I grew up in the South. I have some manners." He winked and slid his shades back over his eyes. "Shall we?"

73

10

AVERY

The preschool handled all the paperwork without batting an eye. Wyatt completed a form and provided a copy of his photo identification for them to scan into their records.

No one seemed to recognize him, but they were definitely intrigued by our request not to disclose his paternity to Jamie. It likely wasn't every day a father requested to remain anonymous to his child.

"Garrett will want them to sign NDAs this week," he murmured as we walked toward Jamie's classroom.

"NDAs, as in nondisclosure agreements?"

"Yes. It's more to protect Jamie than it is to protect me. This is complicated enough already without the tabloids breathing down our necks."

I hadn't considered any of that, even after I learned of Wyatt's family identity. It wasn't a lifestyle I knew anything about. "What will Jamie's life be like after they find out?"

"He'll be well protected, but his world will be changed irrevocably. It's part of the reason I agreed to let him stay with Jean. I didn't want to remove him from a normal life. No child deserves that."

Interesting. "So you had no idea she wasn't actively involved with him?" I asked as we paused outside the classroom door.

"She provided me with regular updates that I'm starting to believe came from you."

My hands fisted at my sides at the very real possibility that she'd used my words to update the father—a man I never knew existed. "I texted her photos and comments almost every day."

"And she must have forwarded them to me."

A low growl of disapproval emanated from me, born of frustration and fury. "If she were still alive, I'd strangle her."

He chuckled. "I do believe I'd enjoy seeing that."

Of course he would. Men loved catfights. "It wouldn't end in our underwear. I promise you that."

"Pity." He pressed his lips to my ear. "I think I'd rather enjoy seeing you in nothing but a thong and maybe a bra. Preferably lace."

Heat rushed up my neck in response. *This man!* How the heck did I respond to that? I had no idea if he meant it or merely wanted to rile me up.

The door opened, saving me from having to reply, and Miss Greene smiled up at me. "Hi, Miss Perry." Her hazel eyes flickered to Wyatt and widened. "Oh. Hello."

"This is Mister Mershano." I gestured toward him like she wouldn't know whom I was referring to and lamely added, "Miss Greene is Jamie's teacher."

Wyatt held out his hand. "Wyatt."

"Gretchen," she replied, her cheeks flushing as she pressed her palm to his. It seemed to be the way all women reacted in his presence.

No wonder he'd laughed at me for saying he paid for sex. I hadn't meant he needed to purchase pleasure, just that he spent a lot of time with escorts, models, and would-be hookers. Or so the gossip magazines claimed, anyway. From what I'd observed this week, he seemed like a normal guy. Well, a normal guy with a hefty bank account and a swagger most men would envy.

"Nice to meet you." The low, sexy quality of his voice seemed more appropriate for the bedroom, not the preschool hallway. Paired with the seductive grin flirting over his lips, it was a wonder Miss Greene hadn't fainted.

Her mouth opened and closed, words escaping her. I understood the feeling.

"Rebel friend!" Jamie came running toward us with his book bag hanging off one shoulder. His brown eyes were on Wyatt, his grin wide; then it morphed into a glorious smile when he realized I stood beside him. "Auntie A! I missed you!"

I bent just in time to receive his hug and pressed my nose to his mop of brown hair. He'd need a cut soon, but it could wait another week.

"We played more goose games today. It was sooo awesome. And I made you something. Hold on." He pulled his pack off and unzipped it eagerly. A paper appeared before my nose. I had to crane my neck back to see the stick-figure drawing properly. "Miss Greene said it's Friday, so I drew a pizza with you, rebel friend, and me." He sounded very proud of himself.

"It's beautiful. Why don't you show Wyatt?" I stood and fixed my freshly wrinkled shirt.

Jamie eagerly lifted the drawing for Wyatt's perusal. "See!"

"Wow, I had no idea you were an artist, Jamie." Wyatt's expression and voice radiated approval, just like a dad's should. "Is that a pepperoni pizza?"

Jamie beamed. "Yep. Because it's pizza day!"

"We just had pizza on Wednesday," I reminded him.

"Oh." Jamie's face fell. "But it's Friday. We alllways have pizza, Auntie A. Can't we have pizza again? Maybe cheese instead of pespers-onis?"

"Pep-per-oni," I corrected him slowly.

"Pepser-onis." He grinned proudly, assuming he'd said that correctly. "Pleeeaasseeee!"

Wyatt gave me a bemused look. "He really loves pizza."

"You have no idea." I never should have started the Friday night pizza tradition. It seemed to be his sole focus for food, and he always wanted to know how many days until Friday.

"I'll leave you all to sort your dinner plans," Miss Greene said, smiling. "Nice to meet you, Wyatt."

"Likewise." He flashed her a polite smile before shifting his focus to Jamie. "So, what's the best way to talk your aunt into having pizza again tonight?"

Jamie grinned and waggled his finger at Wyatt, indicating he wanted him to bend down so he could whisper in his ear. "I'll show you," he said far too loudly to be stealthy.

Wyatt smiled. "Okay."

A pair of beautiful brown eyes gazed up at me with the most pathetic, pleading expression ever. "Pleeease, Auntie A. Pleeeaassseee." Jamie added the lip wobble.

Clever kid.

Manipulative, too.

I shook my head, charmed despite the obvious ploy to trick me into another pizza night. "Fine, but I'm picking the toppings." I never could deny this kid. He was too damn cute.

"Yes!" He danced around and nearly tripped over his bag. Wyatt caught him and set him upright while chuckling.

"Your aunt is that easy, huh?" Humor touched his dark gaze as he glanced at me. "I'll remember that trick."

I rolled my eyes. "It won't work for you."

"Perhaps not that particular one, but I have several others at my disposal, Miss Perry. Consider that your only warning."

My heart skipped a beat at the promise in his voice. He must have heard it, because his dimples deepened.

"There's that flustered look again," he teased.

Jamie managed to put his bag back together on his own,

hopefully with the picture inside. As it wasn't lying on the ground near us, I assumed he remembered it. He put both arms through the straps this time and held out his hand for mine. "Ready!"

"Good job, Jamie." He was a good kid, minus the pizza obsession. "Let's go home and order some pizza."

* * *

Wyatt played cars with Jamie while I finished up a few work emails. For the first time since Mershano's arrival, I saw the benefit to him being here.

This was no longer a one-person job.

I had someone in the house to help me.

The novelty of it struck me again after dinner when he offered to clean up.

And again when he offered to read Jamie a bedtime story. I stood in the door watching as the two of them lay on the twin bed, snuggled up in obvious contentment.

Wyatt's deep voice provided a new quality to the story-time routine that seemed to have Jamie entranced.

I couldn't really blame him.

Wyatt's changing tones and smooth transitions hypnotized me as well.

As did the sliver of skin peeking at me along his hip bone. His shirt had inched up just enough to provide a glimpse of the goods, and my eyes refused to ignore it.

Mmm.

I tried to remind myself that he slept with my sister, but his comments about not remembering any of it hindered my ability to feel disgusted by that thought. If anything, my disgust was at her for drugging him.

Assuming he'd told me the truth.

Why would he lie?

I spent hours last night debating the veracity of his words and couldn't find a single reason for him to make up such a story. His demeanor had been flat but genuine. And it explained the hatred I picked up from him whenever he mentioned Jean.

What did you do to him? I wondered, not for the first time. *And why didn't you tell me?*

"Good night, Jamie," Wyatt whispered as he slid out of bed.

Jamie didn't reply. He'd fallen asleep while listening to the story, and his peaceful expression warmed my heart. It seemed to match the one his father wore as he stepped into the hallway.

Like father, like son.

My goal of proving Wyatt to be an unfit parent seemed to be hanging by a loose thread. I couldn't deny how good he was with him, though we were only on day two. Everything could change after a week, or even a month.

He softly closed the door and turned to lean back against it. He didn't say anything, just stared down at me with an unreadable expression, waiting.

"Thank you." The words sort of tumbled out without my permission, and I wasn't quite sure what they meant, but they sounded right.

He grinned. "If anyone owes a debt of gratitude, it's me. To you."

I swallowed as he stepped into my personal space. His shirt brushed mine, causing me to retreat until my back hit the wall. He rested his forearm over my head and captured my gaze with his smoldering irises.

"Do I make you nervous, Avery?"

"N-no."

His eyes dropped to my lips. "No?"

I shook my head because my mouth refused to voice the word again.

"Then I'm not doing my job right," he murmured, moving even closer. His arm remained above my head while his opposite hand caught my hip, holding me in place. "How about now?"

My pulse raced, but still, I shook my head. *Nervous* wasn't the word I'd use to describe the way he made me feel.

Hot. Excited. Terrified. All far better adjectives.

"Mmm. I think you're lying, Avery." He skimmed his nose along my cheekbone, and my breath halted. "You're shaking." He continued his path down my neck and up to my ear. "Perhaps *aroused* is the better term."

I wanted to call him presumptuous or cocky, but the words stuck in my throat. My thighs clenched—accepting his summarization without preamble—while my brain fought for reason. I shouldn't be allowing this… or enjoying it.

His thumb slipped beneath my shirt to caress the skin just above my jeans near my hip. Electricity zipped through my veins at the soft touch, stirring an erratic rhythm inside my chest.

More, my body demanded.

He chuckled. "More, hmm? What did you have in mind?"

Shit. I must have said that out loud. "I… This…" *Words, Avery. Use them.*

But I had nothing.

I shouldn't want him, but I did. Maybe because I hadn't been with a man in far too long. A little adult time was extremely overdue.

His mouth skimmed mine, melting my insides. I swore he grinned, as if sensing my crumbling resolve.

It felt forbidden. Wrong. Scandalous.

I barely know him.

Who cares?

"You're not ready," he whispered. "But I'm not known for my patience."

His tongue parted my lips in an unforgiving kiss that stole my breath. He didn't wait for me to accommodate, just took what he wanted without remorse. It was domineering, hard, and exactly what I craved.

He kissed me deeply, exploring every inch of my mouth. Confidence poured out of him. He knew how to move his tongue and proceeded to prove it with a severity that left me quivering against him.

Flames danced along my skin, shooting sensations through every inch of my being.

Ready or not, I would have given in to whatever sexual act he desired in this moment.

Because wow.

I wasn't inexperienced, but he left me feeling like a woman receiving her first kiss. He had moves I didn't know existed.

My panties soaked straight through under his assault, preparing my body for whatever he had in mind. I'd take whatever he offered, however he offered it.

His thumb continued to stroke my hip while his other arm remained above me. This was all about his mouth and retraining my tongue to meet his preferences.

He broke the kiss as suddenly as it had started and pressed his forehead to mine. I panted against him, shaking with need and the desire for so much more. When I angled my face to resume our kiss, he pulled away to study me with his grinning eyes.

"I'm going to retire to my room early. If you want to join me, you're welcome to, but give yourself ten minutes to decide first." He pushed off the wall and opened the door beside me. "Consider it an open invitation."

Wyatt left me gasping for air in the hallway.

Holy shit.

I closed my eyes and focused on remembering how to breathe. Slowly, sanity returned, reminding me of all the reasons why stepping into his room was a bad idea.

Jamie.

Jean.

It would make everything more awkward.

Wyatt's a notorious playboy who only wants sex.

But we are consenting adults, and I could use a few decent orgasms in my life.

Not from him. He could take Jamie from you in a heartbeat.

This could all be a test.

Would he do that?

I barely knew him. He could be capable of anything. Another reason not to sleep with him.

I scrubbed a hand over my face and slid to the ground with my knees tucked to my chest.

God, that kiss… It served as an introduction to his methods and skill.

He'd blown my mind, and I had no doubt that would translate in bed. But was a night of pleasure truly worth it? With a stranger who had the ability to relocate Jamie and keep me from seeing him?

No.

I couldn't risk that. Not for anything. No matter how good it might feel.

Jamie meant so much more to me than that.

Wyatt could so easily have ulterior motives. Not that he needed them in order to leave with his son.

I pressed my forehead to my knees, conflicted and confused. Sleeping with him tonight couldn't happen. I needed to learn more about him, beyond the research from the other night.

I wanted to know the real Wyatt Mershano, not the one defined by the tabloids. But the man who cuddled Jamie and read to him with his heart in his eyes.

The one who offered to help me around the house, who studied me with an intensity denoting intelligence and astuteness, and who kissed me as if my body depended on him for survival.

An evening in his bed wouldn't be enough. I wanted all or nothing.

"Good night," I whispered to his door as I pulled myself off the floor to head toward my room. His bed offered mind-blowing orgasms, while mine offered safe ones.

I'd just have to rely on the safe option for tonight.

11
WYATT

God, I loved power tools.

Avery owned only the bare minimum, a fault I corrected this morning after running to the hardware store to gather some supplies. Her garage appeared brand new, thanks to my handy touch.

All the gardening items were in their own section on the wall. The tools, including the new ones, also had their own section. And everything else was partitioned off appropriately, including Jamie's two little outdoor riding toys.

They appeared to be a bit small for him, suggesting they were purchased last year. I'd have to rectify that this week, but first, I had something else in mind. And now that my work in the garage was complete, I could ask Jamie about it.

I grabbed my shirt from the floor and wandered into the house for a much-needed bottle of water. Avery stood at the sink in a pair of jeans that firmly hugged her ass and a tank top. The woman had a body built for a man's touch, yet she didn't show it off like most females I knew. I liked that about her.

Her back was to the entrance of the kitchen, allowing me to sneak up behind her. She'd been avoiding me all day after our kiss in the hallway. I knew she wouldn't join me in bed last night. She wasn't ready, and I could respect that.

But that didn't mean I was going to make this easy for her.

She shut off the water and turned right into my torso.

"Shit!" she yelled, stumbling.

I caught her hips to hold her upright and cocked my head to the side. "You all right, sweetheart? Didn't mean to startle you."

Her nostrils flared, and she slapped my chest. "You scared the shit out of me, you jackass!"

Jamie gasped loudly from the doorway. "Uh-oh! Those are no-no-no words, Auntie A!"

She blushed fiercely at Jamie's chastising tone while I hid a grin. *Definitely my kid.*

Avery cleared her throat. "I know, but sometimes adults use them in special circumstances."

"Your aunt is right." I pressed my lips to her ear and whispered, "And I can think of plenty adult circumstances for the word *fuck.*"

Her blush deepened, thrilling me to no end. She could fight it all she wanted, but we both knew she'd end up in my bed. And soon.

She grabbed the sink behind her—likely needing it for balance—as I stepped away to address Jamie. "I may have startled your aunt by accident." I crouched to be on his level, resting my elbows on my thighs. "Do you like soccer?"

Jamie considered, his little brow puckering. "I think so."

That meant he wasn't sure, but I'd change that. "It's my favorite sport. Would you want to go outside and kick the ball around with me?"

His expression brightened. "Like, right now?"

"Hmm, that depends on your aunt." The vegetables on

the counter suggested she'd just started preparing dinner. "Maybe we can go play out back while Avery finishes cooking?" I left it open as a question directed at her.

"We don't have a soccer ball," she said, sounding almost disappointed.

I grinned. "Oh, you do now. As well as a few other things." I added a stop on my way back from the home improvement store and picked up some items for Jamie, including a soft soccer ball meant for kids his age. "You mind if we kick the ball around out back? Or do you need help with dinner?"

She blinked as if dazed. "Uh, yeah, sure. I've got this. Just be careful?"

"Always." I winked at her and stood. "Ready, little man?"

"Yeah!" Jamie did a little jig that had me suppressing a laugh.

I snatched a bottle of water from the fridge and led him to the garage so we could grab the ball from the space I created in the corner for his toys. Jamie's eyes widened as he took in my improvements; then they grew to the size of dinner plates when he realized the ball wasn't the only item I had picked up for him.

"Is that a bi—bi-thickle?" he asked, awed.

"Yep, that's a bi-cy-cle." I pronounced it slowly for his benefit.

His brow scrunched. "Bi-sssickle."

"Close enough."

He smiled, pleased. Then frowned. "But I don't know how to ride one."

"Don't worry. I'll teach you." I ruffled his hair. "We'll play soccer first, though."

He nodded eagerly. "Le's go!" He started toward the driveway, but I caught his shoulder.

"Shoes," I reminded him. Mine were still on from working in the garage, but Jamie only had on a pair of socks.

"Ohhhhh." He skipped back to the door, plopped onto

the ground beside the mat, and slid on his Velcro sneakers. Good thing I hadn't tried to pick up cleats for him. They'd be too big, and he probably wouldn't know how to lace them up, either.

Jamie hopped up once he finished and announced, "Ready."

"Follow me." I led him around the side of the house to the reasonably sized backyard. The lack of fences made it appear larger but also removed any semblance of privacy. The trees were nice, though.

I chose a spot out in the middle and tossed the ball onto the ground. My jeans and tennis shoes weren't the best choice for this activity, especially with the sun bearing down on us, but I didn't have a lot of clean clothes left. My shipment from the Mershano Suites in New York City—my preferred residence over all of my inherited properties— would have what I needed. But for today, I'd survive.

"All right, little man. Do you know how to kick the ball?"

"Yup." His foot connected with the soccer ball and sent it about ten feet. Pretty good for a kid his size.

I jogged over and tapped it right back to him. Then he sent it off to my left. So his directional skills weren't great, but those could be perfected over time. Especially with the impressive distance he could kick.

We passed the ball several times, each kick to me a little off and forcing me to move. I paused to pick up the water and took a long drink—something I should have done before—and removed my black shirt. Atlanta was too fucking hot for April.

I dropped both items to the ground behind me.

Jamie kicked again and eyed me curiously. "Do you like my Avery?"

I nearly tripped over my feet at his blunt question.

He's four.

He couldn't possibly mean that the way it sounded.

"Uh." I palmed the back of my neck. "Your aunt is nice, yes."

"So you like her?" His brown eyes shone with curiosity. "I like her lots. She doesn't have friends. Not like me. I have lots of friends, like at my school."

That surprised me. "She doesn't have friends?"

He shook his head. "Nope. Auntie A says I'm all she's got." He sounded quite proud about that. "Well, 'cept Momma Jean buuuuut Auntie A says she's not comin' back dis time. But I dunno. She sometimes visits. Maybe she'll bring some angels." He shrugged as if that all sounded completely normal to him.

I skipped the ball over to him. "So your Momma Jean didn't come by much, huh?"

"Nah. But dats s'okay. She makes my Avery sad. I don't like when she's sad." He kicked the ball and added, "Please don't make my Avery sad, 'kay? 'Cause I like her happy."

Astute kid. He was talking about the other night. "I promise not to be mean to her."

"Good, cause Momma Jean wasn't very nice to my Avery sometimes. She liked to yell so looouddd." He sounded exasperated by it, and I couldn't blame him one bit. I'd been on the receiving end of her yelling more than once. "But you like my Avery, so you'll be nice to her. 'Kay?"

Back to that again.

"I'll be nice to her," I agreed. Same thing as not being mean to her, but I didn't feel like explaining that to Jamie. Nor would I add in what ways I wanted to be nice to her. Far too inappropriate for a kid.

"Oookay." He ran to the side, similar to what I'd been doing each time he kicked, and I booted the ball to him. "I think my Avery likes you, too."

"Yeah?"

"Yep."

"What makes you say that?" I jogged to the side to catch his pass and stopped it with my shoe.

He shrugged. "She lets you sleep over."

Let probably wasn't the right word. "You okay with me staying with you?" I should have asked him that sooner, as in two days ago, but it'd been a whirlwind. Moving in hadn't been my plan when I arrived in Atlanta on Wednesday morning.

"Yeah, I like it. You play with me."

"Avery doesn't play with you?"

Jamie zigzagged a little unsteadily as the ball came toward him. "Avery's the only one who plays with me." He eyed the black-and-white-spotted sphere. "Momma Jean never did. She wasn't very nice. I like you better."

"I like you, too, little man," I replied, my throat itching with emotion.

His words both pleased and infuriated me. A son should love his mother, but he spoke of her as if he barely knew her. As if she were a passing friend of Avery's whom he didn't really care one way or the other about. No wonder he didn't mourn her.

Shit.

I like you better. Those words kicked me in the heart.

I wanted him to like me, even though he had every reason to hate me. I'd essentially paid someone else to care for him until now.

Of course, I'd been operating under the assumption it was the right thing to do. I knew from experience how much it hurt to be ripped from a loving mother's arms. No child should experience that.

I'd also wanted to protect him from the Mershano family life because there was nothing charming about it.

Seeing him grin now as we played a child's version of soccer made me realize how much I'd missed of his little life.

How stupid I'd been to give all that up to a woman I barely knew.

I thought it was the best decision for Jamie, but clearly, Jean hadn't upheld her side of the bargain.

Or maybe she had, just in a way I hadn't anticipated. Jamie didn't call Avery his mother, but his actions and words showed how much he cared about her. She'd been the one to raise my son in the way I should have from the beginning, and I would have, had I realized Jean's intentions.

All those calls where she threatened to tell the tabloids suddenly made sense. I'd wondered why a mother would willingly subject her son to that lifestyle, and now I knew. She hadn't worried one bit how it would impact Jamie, just wanted the bottom line: my payment for her silence.

I should have followed my gut and looked into it, but instead, I had chosen to pay her so she'd shut the hell up.

It's for Jamie, I had thought. *In the end, it's the right thing to do.*

But she'd never given Jamie or Avery a dime. I felt sure of that now, despite only knowing them for a few days. Garrett's friend would provide proof soon enough. Although, it wasn't Avery's honesty I wanted to know more about now but Jean's secret life.

Where did all that money go?

12
AVERY

Wyatt Mershano was shirtless.

In my backyard.

Playing with Jamie.

My brain understood this, but my mouth seemed frozen in an open position, refusing the words I needed to say. *Dinner. Is. Ready.*

Three words.

Simple.

Why couldn't I shout them from the back door?

Wyatt laughed at something Jamie said, further dropping my jaw. I knew a decent body existed beneath the clothes, but a glistening six-pack in the early evening sun hadn't been part of my initial consideration.

It would certainly be ingrained in my memory now.

All that tan skin rippled as he moved, showcasing an athletic form crafted by God himself. I leaned against the door frame, just as I had last night outside Jamie's room, and shamelessly watched Wyatt jog to the ball.

My lips tingled with the memory of our kiss. I wanted to experience it again… and more. His abs would be fun to explore with my tongue, especially that little dip by his hip bone.

Mmm. Yes, please.

Electricity hummed through my veins, urging me to do something dangerous.

One night.

Not a good idea.

Who the hell cares with a body and a face like that?

Fair enough. I drew my thumb across my bottom lip as I considered all the ways I'd enjoy him. His dark eyes met mine, as if sensing my thoughts, and his mouth quirked at the corner.

He'd definitely caught me admiring him.

Oh well. The man was beautiful, and he knew it. Hence the saunter toward me now.

"Enjoying the show?" he asked, his voice deep and sensual.

"Yes." No point in denying it. Dinner was probably cold now. Maybe we could heat it up on his flat, hot stomach.

He held my gaze as he bent to pick up his shirt from the ground. His comment about a striptease the other day came back in a flash. I'd definitely be up for that with the way he moved—so sensuous and confident.

Wyatt stopped in front of me, still shirtless. "You're welcome to another one later, sweetheart."

"You two are being we-ord." Jamie pushed his way between us. "I'm hungry."

"He's hungry," Wyatt repeated, grinning. Then he cocked his head to the side. "What about you?"

I looked him up and down, emboldened by his flirtation. "Starved." This time, I winked at him and wandered inside after Jamie.

Wyatt's chuckle followed me, stirring butterflies in my belly.

I'm so screwed.

I nearly gave in to him last night. Had he not given me the space to think, I would have probably started stripping in the hallway and happily gone to his bed.

And regretted it in the morning.

Maybe.

I shook my head and focused on finding water for the boys while they washed up for dinner. They were both seated at the table by the time I turned around. I was only slightly disappointed to find Wyatt wearing his shirt.

Okay, more like full-on disappointed, but all that exposed skin would have me wanting to eat him instead of dinner. Better to hide the temptation.

Jamie dug in without preamble, mumbling his approval while Wyatt and I ate in silence. It wasn't so much awkward as it was peaceful. Almost as if we did this every night.

Could it be that easy?

No.

This was only temporary. Two months. Then who knew what would happen next.

Proving Wyatt to be an unfit father wasn't going to happen if the last two days were anything to go by. Despite the bad-boy façade he put on, he knew exactly how to talk to his son.

They were bonding faster than I could ever have anticipated. Maybe because Jamie needed a father figure in his life, or maybe because their souls already understood each other.

I couldn't compete with that. I loved Jamie more than anything and considered him mine, but he wasn't. Not fully. And he never would be now that Wyatt had entered our lives.

I set my fork down, no longer hungry.

"You all right?" Wyatt asked, his expression radiating concern.

"Yeah, just tired." Not exactly a lie. Thinking about our kiss in the hallway had kept me up half the night. I shook my head and forced a smile. "My eyes were bigger than my stomach."

"Hmm." He picked up his empty plate and stood. "Then I'll do the dishes while you relax."

"Oh, no, you—"

"It wasn't a request," he interjected. "You done, little man?"

"Yep!" He'd even finished all his vegetables without me forcing him. Not bad.

Wyatt grinned at his son and grabbed Jamie's plate. "I'll come back for yours, Avery. Just in case you want to eat more." He wandered off to the kitchen with me gaping after him.

What just happened?

"I like him," Jamie announced in one of his not-so-quiet whispers.

"Yeah?" It came out hoarse and startled. I snagged my glass, needing a drink. Too bad it wasn't wine.

"Yep." Jamie sounded quite pleased. "He plays with me. We're friends. You should play with him, too."

I choked on my water. He meant it innocently, but a not-so-innocent vision flashed behind my eyes. One that involved a very naked Wyatt.

"You're acting we-ord, Auntie A. And you're all red." His frown puckered his brow. "Are you sick?"

I cleared my throat. "No, I'm okay. Just..." Yeah, I had nothing else to say on that. "So you like him, huh?"

"Yep." His eyes brightened with his tone. "I think he's my new best friend 'cause he's older and knows stuff."

"What kind of stuff?"

"Like how to ride bikes. And kick the ball sup-per far. Oh! And he reads real good." He tapped his jaw. "Can rebel friend read to me again tonight? 'Cause I like his voices."

I like his voice, too. "You'll need to ask him." And what was that about riding bikes?

"'Kay." Jamie hopped off his chair and ran to the kitchen to tug on Wyatt's shirt.

"What's up, little man?" he asked, his lips curling in

amusement.

"Can you read again tonight? Pleeaasseeee?" He bounced a little with the words, and I knew he was giving Wyatt his best begging face.

"What'd Aunt Avery say?" He glanced at me with the question.

"To ask you," Jamie said, exasperated. "Pleeassse?"

"If she says it's okay, then I'd be happy to read to you again."

"She says it's okay," I told them both. But unlike last night, I'd avoid listening. No way did I want to get caught in the hallway again. I stood and took my plate over to Wyatt at the sink. "Thank you for cleaning up."

"You cooked. It's only fair." He winked and went back to his task.

Jamie tugged on my hand and asked to watch his favorite movie of the month. Again. For the fifteenth or thirtieth time. I'd lost count. There was no sense in asking him to change his mind, so I rolled with it and turned on what he wanted.

With him settled into his favorite seat, I wandered into my office to review some emails from yesterday. My work projects weren't behind yet, but I felt the deadlines sneaking up on me. I would be pulling some late nights this week.

There were a few items I could tick off the list now, though.

I cracked my knuckles and went to work and was surprised when Jamie popped into my office to kiss me good night. A glance at the clock showed I'd spent two hours updating the project proposals from two departments.

Damn.

I'd completed a lot, but time really did pass by quickly. After a hug and a kiss with Jamie and assurance from Wyatt that he would handle the nightly routine, I set about sending a final email. Then I forced myself to shut the computer down and enjoy what was left of my Saturday night.

Adult time on the couch.
Wine.
Popcorn.
Yes, please.

I crept upstairs, past Jamie's room, where Wyatt was still reading, and changed into a pair of yoga pants. My tank top from earlier suited the evening just fine, so I kept it on and quietly slipped by them again on my way back downstairs.

Five minutes later, I was curled into the corner of the couch with a bucket of freshly popped deliciousness in my lap and a glass of wine on the end table.

A scroll through my saved programs brought up the show I'd been binge-watching—or trying to, anyway—and selected the next episode.

So much better than Jamie's current sing-along obsession.

Eye candy, mystery, and action.

The perfect way to unwind for the evening. *Finally.*

13
WYATT

After a much-needed shower, I pulled on a pair of sweatpants and a white shirt. If my shipment didn't arrive Monday, I'd need to venture out for more clothes and then figure out how to use Avery's washer and dryer.

Living out of hotels most of my life had some benefits, like laundry service. Room service was also another key advantage, but I did enjoy Avery's home-cooked meal earlier.

Dinner drifted through my mind with a frown. Everything had been fine until it wasn't. Avery had flirted, even smiled. Then her playful side had just disappeared.

Whatever thought had killed the seductive air floating between us was about to be challenged. Because I wanted her. I shouldn't. But I did.

I wasn't the kind of man who ignored my needs, even when reason demanded me to. Perhaps that, even more so, was why I craved her. It was wrong, which made it far more fun.

I swept my fingers through my damp hair on my way down the stairs.

Avery glanced at me as I approached her on the couch, and ran her eyes over my attire before training them studiously on the television.

The faint hint of a blush touching her cheeks suggested she liked my casual outfit but not nearly as much as she enjoyed me shirtless outside. Interest had practically oozed from her from the back door, a look I understood well.

I settled beside her without a word and stole a piece of popcorn from the dish in her lap. She shot me a glare as I tossed it into my mouth.

"Sure, you can have some of *my* popcorn." The hint of irritation in her tone caused me to smile.

"Thanks, sweetheart." I draped my arm over the couch behind her head and leaned in to grab another kernel with my free hand. She jerked the bowl away, forcing me to reach across her to complete the action. It put my face beside hers, right where it belonged. "There are more polite ways to ask a man to cuddle, Avery."

She sputtered as I guided the dish back to her legs and grabbed a handful of her snack.

"There are more bags in the kitchen. Go heat up your own." Her nostrils flared, and her cheeks reddened. My sudden nearness appeared to make her uncomfortable. Too bad. She invited me over with that stunt, and I had no intention of moving now.

"I spent the afternoon reorganizing your garage and the early evening entertaining Jamie, I cleaned up after dinner, and I tucked Jamie in for the night. And now you want me to heat up my own popcorn?" I *tsked* and shook my head in mock disapproval. "I suppose that, next, you'll tell me I have no say over the television choice, either, right?" Not that I minded her pick of shows. I just wanted to rile her up. "What's a man have to do around here for a little gratitude?"

I meant it completely in jest, but her eyes rounded in mortification.

"Oh God, I'm being really rude. I'm... I'm not used to sharing. And this is all... What I mean is, I'm not... This isn't..." She groaned low in her throat and shut her eyes. Her face darkened to a delectable shade of cherry red that stirred all manner of inappropriate thought.

I lowered my arm from the couch to her shoulders and ran my thumb up the column of her neck. "You're adorable when flustered." And adorable in general. "And you're not being rude. Just protective of your popcorn." I snagged another piece while I spoke and brought it up to her lips. "It is delicious." She opened her mouth, accepting the kernel.

Smoky blue eyes met mine as she chewed and swallowed. I repeated the motion, this time dragging the popcorn across her lower lip first before sliding it inside. She licked the salty area slowly, her gaze holding mine the entire time.

"Thank you," she whispered.

"For?"

"Everything." Bemusement entered her features, and she shook her head, breaking the intensity of our eye contact. "This is all... bizarre. I worked tonight. On a Saturday. While you watched Jamie. I can't tell you the last time, if ever, that's happened."

"Jean never watched him for you?"

She laughed and picked up her wine to take a long sip. "No. When Jean visited, she spent most of her time playing on her phone. She didn't seem to know how to act around Jamie."

I nodded, considering. "He mentioned earlier that she never played with him."

"No. She barely spoke to him."

I studied Avery's profile as she finished her wine. A week ago, I would have called her a liar or laughed at this whole charade. But four days in, her company had me reconsidering everything I knew. There was a sincerity about her that Jean definitely lacked, not to mention Jamie's obvious feelings.

That report from Garrett's contact couldn't come fast enough. Once I had it, things would become even more complicated because I would have to determine the next steps. Letting Jamie go again wasn't an option, but I couldn't exactly take him from Avery, either. Not if her feelings were real.

I wanted to believe her, but the last Perry woman I trusted burned me.

She's not Jean.

No, she's definitely not.

I surveyed her ample breasts, flat stomach, and legs. Avery Perry was all mature woman—in the best way—and very much my type.

I always did enjoy playing with fire.

She set her empty wine glass aside and placed the bowl on the table. "I need to get another drink. Do you want anything?" she asked as my arm slid to her lower back.

I curled my hand around her hip. "Yes."

Avery faced me with a raised brow. "Water?"

"No."

"Wine?"

"I don't drink alcohol."

She swallowed, her gaze dropping to my mouth. "You don't?" she whispered.

"No."

Her brow furrowed. "But, the, uh…" She trailed off, but I knew what she'd been about to say.

"I warned you already not to believe everything you read, sweetheart." I played the media like an instrument, using them to help destroy my reputation because it pissed off Jonah. And pissing off Jonah made me very, very happy. "I haven't touched alcohol in over four years, Avery. Anything you've read or seen is either old or me putting on an act."

"Why?" she asked, her gaze finally returning to mine.

"Why do I put on an act? Or why don't I drink?" They were two entirely different answers.

"Both."

Of course she would say that. Talk about a buzzkill. I relaxed into the couch with a sigh, my hand dropping to the seat cushion near her ass. "Those are two very heavy topics, Avery."

She angled her body toward mine by drawing up her knee and using the armrest to support her back. It left my hand near her upper thigh, a place I wanted to explore more thoroughly, but it seemed she preferred to talk.

"I don't understand," she said.

No, I supposed she wouldn't. "Let's just say I enjoy irritating Jonah Mershano. And I don't drink because I prefer to keep my inhibitions under control. Particularly, after I lost them with your sister." And wasn't that a nice dose of reality for us both?

Avery's lips parted, then closed, then parted again. Normally, I liked the tongue-tied look on her. But not now.

I withdrew my arm, placing my hands in my lap, the mood completely killed. Thinking about Jean did that to me. Avery being her sister didn't help matters.

What is with me and these Perry women? Why do I constantly fall for their antics?

"How did you meet Jean?" Avery asked softly.

She wanted to go for a trip down memory lane? Fine. We could do that.

"We met at Harvard while I was in law school. She and her little sorority friends used to hang around our house on the weekends. We were just acquaintances at first. She liked to flirt. I didn't mind, and she spent a lot of time trying to get in my pants."

Blunt words, but true nonetheless.

"Alas, contrary to what the media says about me, I am actually very selective about who I fuck." I gave her a pointed look with the statement. "And your sister was too young for me, something I told her often. She eventually settled for just being friends." *Or so I thought.*

I reached around Avery for another handful of popcorn and ignored the shocked expression on her pretty face.

"Harvard?" she asked, her eyebrows in her hairline. "My sister convinced you she was a student at Harvard?"

I snorted. "No. She claimed to go to Boston College." One of the many things I later learned was an outright lie. "Her sorority friends never said otherwise, so I didn't think much of it, and she never gave me a reason to look into her background."

I shoved the kernels into my mouth, chewing harder than I needed to. Rehashing my history with Jean reminded me why I didn't trust anyone. Not that I ever really trusted her, either. It was more that I'd led a carefree existence, not giving a fuck about anyone or anything apart from myself. I just never expected her or anyone to betray me in the way she had.

But she'd played every part perfectly, worming her way into my life and digging her claws in deep without my knowledge. While not cluing me in to her asinine plans until it was too late.

"So you were friends?" Avery summarized.

"Yes, sure. I mean, we weren't close by any means, but I had her pegged as a bored girl who just wanted to have a good time." Little did I realize she was stealing from her drunk-ass friends and essentially impersonating them to fit into the lifestyle.

I refocused on the television, my mind darkening with the memories I hated to relive. But Avery wanted a story, so I'd give her one.

"Your sister had me fooled, and several others, too. Which is why my buddy Powell didn't really question her intentions when she came to visit us in New York City about five years ago, claiming she needed a place to crash."

Biggest fucking mistake of my life.

"She brought some friends. Alcohol was flowing. Typical Friday night." My hands curled into fists, the memory clear in my mind. Until it wasn't. "They warn women not to accept drinks from men they don't know, but they rarely warn men. Well, your sister played me very, very well." Because I'd accepted the drink she'd handed me without a thought. Noted the sour element to it, but I drank it anyway.

And woke up the next morning with the world's worst hangover.

Avery gasped, her mind piecing the clues together. "And that's when she drugged you." Not a question but a statement. I'd already given her the brief version. This was just the elaborated one.

Rather than confirm her statement, I stood, needing something cool to soothe my suddenly dry throat. I found a bottle of water in the fridge and grabbed the wine from the counter for Avery, knowing she'd intended to pour herself another glass.

She couldn't meet my gaze when I joined her on the couch again, so I left about a foot of space between us.

Dredging through the past killed whatever desire I harbored. Which was good. I needed to remember this shit because I'd been about to let my dick lead me down a similar path.

I knew nothing about this woman apart from her ancestry.

She was a fucking Perry.

They were skilled in the art of deception.

I knew that from experience. And wow, I'd almost been played. Again. What the fuck was wrong with me? I needed to give myself some space, to stop allowing my hormones to make decisions for me. What if Avery wanted to trap me, too? Create another kid to double the child support?

She didn't know anything about the money.

Or so she claims…

I glanced around her home again, frowning. None of it added up. The only logical explanation was that Avery really knew nothing, and her reactions now were one of disgust and shock, which suggested Jean had never told her this horror story.

But she could still be acting.

Right?

I ran my hand over my face, then downed the water from my bottle and shook my head. "This was a mistake." I couldn't seduce a woman I had so many concerns about. Trusting Avery might not be required to lure her into the bedroom, but I needed to be able to trust my own reactions to her afterward. And as of this moment, I couldn't.

"What?" she asked, the color draining from her face. "What do you mean?"

"Nothing." I stood, shaking my head again. "Nothing, Avery. I'm retiring for the night. I'll see you in the morning."

14
AVERY

I hit Send on my final work email of the day and checked the clock—four in the afternoon.

"Holy crap," I breathed, shocked.

It was the first time in months I felt caught up. All of my project spreadsheets were updated, every single task completed ahead of the due date, and my meetings for the next phase were already scheduled.

This had to be the most productive two weeks in the history of my employment.

I powered off my laptop and tucked it into my bag. Wyatt would be picking up Jamie right about now, a task he seemed to have adopted over the last fourteen days. I went with him the first Monday, only because I worried about the change in routine. However, he proved capable and offered to go alone the following day. And it'd become our routine ever since.

Which had afforded me the rare opportunity to return to the office for more than a few hours a week. Hence my clean desk and work-free weekend ahead. I couldn't remember the last time that had happened.

I slid on my jacket, pulled my laptop bag and purse over one shoulder, and locked up my office. My phone rang just as I turned on the car.

Recognizing Wyatt's number, I picked up the call. "Hello?"

"Auntie A!" Jamie's voice sang through the speakers of my SUV. "Guess what?"

"It's Friday," I said, knowing exactly where this was going. "Pizza day."

"Yesssssss, but tha's not ittttt," he sing-songed.

"More goose games?"

"Nope."

"Hmm." I drew out the hum while I worked on navigating out of the parking lot. Fortunately, my office wasn't too far from home, so I wouldn't be playing in Atlanta area afternoon traffic for too long. "Did you draw something new today?" I guessed again, turning right onto the four-lane road.

"Nope."

"I think you need to give her a hint," Wyatt said, his deep voice amused. Just hearing it sent a flurry of goose bumps down my arms. He'd been the epitome of professional roommate these last two weeks, giving me space and helping as needed while keeping his hands to himself. It was as if that conversation about Jean had flipped a switch between us, one that defined any flirtation as forbidden and wrong.

Which I appreciated, especially after catching him in the hallway in nothing but a towel—twice. But I couldn't seem to stop *reacting* to him.

Whenever he stepped too close, my heart rate escalated.

His voice warmed me in a way it shouldn't.

His smile tempted me.

His body, well, it was a work of art. The man liked to run every morning, and I'd made it part of my routine to watch him whenever he returned because he usually showed up shirtless. Wrong, perhaps. But fuck, he was hot.

Ugh, I hated feeling this way about him.

He slept with Jean. Sure, it hadn't exactly been consensual, but it still seemed wrong to lust after him. And he clearly didn't feel the same way. Whatever game he'd been playing those first few days had died, and all he'd done since was act as the perfect father to his child. Something I adored and hated at the same time.

There was absolutely no way I would find him unfit as a parent.

None whatsoever.

Yet, he could take Jamie whenever he wanted. A concern that—

"Auntie A!" Jamie yelled through the speaker.

I shook my head, clearing it. "What, dude?"

"Why aren't you guessing?" he demanded. "I tolds you tha' we're going on a thing that flieessssss. Highhhhh up, Auntie A. Can you guesssss? Guess? Guess…" He started to chant loudly, causing me to frown.

"Fly?" I repeated, my heart skipping a beat. "Like on a plane?"

"Yesssss!" he cheered. "Zoom! Zoom!"

"Like, right now?" I asked, my voice cracking at the end. This couldn't be happening.

He'd just misunderstood whatever Wyatt had told him. It's fine.

They weren't actually going—

"Nooooow, Auntie A. Yesss. Are you not listenin'? 'Cause I already explains it to you."

Wyatt chuckled in the background while my hands gripped the steering wheel. "You're going on a plane? Right now?"

"Yep."

My lungs burned from the lack of air, my eyesight blurring. I pulled off the road into a complex and parked the car, my heart in my throat. "Where are you going?" I asked.

"New…" His voice trailed off. "How you say, again?"

"New Orleans," Wyatt said slowly.

"New Or-lenssss," Jamie repeated, confirming my worst fears.

"When?" I squeaked.

"Now, Auntie A. She's not hearing good. Here. You explains better." There was a fumbling of the phone, a swish of sound.

And the line went dead.

"Jamie?" I knew he couldn't hear me, but his name left my lips anyway. And again. Twice more. Before my brain kicked in and I dialed back Wyatt's number.

It went straight to voicemail.

This had to be a misunderstanding, some sort of fucked-up joke.

We were fine.

Everything was fine.

We were even getting along. Or so I thought. Why would he…? No. No, he wouldn't. He'd… He'd talk to me, right?

His lawyer's words replayed through my thoughts…

"Wyatt can void the agreement at will should he decide the arrangement is no longer suitable, and he maintains full custody of his son. You, Miss Perry, are in no way considered the primary caregiver by law, meaning Wyatt can remove Jamie at any time."

"But he would tell me…," I whispered to no one. "He'd tell me if he was taking Jamie."

I tried his phone again.

Still voicemail.

"This is all just a misunderstanding," I told myself. "A mistake. They'll be home when I get there."

Except they weren't.

Wyatt's SUV was nowhere to be found when I pulled into the garage twenty minutes later, my hands clammy, my eyes refusing to blink.

My heart stuttered as I entered the house, Jamie's name falling from my lips on autopilot as I checked every room.

I called again. And again. And it never fucking rang. Just a monotone telling me I'd reached the voicemail of Wyatt's phone number. I left a message. It was incoherent. So I hit Redial and tried again. But words seemed to be failing me.

Jamie's stuff was still in his room.

Wyatt's, too.

But they were gone.

Nowhere to be found.

I ran through the house, checking the garage again. Nothing. This… I couldn't… *No*.

A paper on the kitchen counter caught my eye. My name was at the top.

"Try to relax this weekend," I read out loud. "Wyatt." I blinked at the spa schedule laid out beneath it. He'd booked me a massage and pedicure. "Is this some sort of fucking joke?" I demanded, glaring at the offending item.

Had he really just taken the most important person in my life from me and expected me to *relax*?

I grabbed my phone and dialed Scott, which, of course, went to his voicemail as well.

Was no one in this world available?

I can call the police.

And tell them what? The father of my sister's child had taken him from me? I had no legal rights. That was the whole purpose of the adoption that never happened because Wyatt showed up.

My knees buckled beneath me.

I landed hard on the kitchen floor, the spa schedule in one hand, my phone in the other.

"What do I do?" I whispered. "Jamie…" I wasn't ready to say goodbye. I… I thought we were in a good place. I thought Wyatt would at least work with me on this, not just take my only reason for being from me.

A choked sound left my throat.

Jamie…

He'd been my world for four years. My everything. To have him ripped from me…

"...if I said yes, that I plan to take him with me, what would you do?"

Wyatt's cruel words played through my heart, my head, my being. He'd warned me in his own way this might happen. Then lulled me into a false sense of comfort, just to cruelly rip apart my world in the span of seconds.

I curled on the floor into a ball, tears rolling down my cheeks as I fought to remember how to breathe. But the ache in my chest made it impossible.

"Jamie..." I thought I'd at least have a chance to say goodbye before this happened, could have at least spoken to him... explained. Told him how much I loved him. Worked out a deal to see him.

But I didn't even know where Wyatt would take him in New Orleans. Didn't have another number to reach him... and the one I had refused to fucking ring! "How could you do this to me?" I begged, sobbing. I didn't know if it was to his voicemail or to the room, and I couldn't bring myself to care.

Why did it always fall on me to pay for my sister's sins? Because this had to be what it was about, his cruel chance at revenge.

And yes, what she did to him was horrible. "But it wasn't me... It's not me... I love him... my Jamie..." My stomach heaved from the onslaught of emotion, my body shivering and heating at the same time. "*Why*?!"

The phone began to buzz, and I answered immediately. "Jamie?"

"No, it's Scott. What's going on, Avery? Your voicemail was incoherent."

My chest deflated, all my hope gone. "He took him," I whispered. "He's gone."

"What?" Scott's confusion came through in that single word. "Are you talking about Jamie?"

"He took him," I repeated, unable to say anything else, my heart broken beyond repair.

"Wyatt?"

I nodded, then realized he couldn't see me and muttered something in the affirmative. Or, at least, I tried to, but it came out more like a cry.

"I need you to take a few deep breaths and tell me what's going on, Avery."

Deep breaths. I almost laughed, which created another strangled sound.

"Avery, honey, I can't help you if I don't know what's going on. Where did Wyatt take Jamie?"

"New Orleans," I managed, my voice soft and broken. "He took him to New Orleans."

15
WYATT

"Why the hell are you ignoring my calls?" Garrett demanded as he entered my New Orleans condo without knocking. He'd mentioned his plans to fly in from Houston for the weekend, but I'd expected him to bother my brother upstairs. Not pester me.

This was why I hated family gatherings. No one understood the importance of personal space.

"You're not planning to brood all weekend alone with the kid, are you?" he asked, sounding exasperated. "Because that's boring as hell."

"Could you keep your voice down? I just got Jamie to fall asleep." The kid had been all amped up after the flight and dinner. He'd wanted to call *Auntie A* to tell her all about his night, then started crying when I reminded him why he couldn't. It took thirty minutes to calm him down and convince him I wasn't mad. "As to why I'm not answering, Jamie dropped my phone at the airport."

Where it had shattered into pieces.

Technically, we could have used a landline to call Avery tonight, but I really wanted to give her the weekend off. The woman worked so damn hard. She deserved a break.

"The kid is in bed already?" Garrett glanced at his watch. "It's only nine."

"Yeah, his bedtime is seven thirty," I replied. "*Eastern.*" Avery would be pissed if she knew how late I'd let him stay up. After observing her over the last two and a half weeks, I'd learned a few things about the habits she'd instilled in Jamie. She was, quite simply, amazing with him.

Which was why I'd decided on this spur-of-the-moment trip.

I needed a vacation away from Avery Perry before I did something stupid. Like kiss her again. And then fuck her up against a wall.

The damn female chipped at my resolve more each day, proving with every second how different she was from her sister. But my past left me conflicted, unable to trust, and Avery deserved better than that.

Nothing between us could be just a fling. Not with Jamie sitting right in the middle of our future.

Hence, I'd agreed to travel here for a tux fitting—for a wedding I still didn't want to attend—because I needed a distraction. I couldn't handle two full days of Avery being in the house and easily accessible. Not with my impulses running so damn hot around her.

She was probably home right now, watching a movie in those sexy-as-sin yoga pants and tank top. If she wore those around me one more time, I couldn't be held liable for ripping them off to explore the curves beneath.

Just thinking about the prospect of it made me hard as a rock.

I'm so fucked.

"Bedtime?" Garrett's mocking tone brought me back to him in the living room. "Look at you, sounding like a dad."

Asshole. "I *am* a dad." Something that had become increasingly evident over the last few weeks—an experience

I wouldn't turn down for anything in the world.

"True." He collapsed onto one of the recliner chairs near the floor-to-ceiling windows and braced his elbows on his knees. "Speaking of which, Kincaid is on his way here to deliver the details on the Perrys. Something I would have given you more of a notice about had you answered your phone."

"Ordering a new one is on my task list for tomorrow." Assuming I even had time. I left Garrett for the freshly stocked fridge and grabbed a water and a beer. Finding a bottle opener, I popped off the bottle cap and returned to the living area.

"Thanks," Garrett said, accepting the beer and taking a long swallow. "It's weird meeting with you here."

I snorted as I sat on the couch across from him, kicking up my feet onto the coffee table. "Tell me about it."

I hadn't set foot inside this property in almost five years, despite owning it. This was, after all, one of the family residences inside the Mershano Suites home location in downtown New Orleans. Evan owned the penthouse on the top floor, while Jonah had assigned me to the floor just below it.

Garrett's phone rang, causing him to answer with a "What?" He listened, his expression darkening. "What part of *I'm taking the weekend off* didn't you get?" He shook his head. "No. That was a rhetorical question. I pay you to field calls. So field them. I'll handle things on Monday." He paused again, sighing. "Is someone dying?" He arched a brow. "Have any of my clients been arrested?" He snorted. "Then it can wait until Monday. Goodbye, Alicia."

He hung up before his poor assistant could say another word.

Why the sweet woman tolerated him, I didn't know. Actually, I wasn't sure why most people tolerated Garrett Wilkinson. They called him The Devil inside the courtroom and outside of it. Oh, he could put on the charm better than anyone I knew, but beneath the expensive exterior lived a man who thrived on cruelty. Definitely a sadist. And the women loved him. Including his sweetheart of an assistant.

"She's going to quit on you one of these days," I said, amused. *Or, at least, she damn well should.*

"Alicia?" Garrett scoffed and took another swig of his beer. "I pay her very well. Which is why she should know better than to bother me with irrelevant details."

"Maybe it was important."

"All my clients are healthy and not currently seeking legal help. The rest can wait, including whatever message she received that *sounded* urgent. I'll judge that on Monday." He shrugged and relaxed back into his chair with a bored expression.

Fair enough.

I gulped down my water while he enjoyed his beer, the silence companionable and over too quickly as the elevator opened in the foyer. "Did reception forget that I live here and that they should call before sending people up?" I wondered out loud.

"Skeleton key," Evan replied as he entered with a woman at his side. "You know, since I own the hotel."

"And here I thought this was *my* floor," I drawled, not bothering to stand in greeting.

"Just as charming as ever," my big brother said, sarcasm thick in his voice.

"At least he's sober," Garrett pointed out, grinning as he set down his empty bottle.

"That's something," Evan agreed.

I didn't bother commenting. They both knew I didn't drink anymore, even though the media enjoyed saying otherwise. I eyed the dark-haired beauty beside Evan. "You must be my future sister-in-law." She was pretty enough, I supposed. But she lost significant points for being desperate enough to go on a reality dating show to secure a husband.

She arched a brow. "And you must be my future brother-in-law. I hear you're a real rebel."

I smiled, not at all bothered by the jibe because I already

had a return comment waiting and ready for her. "Better a rebel than a gold digger, sweetheart," I replied, lifting my bottle in mock salute.

Evan's expression morphed into one of pure rage. "You will not—"

His future bride pressed her palm to his chest. "Oh, I've got this." She turned a succulent smile my way, her smoldering dark eyes giving away her true intent. "From what Evan tells me, you're fully aware of how the media can twist a story. So you'll understand when I tell you not to believe everything you read."

"Does that mean you didn't meet my brother as a contestant on *The Prince's Game*?" I asked, knowing full well that was how they met.

"Are you aware that I have an identical twin sister?" she countered.

"Garrett may have mentioned it." Something about not desiring her, which I didn't understand. Sarah wasn't bad to look at, which meant her sister would be just as appealing. At least physically. And Garrett typically only cared about the exterior.

"Abby—Sarah's sister—auditioned on her behalf," Garrett explained, ruining the woman's punch line and earning a glower from her. "I drafted the contract between them during the show. They essentially staged everything except for their clear feelings for one another." He sounded disgusted by the end of his explanation, earning him a look from my big brother.

"The whole thing was a gambit?" I asked, actually intrigued. "And no one thought to tell me until now?"

"Not like I see or speak to you very often," Evan drawled.

"Yet, you want me to be part of this farce of a wedding party and play the loyal little brother." I smirked. "I'm so honored."

"You're family," Evan replied. "I want you there."

"You want me there, or Jonah wants me there?" I

searched his expression and smiled when I caught the flicker of hesitation in his brown eyes—eyes that rivaled my own. "Yeah, that's what I thought."

"Look, it's not—"

I waved him off. "I don't need an explanation, big brother. I'm here for the tux fitting, and maybe I'll show up in a few weeks." I shrugged. "Or maybe I won't. Either way, you can tell our *father* that you tried."

Our eight-year age gap had always weighed heavily between us. Evan was twelve when my father first brought me home. He'd been an only child for over a decade, and I'd quickly become the ugly thorn in his parents' side. The bastard child our father forced Evan's mother to claim as her own. Even had her name put on my birth certificate.

It made me the enemy from day one.

Which only worsened when Jonah forced me to live at the Mershano estate full-time at the ripe age of five. It broke my birth mother's heart. I learned later that she died shortly after, something Jonah never told me.

Because he was an asshole.

Regardless, it stood to reason Evan never cared for me much. And Jonah didn't help matters by constantly lording my existence over his head.

Hell, it was my fault Evan had to go on the damn dating show to begin with.

The stupid Mershano inheritance clause said the eldest had to produce an heir by his thirty-eighth year or forfeit his claim. It would have been a moot threat had I not created Jamie. Naturally, Jonah held my son over Evan's head, forcing my big brother to engage in a compromise that led to *The Prince's Game*.

Thus, the resulting engagement.

And now, as he'd just turned thirty-seven, the two lovebirds would finally wed, thereby securing his claim to Mershano Suites.

As if I desired a future in hotel management.

I just wanted to be left alone.

"Can you both give us a moment?" Evan asked, glancing at his bride-to-be and Garrett.

Oh, great. Big brother wants to have a chat. These never ended well.

"I need another beer anyway," Garrett said, hopping up and hooking his arm around Sarah's shoulders. "Gives me a chance to have the best-friend chat with the bride, too."

"How exciting," she deadpanned. "Are you going to try to force another prenup on me?"

He chuckled as he guided her away. "Your fiancé won't let me."

"Damn straight," my brother called after him. "Jackass," he added under his breath as he took over the chair Garrett had just vacated. Evan hooked his ankle over his opposite knee and stared at me.

I finished my water while I waited, setting it aside and mimicking his position with an arched brow. If he thought I intended to speak first, then we'd be playing the silent game for a while.

"*I* want you there," Evan said slowly, his gaze intense. "Not because of our father but because of me. I gave up trying to please that man a decade ago. And before you say I went on that damn charade of a show to appease him, I didn't. I agreed because I wanted to protect the company. Not from you but from *him*."

"He would have just put you in charge anyway," I pointed out.

"And you would have done everything in your power to rebel. Right?"

I lifted a shoulder. "I guess we'll never have to know, will we?"

"You know I'd share all of this with you; just say the word."

"I don't want it."

"I know."

"It was never mine," I added. "This whole life. I never wanted any of it."

117

"That doesn't stop you from enjoying it, though, does it?"

I snorted. "You think you understand me and what I do. But you don't."

"I understand a lot more than you give me credit for," he retorted. "Everything you do is a *fuck you* to the old man, but deep down, that's not who you are at all. You're brilliant. You're caring. And you're loyal to a fault."

"And here I thought you knew nothing about me," I drawled, deflecting.

"Cut the act, Wyatt. You can pull this shit with Jonah but not with me. I'm telling you I want you at the wedding as my brother, not because I'm being told to, not because I have to, but because I *want* to. And if you would take five minutes to get to know Sarah, you'd see that this wedding is all about what we want, not what anyone else expects."

"Is that why it's a two-week affair?" I asked, actually curious. Because who required attendees to stay for fourteen fucking days?

His eyes narrowed. "Sarah wanted a vacation more than a wedding. We compromised."

"A vacation?"

"She thinks I work too much."

"You do," I agreed.

Evan sighed and ran his fingers through his hair. "Well, you know, if I had more help…"

"No." He'd done this to me before, offered to share the company with me. "I'm not interested."

He stared me down for a long moment, then shook his head. "I'm not our father, Wyatt."

"I know."

"Then why do you hate me as much as you hate him? You don't think I suffered, too? That I didn't hate every moment of our childhood?"

"You had Will."

"And you had Mia," he tossed back, not missing a beat. "We both had our escapes, but we should be allies here.

118

Jonah Mershano is the devil. Not me."

I fucking hated this argument. We had it almost every time I saw him. Granted, the last time was about five years ago in this same fucking room. And it had ended with me throwing one hell of a party, one the media caught wind of and plastered all over the gossip mags. Jonah had been furious. I'd been quite pleased.

But that sort of reaction no longer appealed. Especially with Jamie in the other room. *My son.*

Thinking about him curled my lips at the edges. What would he think of Evan? Would he find him to be a suitable uncle? Perhaps he'd prefer him. Evan was older, more mature, more successful.

An ideal candidate to be a dad.

My smile fell.

What did I truly offer Jamie aside from a hefty bank account? *Isn't that the only thing Jonah ever gave me?*

"What?" Evan demanded, catching my scowl.

"Nothing." I shook my head, rubbing a hand over my face. "I, uh, I brought Jamie with me."

Surprise flickered in Evan's features. "As in, my nephew?"

I nodded. "Yeah. He's asleep. But I think… I think he'll like you." *Probably more than me.* Which he should. Evan was a good role model. He worked hard, managed a billion-dollar company, had a strong moral compass, and put up with my shit on a regular basis.

"Is the, uh, aunt here?"

"Avery," I corrected him, my chest warming with her name. "Nah, I gave her the weekend off. She works too hard. I actually scheduled a spa weekend for her." For whatever reason, I'd wanted to take care of her, to give her a way to relax. Hopefully, she would enjoy it.

Evan's brow furrowed. "I thought she just wanted custody for financial reasons?"

I grunted. "Garrett's a dick." Because I knew he was the one who had said that. Of course, I thought the same only

119

three weeks ago. "Avery isn't Jean." Far from it. Avery was caring, hardworking, and dedicated. While her sister, well, she was not any of those things.

"You'd like her," I realized. "Avery, I mean."

His eyebrow arched upward. "Maybe you should bring her to the wedding."

I gave him a look. "I haven't even decided if *I* am going yet."

"You're going."

"This again." I spread my arms out across the back of the couch. "We both know the harder you push, the more I'll rebel."

"The old you, yes." His gaze ran over my T-shirt and jeans. "But you're wiser now."

"Am I?" I mused. "Says who?"

"No one." His lips curled slowly. "But your actions tell me everything I need to know." He glanced at the closed bedroom door, then back at me. "Can I meet him tomorrow?"

His words surprised me. "You want to meet Jamie?"

"Of course I do. He's my nephew." Emotion softened his gaze. "Sarah and I have discussed kids, you know, for the future. But I worry about how that will work with our conflicting schedules." He frowned. "Well, anyway, yes, I'd like to meet him. If you're comfortable with it."

"Yeah, I mean, sure. But he doesn't know…" I trailed off, palming the back of my neck. "He thinks we're friends."

Shock registered in Evan's features. "You haven't told him…?"

"Not exactly sure how, if I'm honest. Especially considering the complications with his, uh, aunt."

"What about her?"

"She's pretty much raised him as her own," I admitted softly. "Taking him away from her…" I trailed off, unable to say the words out loud. *It would make me no better than our father.* A boy needed his mother. I knew that better than anyone.

I couldn't do that to Jamie.

But I also couldn't let him go.

He was mine. My responsibility. My *son*.

There had to be some sort of middle ground. A compromise. A way to make this work.

"Hold that thought," a deep voice said as a man with a beard appeared in the living area.

"Where the hell did you come from?" Evan demanded, clearly familiar with the intruder.

"The stairs," he replied. "I went to your penthouse first. It was empty, so I came down here."

"How'd you get the code?" I wondered, confused. Yes, there were stairwells—a fire safety precaution. But this floor had restricted access. As did the top floor.

The man grinned. "You'd be surprised what I know, Mister Mershano. Which is exactly why Garrett hired me." He set a file on the coffee table. "We need to talk about Avery Perry."

This must be Kincaid. I sat forward, intrigued that he wanted to get right to the point. "What did you find out about her?"

"Well." He crossed his thick arms over a chest of solid muscle. "Either Miss Perry is a brilliant liar or she's been played even worse than you."

I stared at him, my heart skipping a beat. "Tell me everything."

16
AVERY

Monday.

That was all my lawyer could say. We had to wait until Monday, which was—I grappled on Jamie's nightstand for my phone and looked at the time—four hours from now.

Four hours until midnight.

Then it would be Monday.

Then we could call Garrett's office again and find out what the hell Wyatt was thinking. Why he'd chosen to rip Jamie from my life. What grounds he had to find me unfit as a guardian.

Of course, Scott said it could have nothing to do with me and everything to do with Wyatt. Jamie was his son; he could do whatever he wanted—

"Auntie A!" The familiar voice sing-songed through my thoughts, causing me to wince.

And now I'm hearing things.

This had been the weekend from hell. I tried calling Wyatt almost nonstop all of Friday night while I read

122

everything I could on the internet about my rights as legal guardian.

News flash: I had none. Wyatt being a fit, capable birth father superseded any rights I might have possessed as an aunt. Even if I did take care of Jamie for the first four years of his life.

I buried my head in Jamie's pillow, inhaling his lingering essence. It mingled with my tears, providing a scent of sadness so profound it stole my breath and shattered my heart all over again.

Four hours.

Monday.

It would only be midnight, but fuck if I cared. I would start blowing up whatever phones I needed to—

"Auntie A!" Jamie's voice sounded louder now, clouding over my thoughts and causing my shoulders to shake harder. I'd slept in his room last night, after I couldn't keep my eyes open any longer, and spent most of today crying in his bed.

Jean's death had hurt.

Losing Jamie rendered me useless. It destroyed me. He'd become my life, my purpose, and I loved him more than anything else in the world.

"Auntie A?" the confused voice came from right behind me, followed by a touch against my arm that had my eyes flashing open. "Are you sleeping?"

I blinked several times. "Jamie?" It came out dry, broken, and nothing like my usual voice.

"Are you sick?" he asked, giving my arm a shake. "Do you need soup?" His hand left. "I think she needs soup, rebel friend. That's what I get when I'm sick. Can we make her soup?"

"I can make her soup," a deep voice replied, sending a chill down my spine. "But you need to go to bed. It's already late, and you have preschool tomorrow."

"But Auntie A doesn't feel good, so I has to take care of her. S'my job."

Is this real?

"It can be my job for the night, little man. You need sleep. You've had a busy weekend."

Jamie nudged my arm again. "Auntie A?"

I finally rolled over to look at him, half-afraid he might be a figment of my imagination, but his adorable little face filled my vision. *He's here. He's really here!*

"Jamie…" I pulled him into a hug and buried my face in his neck. "You're here." I couldn't believe it. But he was real. And standing in his room.

"Yeah, I'm here." He patted my bicep. "You sick, Auntie A?"

God, that little voice. I'd missed it so damn much. "I thought I was never going to see you again," I whispered, reeling from the feel of him in my arms. I hugged him tighter, inhaling his sweet scent, memorizing him, and adoring him.

My Jamie.

My life.

"Oh, oh, oh! Gift!" He tapped my arm again. "Lemme go. I wanna get it."

But I couldn't release him, too afraid he might disappear again.

"Auntie A," he whined, stomping his foot. "I wanna get your present!"

"I'll grab it, Jamie," Wyatt replied, reminding me that he stood in the doorway.

I refused to acknowledge him, too afraid of what I might see in his expression. Had they returned just for Jamie's things? To leave again?

"You get ready for bed while I grab the gift," Wyatt added.

"Ugh, do I have to? I'm not even tired." The familiar grumbling almost had my lips curling, but it was the words being exchanged that gave me true pause.

They're talking about getting ready for bed.
Does that mean they're staying?

"It's past your bedtime, Jamie." Wyatt sounded stern.

"You know how Auntie A feels about bedtime rules."

"But she's sick. We gotta make her soooouuuup," he drawled.

"Do you want soup or her gift?" Wyatt asked.

"Both." Jamie tried to move out of my arms, maybe to face the door, but I still wasn't ready to release him.

"Can't have both, little man."

"I don't like you right now," Jamie pouted.

You and me both, I thought, finally braving a glance at the man in the doorway. His smoldering dark eyes narrowed, his brow furrowing with the look.

"Tell him it's bedtime," Wyatt demanded.

Fuck you, I wanted to throw back at him. "Is he staying here?" I asked instead, my voice hoarse from hours of crying.

Damn, I probably looked like a hot mess from not showering today… or yesterday. And essentially living in Jamie's room, mourning him as if I'd lost a child.

"Yes," he said slowly, his forehead crinkling in confusion. "Doesn't he have preschool tomorrow?"

"Does he?" I wondered out loud. In New Orleans? Here? Where did he plan to send him? I had no say in it, just as Scott reminded me.

No control over the life of the little boy I'd raised as my own.

Because his father maintained all rights.

"Jamie, go brush your teeth and get ready for bed. Avery and I need an adult moment."

"No." I pulled Jamie back to me, afraid to let him out of my sight ever again. *He might not come back.*

Wyatt's eyebrows lifted. "All right. Why don't you help Jamie get ready for bed and tuck him in? I'll be downstairs." He left before I could reply, causing me to frown after him.

What just happened?

Oh, who cares, Jamie is back!

I hugged him again, earning me a groan that I adored far more than I should. "I missed you," I breathed. "I missed

125

you so much."

"Next time, you come, too, 'kay? 'Cause I think you'd like Sarah lots. She'd be a good friend for you."

"Sarah?" I repeated, frowning.

"Yep. She's my new best friend. I like her more than rebel friend 'cause she's funny. Well, rebel friend is funny, too. But in a different way." Jamie pulled back, his little face thoughtful. "Can someone have two best friends?"

My heart was breaking over each word, but I couldn't let it show. I'd already given away too much by being "sick" in his room when he got home. Clearing my throat, I finally sat up, swallowing the dread climbing up my throat.

"You can have as many friends as you want," I finally managed to say, my voice softer than I intended. "Whatever makes you happy."

"Ah, good, 'cause I like them both lots." He brightened. "So next time, you come and meet them, 'kay? You need more friends, too. Lots of them."

His words were a knife to my chest. He didn't mean them that way, but I'd learned the truth of that statement over the last two days.

I had no one.

No one aside from Jamie.

Everyone I used to talk to sort of left after I took Jamie in, mostly because our lives didn't gel anymore. It was hard to remain close when I had a son to take care of, especially one who wasn't truly mine. A lot of my so-called friends told me to put the weight back on Jean, to force her to step up, but I couldn't do that to Jamie. He deserved better.

However, it had left me alone.

Very, very alone.

"Auntie A sad," Jamie said, his brow puckered. "Why sad?"

"I just missed you," I whispered. "But I'll be fine."

Lies are bad, I always told him. Well, I'd just told the biggest one of all.

Because if this weekend showed me anything, it was that

I would not be okay.

Not when Wyatt finally took Jamie away for good.

When will that be? Later tonight? Tomorrow? This week? Only Wyatt could answer that, and something told me he wouldn't. Because he didn't have to. At least, not in his mind.

It didn't matter that I'd essentially raised his son for him these last four years. I was just an inconvenience related to a woman he clearly despised.

"You sure?" he asked, studying me intently in that eerily intelligent way of his. He saw far too much for a child his age.

"Yeah, I'm sure." I gave him my best smile, which probably appeared watered down and ugly.

His mouth twitched to the side. "You don't need soup?"

If I didn't feel so destroyed, I might have laughed. I probably did need soup considering I hadn't eaten much since Friday, but food didn't appeal to me at all. "I'm okay, dude. I don't need any food."

"'Kay." His gaze brightened. "Gift time?"

That required going downstairs and facing Wyatt, something I was not ready to do. "What if I promise to open it tomorrow after you sleep? It's past your bedtime."

He sighed. "Bedtime, bedtime. I hate bedtime."

"I'll read to you," I offered. "If you want." He'd requested Wyatt the last few weeks, saying he enjoyed his voices better. I found it cute, so I didn't mind. Tonight, however, I would mind if he turned me down.

Jamie glanced at his bookshelf and back at me. "I get to pick the story?"

"Of course."

"And you'll read to me?" he asked, warming my heart to where it almost beat again.

"I would love to."

"Oooookay."

Fortunately, that seemed to appease him, because he nodded and led me to the bathroom, where he brushed his teeth and went through his bedtime routine under my supervision. Then he picked out a book for me to read, just like old times. And fell asleep beside me.

I watched him for far too long, engraving every second into my thoughts in case this never happened again.

"I love you," I whispered. "I love you more than you'll ever know, Jamie. I love you like you're my own. No matter what happens." A tear slid down my cheek, meeting his neck and causing him to stir. Or maybe it was my words. Or the way my body had begun to shake with a barely controlled sob.

I need to move before I break down right here and wake him.

With my hand over my mouth, holding in the sounds, I quickly crept out of his room and shut the door. Then I went straight to my room to take a shower.

That was the one place I could truly cry.

The sounds hidden by the running water.

I set the baby monitor up on the counter so I could hear Jamie if he needed me—could hear if Wyatt tried to take him again—and stepped inside the steaming marble.

And collapsed.

My heart and soul somewhere on the floor.

My life in ruins.

My future unknown.

17
WYATT

What. The. Fuck?

I'd expected to find Avery well rested and excited to see us, not... *broken*. The way she'd clung to Jamie brought back so many memories of my own mother holding on to me.

Begging.

Pleading with Jonah not to take me.

But he always won.

His checkbook too big for her to argue. She needed him to survive, mostly because she'd given up everything to have me. She'd been too young, an innocent hotel clerk ensnared by a powerful man who refused to let her work anywhere in his industry again after getting her pregnant. Rather than fight him, or to try to find a new job, she gave in and agreed to his financial terms.

A deal with the proverbial devil.

One that he ended at his leisure, taking me from her arms and leaving her to perish.

Avery's expression tonight resembled my mother's on

the last day I saw her.

"I thought I was never going to see you again," Avery had said. And later…

"I love you like you're my own. No matter what happens."

I shouldn't have eavesdropped, but I wanted to understand. To find out what had put that shattered look on her beautiful face.

Had she thought we were gone for good? Didn't she know I would tell her if I planned to take Jamie away from her?

No, better question—didn't she realize just how impossible that would be?

He adored her, hadn't stopped talking about her all weekend to everyone he met, saying over and over how much he wanted her to be there. It was why we'd bought her a souvenir—a gift that now sat on my dresser because I didn't know how to give it to her.

I ran my fingers through my hair for the millionth time and blew out a breath. I'd left my door open, assuming Avery would want to talk. But she'd disappeared into her room over an hour ago. The water had run for thirty minutes, then the last half hour was too silent.

It was too early for her to go to bed.

So why hadn't she come out yet? We clearly needed to discuss this.

I sound like a woman in a relationship—we need to talk.

"Shit." I flopped onto my back, staring at the ceiling. Then sat back up again. "Fuck it."

I needed to understand what was going through her head, and the only way to find out was to ask. It wasn't like I just took Jamie away for the weekend without telling her. And hell, I'd booked her a spa package with a note suggesting she take the weekend to relax. So whatever had her all riled up was a misunderstanding, one we needed to address. Right now.

I didn't bother putting on a shirt and, instead, wandered down the hall in just a pair of sweatpants. Avery's door was ajar, her light still on inside.

I knocked softly. "Avery?"

No reply.

I nudged the door open just enough to see if she'd fallen asleep with her lamp on and found her sitting on her bed in a towel, staring at the wall.

"Avery?" I repeated.

Nothing.

"Are you seriously playing the silent game?" I demanded, shutting the door behind me and not giving a damn that she wasn't properly dressed. Because fuck this shit. "What the hell is going on? Why are you so angry?"

Her head twisted slowly, her vacant eyes finding mine. "Excuse me?"

"You heard me. What the hell is your problem?" I'd given her the weekend off. It was meant as a gift, one she clearly didn't appreciate. And I had no idea why.

"My problem?" she repeated, standing, the first signs of life returning to her expression. "You want to know what my problem is?"

I folded my arms. "I—"

"My problem is that I have no rights," she said, talking over me. "It doesn't matter at all that I raised Jamie for the last four years. That I've cared for him as my own. That I've sacrificed everything for him. He's not mine. He's yours. And so, you're allowed to just take him. Leaving me with nothing." Her shoulders fell, tears brimming in her eyes.

I hated that look. Hated more that I'd put it there. "Sweetheart, I didn't—"

She charged at me, shoving me hard in the chest. "Don't call me that!" she yelled, shocking the hell out of me. "Don't belittle me. Not now. Not over this. Not after…"

She cringed, her face etched in pain, her eyes an image that would haunt me forever. *What have I done?*

"You've ruined my life," she whispered. "You've taken everything from me. He was mine. My world. And you took him." Her fist slammed against my pec. Not hard enough to hurt, but it definitely grabbed my attention. More punches followed, each one more defeated as she repeated, "You took him. You took him. You took him!"

I wrapped my arms around her, catching her as she collapsed on a sob. The sound of her anguish pierced my insides, destroying me on a level I didn't know existed. "Avery…"

"I hate you." Her broken voice destroyed me, along with her heartfelt claim. "I… I…" She buried her head against my shoulder, her body shaking so violently from the onslaught of her emotions that it was a wonder her towel hadn't fallen yet.

I carried her to the bed, holding her as she completely fell apart.

All her sadness, her anguish, and her fear poured out of her in hurtful waves that dragged me into the depths of the ocean with her. I absorbed it all, lent her my strength while she cried, and listened when she finally decided to speak.

Her words.

Her statements.

They left me at her feet, undone by her raw honesty. The pain I'd unknowingly caused. The burdens of her past.

She told me about Jean, how she constantly threw every burden and problem at Avery. Because Avery always fixed everything. She took care of others, including Jamie. And she adored that child, had loved him with all her heart, only to find out I existed.

"He's the only one I have left," she said, more than once. Apparently, this weekend had truly driven that point home because there'd been no one who could help her. She thought Jamie was gone, and she had no one to call apart from her sad excuse of a lawyer.

Hearing her side, understanding what she thought had happened, killed me. I had an explanation, one that would make this better, but she needed to confide in someone, and so I let her.

It was as if a dam had opened, allowing her to speak

freely for the first time in years. Her wall of courage had crumbled, and she needed someone to help her restore it. And for some wild reason, she'd chosen me. Even though I'd been the one to destroy her, to bring her to her knees, it was my strength and reassurance she sought now. And I gave it to her in spades.

I gave her everything.

Because it was what she needed, what she deserved.

Since when do I care about others? I thought at one point. Then realized that was the very reason we'd landed in this mess. I hadn't considered what my last-minute trip with Jamie would do to Avery. I made assumptions, thinking she'd be fine. Hell, I expected her to be *happy*.

How wrong I'd been.

"I'm not used to considering consequences," I admitted what felt like hours later.

Avery had finally calmed down, her body cocooned against mine beneath the sheets, her head on my shoulder. It was probably the last place either of us expected to be tonight. Yet it felt amazingly right, apart from her damp face against my skin. I never wanted to make her cry again. Although, this hadn't all been me.

The woman had been carrying the weight of the world on her shoulders. She *needed* a break, she needed someone else to shoulder her burdens for her, at least for a little while. And I happily volunteered myself for the job. It was the least I could do after everything she'd done for me, for Jamie, and even for Jean. Avery deserved so much better, and a foreign part of me longed to give it to her.

My desire to destroy the woman I thought wanted to illegally adopt my son felt like a lifetime ago. I'd spent the entire weekend defending her, stating over and over that she couldn't possibly be the woman Kincaid depicted in those documents.

Garrett said I was blinded by my dick.

He was wrong.

Avery had more than proven herself to be a

hardworking, dedicated mother to my son. And tonight only further confirmed that my feelings about her were accurate.

She's not Jean. Not even close.

No, Avery was, quite simply, amazing.

"Jamie broke my phone," I told her now while combing my fingers through her long, blonde hair. "That's why your calls went unanswered. I thought we were giving you a weekend off, to relax." I understood now that we should have called her from Mershano Suites and given her an update. Jamie had asked several times. If only I'd listened to him, her pain could have been avoided. "I'm sorry, Avery."

"It wasn't very relaxing," she whispered, her voice hoarse from all the crying.

"I see that now. But I hadn't meant the spa appointments as a taunt. They were supposed to be a gift, a way to thank you for everything you've done." And wow, *that* had backfired. She thought it'd been a cruel joke. "I'm not used to answering to others, to having to think about how my actions may impact another person. It sounds selfish and conceited, and I suppose it is, but it's how I've lived for so long. I was more concerned with making Jamie comfortable than anything else, and I didn't think it all through. But I never meant to take him from you."

She remained quiet for so long that I thought maybe she'd fallen asleep. Until she cleared her throat. "And what about…? What about the future? When do you plan to take him?"

Avery had already admitted to not being ready to let Jamie go, to not knowing how to live without him, that he'd become her world. And each statement had reminded me of my own mother, what she must have gone through when Jonah took me from her.

"I won't be doing anything without talking to you," I admitted, brushing my lips over her forehead. "Which reminds me, I want to go on a field trip tomorrow." Or later today, if I was reading that clock right. We'd been up half the night already. Normally, if I were up this late in a woman's bed, it was to do something very different than holding her while she cried.

"Field trip?" Avery repeated, tilting her head back to stare up at me. "Where?"

I shook my head. "I don't want to go into it now." Mostly because I didn't have the energy to tell her everything Kincaid had found. Besides, it would be easier to show her. Garrett would be making the arrangements for me. I just had to show up at noon. "Are you able to take the day off work?" I'd meant to ask her that when I first arrived, but things had derailed swiftly.

"I've already called off," she admitted. "I, well, I expected to spend the day with my lawyer."

Hmm, yes, though I wasn't sure how he could have helped her. Fortunately, it would no longer be necessary. "I know you don't have a lot of reason to trust me—especially after this weekend—but I promise to talk to you before I make any further decisions about Jamie."

From what I'd observed, there was no way I could take him from her. Ever. However, that didn't mean I intended to give him up. It meant I wanted to find a way to *share* him.

"We should get some sleep," I murmured. "It's been a long day for us both, and Jamie will be up in a few hours."

Her fingers dug into my side, as if she worried I would pull away from her. "I…" She swallowed, her arm stiffening across my abdomen. "Can you, um, stay a little longer? Just until I fall asleep?"

Was she afraid I might sneak off with Jamie in the night? Or was it my comfort she coveted? The questions refused to voice themselves, likely because I didn't want to know the answer. I feared the former and craved the latter. She had every reason not to trust me, but I wanted her to anyway, and I also wanted her to desire my touch.

This woman had me all tied up in knots.

And oddly, I didn't feel the urge to free myself. Neither from her arms nor the figurative bindings weaving us together.

I like her.

A fact I already knew but truly understood now. The way she'd fallen apart in my arms had connected us on an intimate level, securing our fate.

"I'll stay," I promised, kissing her forehead once again and tightening my hold around her. "I'm not going anywhere."

"Thank you..." The soft words were a puff of air against my skin, her towel-clothed body already curling into mine. Where it seemed to fit perfectly.

"Good night, Avery," I whispered.

She didn't reply, already asleep.

I smiled. *Sweet dreams.*

18
AVERY

Light streamed through my window, bathing me in an addictive warmth that had my toes curling as I stretched my legs.

It caused me to slide against something hot and hard.

And decidedly male.

Wyatt.

My calves were tangled with his, my breasts against his side, and one of my thighs was... *Oh...* Yeah, that was definitely his groin.

His very *aroused* groin.

My lips parted, realization heating my skin. The towel had disappeared, leaving me naked against him. *When had I fallen asleep? What time is it?*

A glance at the clock said I had at least thirty minutes before Jamie would be up. I always seemed to rouse before him. In this case, it was likely because of the hot body pillow pressed up against me. And the very excited response that stirred between my legs.

Wyatt shifted, his hip brushing my sensitive center and eliciting a groan from my throat that I couldn't swallow fast enough. Because damn, that felt good. *Too* good.

Oh, I wanted more.

It'd been so long since I'd last awoken with a man beside me. Five... no, six years ago.

I whimpered as Wyatt moved again, the fabric of his sweatpants taunting against my weeping core. God, this was embarrassing. As if last night's sob fest hadn't been enough, now he had to see me needy and turned on. *Great. Just fucking great.*

Him being awake meant I couldn't just slip out of bed undetected. I had to say something. To lift my head, meet his gaze, and excuse myself. Heat crept along my spine as he drew his fingers upward to wrap his palm around the back of my neck. I quivered against him, fighting the desire to arch into his hip one last time.

This can't happen. Not after he witnessed me fall apart.

I was supposed to hate him.

Yet, I couldn't, especially after hearing his explanation. It wasn't that I overreacted. No, he'd definitely fucked up. However, he owned up to it and apologized. Several times.

Confusion mingled with heat, causing my insides to twist and turn as his grip tightened.

"Look at me, Avery." His low voice had my thighs clenching around him, the demand very much *not* a standard morning greeting. And yet, I tilted my head back as requested, my body bowing to his will on instinct alone.

Dark, intense irises stared down at me, a knowing gleam glimmering in their depths. He searched my features as I snagged my bottom lip between my teeth. I didn't trust myself to speak. It'd probably come out as a needy groan, which was the last sound I needed to make in this state.

This is so wrong.

I tried to remind myself of how I felt last night, how lost and broken I'd been, but this strength seemed to surround me, holding me in the present. Forcing me to acknowledge the very beautiful, hard body pressed up against mine.

Why did he have to be so damn good-looking?

My heart skipped a beat as he pushed me to my back, his palm hot against my side while he went to his elbow beside me. "Wyatt…"

"Shh," he whispered, his gaze stroking over every inch of my exposed skin. "I'm admiring."

I swallowed, my throat dry. I'd never been shy about my body, but his perusal was far more intense and thorough than that of anyone of my past. It felt like a brand against my skin, searing me as *his*. He might as well have been carving his name across my breasts, because I was pretty sure no one would be allowed to look at me after today. Not without knowing he had claimed me first.

And wow, that was arousing as hell.

It had my legs clenching, my body pleading for him to do something other than stare, and my nipples beading into harsh points.

This man undid me in a way no one else ever had.

He destroyed my ability to think, to consider the consequences of what this might do. Because I had desired him for days—weeks, even—and now that he was lying in my bed, I never wanted him to leave.

"You're even more gorgeous than I imagined." The husky quality to his voice sent a shiver across my skin, eliciting goose bumps in its wake. He traced the column of my neck with the pad of his finger, then traveled all the way down the center of my body to the tip of my pelvis. "So soft and perfect."

My lips parted, words failing me, but they weren't needed. Because he was there, his mouth taking mine before I could even breathe. I grabbed his shoulders, not to push him away but to pull him closer.

His palm returned to my throat, wrapping around it as he possessed me with his tongue. No one had ever kissed me like this—so demanding, so skilled, so overwhelming.

I groaned. *This has to be a dream.* No one could be *this*

good. It was physically impossible. But of course, that meant I could take advantage of it, right? If this wasn't real, then I could play.

Oh, yes…

I liked the sound of that.

My fingers roamed over his bare back, stroking the lean muscle all the way down to his firm ass. He bit my lower lip as I squeezed him, loving the way he felt. Hot, sexy, hard. *Mmm…*

His mouth trailed kisses down my neck, nipping, licking, suckling, until he reached my breast. He took my nipple between his teeth, his tongue teasing the tip, causing my back to bow off the bed.

"Wyatt," I breathed, threading my fingers through his hair to keep him there, my other hand returning to his shoulder.

He murmured his approval before switching to nibble my other stiff point, his palm sliding down my side slowly, purposefully. "When was the last time you let go, Avery?" he asked softly, his dark eyes glimmering up at me from my chest. "When was the last time you came?"

"On my own or with someone else?" Because they were very different answers.

"Both."

I shuddered as his stubble tickled my hard peak. *Such a tease.* "On my own…" I paused to swallow a moan, my legs tensing as he slid his thigh between mine. *Yes, friction. Please. Yes…* He applied the perfect amount of pressure, his muscles flexing beneath the fabric of his sweats. "More…"

"Answer my question first."

Question? "What question?"

"I want to know the last time you orgasmed, sweetheart." He laved the tip of my breast. "By yourself."

I had to clear my throat to speak, my breathing coming in pants. "Thursday," I admitted.

"Did you think of me?" The vibration of his voice against my overheated skin practically lit my blood on fire.

"Wyatt…" I needed more. "Please."

"Tell me if you thought of me and I'll give you what you want."

"You know I did." I hadn't been able to stop thinking about him for weeks. "Every time since we met."

I felt him smile against my nipple. "Good." He began licking a path downward, pausing to dip inside my belly button on his way to the apex of my thighs.

Oh, yes, definitely a dream. Because I hadn't experienced a man's intimate kiss in years, but I certainly had imagined Wyatt tasting me in this manner several times.

"I've thought of you every time as well," he murmured, his mouth hovering right above my slick folds. "And I've been dying to taste you."

My fingers—still in his hair—tightened as he lowered to lick me long and deep. His rumble of approval vibrated between my legs, heightening the sensations and tightening the heat inflaming in my lower abdomen.

Part of me registered that this was really happening, some flare in my brain throwing up signals. But the rest of me refused to listen, too caught up in Wyatt's expert tongue to care about anything else.

His name left my lips on a wave of worship, my limbs spasming in delight.

It'd been so long.

I missed this.

I dreamt of it.

I fantasized about it.

But the real deal blew my mind. Maybe because I forgot how it felt, or, more likely, because it was Wyatt's skilled kiss against my center. He knew exactly how to stroke, how to suck, how to nibble. And when he added his fingers, sliding them inside me and finding that place I craved on one upward sweep, I was done for. Lights flashed behind my eyes, the world unraveling around me, as a tight bundle of nerves expanded and grew inside.

And exploded.

Shattering me without warning.

I pressed my hand to my mouth to keep from screaming, the orgasm so powerful I had to bite my palm. Which earned me a growl from Wyatt.

Another sweep of tremors rocked me to my core, causing me to groan deep in my chest and arch my back off the bed. *Too much…*

But oh, I accepted it. I had no other choice, my body convulsing with the onslaught of what felt like a second orgasm. Or was perhaps the first one just expanding. I didn't know. I just dove headfirst into the experience of it.

Adoring every second.

Groaning.

Whispering "Wyatt" into my hand.

This is oblivion. This is what it feels like to completely let go.

I could become addicted to this sensation. It melted my resolve, leaving me pliable beneath Wyatt as he rose above me, my wrist captured in his hand. He pushed it above my head, holding it to the pillow as he lowered his mouth to mine.

My arousal coated his tongue, providing me with one of the most intimate of kisses that I would remember for years to come. The act itself felt like a domination, his lips commanding mine, memorizing, claiming, adoring. He grabbed my opposite wrist and added it to the one already held in his other palm, effectively holding both of my hands captive over my head.

"We're going to try that again. This time, your hands stay here." He nipped my jaw, his lips sliding to my ear. "I earned that scream, sweetheart. Never keep it from me again."

He didn't understand. I had to stay quiet or we'd wake up…

"Wyatt, but Jamie might…" I whimpered as Wyatt started downward again, ignoring my protest. "I'm not… *Ohhhh…*"

He wasted no time in resuming his task, his tongue almost harsh against my sensitive flesh. I squirmed, but his palm against my lower abdomen held me in place, his eyes two pools of liquid need simmering up at me.

Just that look sent me cascading downward, the ripples of energy already rebuilding. *This shouldn't be possible.* I'd *never* orgasmed twice. Not even with a man. But fuck, this one might do the trick. Especially if he kept… Oh, yes… *that.*

His fingers slid into me again, hooking upward and scissoring in a hypnotic motion that stole my breath.

He's a god.

He's a fucking god.

There was no other explanation. This reminded me of a fantasy, the type of scene one read about but never experienced. The thought that this might be a dream came back to me, but no, was no way. I *had* to be feeling this in reality. Not even my mind was creative enough to fabricate these vibrations, and *shit!*

He sucked my clit sharply into his mouth, causing my hips to undulate beneath him, ripping a cry from my throat. My fingers bit into my palms, threatening to lower, but I held them in place. Because he told me to, and I rather liked the thought of pleasing him. At least, in this.

His name slipped from my mouth, my thighs squeezing around him. "Oh, *fuck.*" This was more intense than the first one. I could feel it building, tightening, threatening to take me into a black hole of no return. "Wyatt…"

"Come for me, sweetheart," he murmured against my arousal. "Let me hear you." His fingers penetrated me deep, his tongue pressing into the spot I desired him most, and the earth shifted beneath me.

I exploded.

So much more powerful than before.

Mind-shattering.

Life-altering.

Ruining me for anyone and everyone else. Fuck, I'd never be able to enjoy my own vibrator again after this. Or another man.

Only Wyatt.

Always Wyatt.

Those admissions left my lips, loud to my ears, followed by foreign moans I didn't even know I could make.

And then Wyatt was kissing me again. His hands cupped my cheeks and angled my head to receive him fully, his adoration palpable. I quivered beneath him, my body slack and useless, my arms limp above my head. I barely even knew how to move my tongue, but he trained me appropriately, deepening our embrace and unleashing a passion I felt down to my very toes.

"That was the sexiest thing I've ever seen," he said against my mouth. "Fuck, Avery. I already want to do it again."

I squeezed my legs together, a groan of protest sliding from my lips to his.

He smiled, his nose brushing mine. "Mmm, I adore that sound. If it wasn't nearing seven thirty, I'd be tempted to force more of them out of you."

He kissed me again, this time slower, more sensuous. Any and all resolve about this being a dream disappeared, but I didn't feel an ounce of regret. It was the perfect way to wake up. And after the horrible weekend I'd endured, I needed this.

Even if it was delivered by the same man who nearly destroyed me.

I hadn't forgiven him, not entirely, but I at least understood now. That was the first step.

Holding grudges only caused torment to those involved, and I preferred to move forward.

His tongue slid over mine, mesmerizing me once again by his seductive prowess, when a little voice from the doorway announced, "It's gift time!"

I froze beneath Wyatt.

"Ugh, are you kissing? Grossssss!" Jamie huffed and disappeared, leaving Wyatt chuckling above me.

"Oh, I can't wait to use that against him in ten years," he said softly. "Make sure you remind me."

He winked and slid off me, his sweatpants a lot tighter than before and revealing his very impressive, uh, girth.

"You shower and put on some clothes—something I never thought I'd demand." He shook his head as if to clear it. "Anyway, I'll take care of Jamie's breakfast. Then he can give you his gift while I get ready for the day. Afterward, we'll drop him off together and go on that field trip I told you about. Sound good?"

I could only stare at him and nod, too flabbergasted by the last sixty seconds of my life.

Jamie finding us in bed together.

His only reaction to say it was gross.

And then Wyatt telling me to remind him of this in ten years, as if he expected me to be there.

"Stop thinking," Wyatt said, leaning over to kiss me once more. "Let's get through today and talk more tonight." The words were a demand against my mouth and were followed with the press of his lips to my forehead. "You taste amazing, by the way. And I very much look forward to you returning the favor later."

He smirked at my dumbfounded expression and left.

"What the heck am I supposed to say to that?" I asked the closed door. Then I groaned at realizing I'd only slept maybe three hours last night, yet I apparently had an entire day ahead of me.

Definitely time for another shower.

This one hopefully far less emotional.

Then, well, I had no idea. Evidently, a field trip. Awesome.

19
WYATT

Avery toyed with her new necklace—courtesy of Jamie via my bank account—while I drove, her lips pinched to the side. She clearly had questions, but every time she glanced my way, her cheeks flushed a gorgeous shade of pink. Similar to the color I'd evoked from her in bed.

Fuck, she'd come beautifully beneath my tongue. If this errand weren't so important, I'd suggest we go right back to her room and pick up where we left off.

Alas, Garrett had messaged me thirty minutes ago to say the meeting was set up and ready to go. I needed Avery with me, not as a test but to provide proof. There was no way she'd believe what I found out about her sister. She needed to see it to believe it.

And so did I.

She licked her lips and tugged the bottom one between her teeth. I nearly growled in response. "You're distracting me from the road, Avery." And considering the midday traffic surrounding us, that was a dangerous ploy.

"What?" She glanced at me. "I'm not even doing anything."

"You're fidgeting." I placed my palm on her thigh, causing her to jump. "Are you thinking about how I made you come earlier, Avery? Is that what has you all hot and bothered over there?" Her muscles tensed beneath my hand, enticing me to smile. "Ah, I see. You're desiring a repeat performance. Well, sweetheart, I can guarantee you it's on the agenda."

"Wyatt…" My name was a breathy whisper, one that had me wanting to turn the car around and take her home to fuck her properly.

"Careful, Miss Perry. Unlike you, I've not experienced a release today, and you're making me want to do very, very bad things to you." I squeezed her leg for emphasis. "So unless you want to blow me in this car, I suggest you stop squirming over there."

She sputtered in reply, her words incoherent and causing my lips to curl into a feral grin.

"I can think of far more useful ways for you to use your mouth, sweetheart. I can recommend a few—"

Her hand grabbed mine. "Okay! You're… This…" She cleared her throat. "Tell me where we're going."

I chuckled. "Looking for a distraction?" Her nails dug harder into my skin, forcing me to go easy on her. It seemed dirty talk made her uncomfortable. Or perhaps it turned her on more. I'd enjoy playing with that later. Or, more likely, all day. "We're going to Buckhead."

"Why?"

"You'll see." A vague reply, but necessary. I released her leg to downshift as traffic slowed before me. "How do you put up with this every day?"

"By not going into the city."

"Doesn't that make you feel trapped?"

"On occasion." She picked at her jeans, her expression thoughtful. "It's not my favorite place to live, but it's affordable, and I like my job."

"Would you ever consider moving?" I wondered.

She shrugged. "Not sure where I would go."

"What if you had an opportunity elsewhere?"

Her shoulders fell. "I mean, my job is something I can do from almost anywhere. My skills are marketable, too, so I wouldn't have a hard time finding a new opportunity, if I had to. But it's a good area for Jamie, and I have to, uh…" She trailed off, her focus shifting to the windows. "Never mind."

"No, don't do that. Finish your sentence." I wanted to know the answer.

"There's nothing to finish," she said without looking at me. "Because I don't know what's going to happen now."

"What do you want to happen?" I pressed. "Where would you live if you had a choice?"

"Somewhere with Jamie," she answered immediately. "Anywhere with him."

"Even if it meant giving up your job here?"

She finally shifted her attention back to me. "I already told you I can work anywhere. So what are you trying to figure out? What do you really want to know? If I'm willing to give up everything to remain in Jamie's life? Because I think the answer to that is fairly obvious."

"I'm asking what *you* want, Avery. Everything you do is for Jamie, and I respect that. But what about you? What are your hopes and dreams?"

"Jamie is—"

"Remove him from the equation," I cut in. "What did you want before Jamie? You're clearly a hard worker. Did you always want your current career in Atlanta? Or did you desire a different opportunity? A different future?"

She shook her head. "I can't answer that without making it sound like I regret Jamie."

I sighed. "This isn't a trick or a test. I just want to know where you once saw yourself going in life."

"And I'm telling you, my former goals no longer apply. I can't see a future without Jamie. It's impractical."

"Okay." I paused to merge onto another highway, heading toward northern Atlanta. We were almost to our final destination, and Avery hadn't shown a single ounce of apprehension, proving my suspicions correct. She had no idea where we were headed.

Garrett had his reservations about my opinion on this matter, but my instincts were rarely wrong. And I would enjoy confirming that to him later tonight.

"If you could do any job in the world—with Jamie by your side—where would it be, and what would you be doing?" I finally asked, deciding this phrasing might work better.

"Life doesn't work like that."

"I'm not asking you to be realistic, Avery. I'm asking you to dream." I spotted our exit ahead and slid into the right lane. "Work with me. Give me a hypothetical response. Tell me a fantasy."

"A fantasy," she repeated, sounding amused. "All right. Well, I wouldn't live here. It's too crowded. I grew up in Pennsylvania. Not that I want to live there again, but somewhere without all the traffic and people. It's exhausting."

"So, the country." Very different from my preference of New York City. But then, did I actually love it there? Or was it my default location due to a lack of a purpose elsewhere?

"Hmm, maybe. I've always loved the mountains. And snow. I think Jamie would love sledding." Her lips curled in my peripheral vision, warming my chest. "But I don't know what job I would do there. I was actually pursuing a master's degree in computer informatics when Jean came to me—pregnant."

She fell silent, causing me to wonder aloud, "Would you want to go back and finish it?"

"No." An immediate reply. "I mean, I enjoyed it, but I only went that route because it pretty much guaranteed me a job, and, well, I found one without finishing. Finishing it now would almost be a step backward. Experience is worth more than a piece of paper at this point in my career."

"Fair enough." I turned right at the exit, our destination only a few miles ahead, according to the map I'd memorized earlier. Avery still showed no signs of recognition, not surprising me in the slightest. "So would you want to keep working in project management? Or do something else?"

She shrugged. "I've honestly not given it much thought. Jamie is my primary focus. But I enjoy my job. It's not glamorous, but it pays my bills, and I'm good at it."

"You never had a dream job growing up?"

"Did you?" she countered. "You went to law school, right?"

My grip on the steering wheel tightened. "I only pursued a legal degree to piss off Jonah." Although, the last few days had me wondering if I should do something with it. Jamie needed a role model, and I hadn't really proven to be one.

I didn't work.

I avoided my family.

I preferred to cause problems rather than fix them.

Not exactly Dad of the Year material.

"Jonah?" she repeated. "That's your father, right? The one you said you enjoy irritating?"

"My sperm donor, yes." I focused on making a left turn before adding, "Defying him has been my ultimate life goal for longer than I care to remember."

She was silent for a moment, causing me to glance at her. I wondered if she recognized our surroundings, but no, her eyes were on me. Studying.

"Why?" she finally asked.

"A discussion for another time," I replied, pulling into the condominium parking lot. Garrett had told me to park in the visitor spots at the front, so that was exactly where I headed. "We're here."

She peered out the windows with a frown. "Uh, okay." Her brow furrowed. "Not exactly what I expected."

You have no idea, I thought, parking the car and killing the engine. I didn't say a word and hopped out. She was opening her door when I reached her side. Grabbing her purse from the floor, she slid off the leather seat onto her heels, her skinny jeans clinging to her curves. Too bad her flowy shirt hid her breasts. Hmm, or maybe not. It provided just a hint of what lay beneath, making it a delectable tease to my senses.

I caught her hips and backed her up into the side of my SUV, needing to say a few things before this show started.

"Wyatt," she warned, her irises scanning the parking lot and front sidewalk.

"Avery," I returned, pressing myself up against her and not giving a fuck about our surroundings. "I've wanted to kiss you for over thirty minutes. So part those lips for me."

Her fingers dug into my sides, clasping the fabric of my black T-shirt. "I—"

My tongue silenced her, the need to ravage her ripping through me. Not just because of this morning's unfinished interlude but because of the emotions tugging at my conscience.

I hated what I was about to do.

I hated that Jean had put us in this situation.

I hated that I couldn't control myself around this woman.

Oh, but mostly, I hated that I couldn't just take her upstairs and fuck her the way she deserved. The way I'd craved for what felt like a lifetime.

I undulated my hips against hers, allowing her to feel my growing arousal, and luxuriated in the moan that trickled from her mouth to mine.

"We're going to have several hours of adult time later," I vowed. "Where I am going to fully acquaint myself with your mouth, Avery. In the best of ways. And then you're going to scream for me over and over. Perhaps at the same time. Because I would love to feel your throat contract around my cock, sweetheart. While we both come together. At the same. Fucking. Time."

Just picturing it nearly had me coming in my pants. Too

bad we didn't have time for me to pull her into the backseat for a quickie.

"Wyatt," she breathed, arching into me.

Damn, I adored that little tell. She'd completely forgotten our location, having lost herself to my touch. Such an intoxicating realization, one that empowered me to kiss her again.

I cupped her face between my palms and devoured her to within an inch of both our lives. Until the clearing of a throat interrupted our interlude.

"I see you're taking my advice well," Garrett said, not bothering to give either of us a moment to pull ourselves together. "I'll meet you inside. Miss Perry." The latter was said as an afterthought, his grin decidedly cruel.

Dick.

"W-why is he here?" Avery asked, her flushed cheeks fading into shades of white. "Wyatt… *Why is he here?*" The query came out stronger, her pupils narrowing into points.

"Avery—"

"No! You can't just *kiss* me like that and then trick me into… into… whatever the hell…? Oh God. Is that why you were asking me about my dreams? Were you tricking me into saying I wanted a life without Jamie?" Tears prickled her eyes, not of sadness but of rage. "You bastard!" She swung her palm at my face, but I caught it before it could connect. Her other hand lifted, forcing me to restrain both her wrists against her chest.

"*Avery*," I growled. "Calm. Down."

"I can't believe you! What was this? A fucking game? A test? Were you just bored?" she demanded, squirming against me. "How could you? What kind of sick bastard—"

I covered her mouth with my own, silencing her.

And she bit me.

Hard.

Right. Not the best plan of action, but I didn't know how else to shut her up. *Now* I cared that she was causing a scene.

Fucking Garrett interfering before I had a chance to

explain.

She fought against me with true force this time, her knee coming dangerously close to my package. "Avery!" I yelled, needing her to calm the fuck down. "This isn't about Jamie."

Her movements slowed. "What?"

"This isn't about Jamie," I repeated, my teeth clenched with the effort of protecting myself while also trying not to hurt her. "This is about Jean."

She finally stopped, her eyebrows coming down over her beautifully fierce eyes. "I don't... Jean?"

"Yes. And Garrett, whether he likes it or not, is here to help you." That was the whole point of today's meeting. Once I proved Avery's innocence to him, he'd have no choice but to agree to assist in resolving this entire fucking mess.

Well, technically, I could force him to anyway. But this method settled concerns across the board. Something all involved parties required.

Because yes, there was a chance my instincts were wrong. A very, very, very minuscule possibility. One that was shrinking by the second.

"Help me with what?" she asked hoarsely.

I shook my head. It would be too difficult to explain. She needed to *see* to believe.

"We're meeting a realtor inside," I said instead of answering her. "She thinks I want to buy a property upstairs." Technically, she thought *we* wanted to purchase one. But that was beside the point.

"A condo?" Avery shifted to glance up at the tall building beside us, her brow crinkling. "Here?"

"Yes."

She returned her focus to me, a glimmer of hope replacing the hurt in her gaze. "Wait, are you thinking of moving here?"

I ran my fingers through my hair. Why did this have to be so difficult? Of course, I knew the answer. Nothing in this world was ever easy. Especially where I was concerned.

"I don't know yet, Avery," I replied honestly. "We need closure on this issue first, then we can begin discussing what's next."

"You mean on Jean?" she inferred.

"Yes."

"I... I'm not sure I understand."

I know. "You will." I took a step back, hating the distance already growing between us but also knowing it to be necessary. "Just... I need you to know one thing."

"Okay." Her gorgeous features contorted in confusion. "What thing?"

"No matter what happens, I've never doubted you in regard to this." And I still didn't. Garrett had the jet on standby, convinced we would be leaving with Jamie tonight. But I knew otherwise.

Kincaid had been right.

Avery was even more of a victim than I was.

And today, she would have proof of it.

20
AVERY

Wyatt said this isn't about Jamie.
Should I believe him?
Maybe. Yes. I think so.

My head spun as I entered the building ahead of him, my heart in my throat. I'd gone from turned on to furious to confused as hell in the span of minutes. Talk about an emotional roller coaster.

Wyatt's palm met my lower back, his touch burning right through the thin barrier of my shirt and marking the skin beneath. *Mine*, it seemed to say. So many mixed signals.

This weekend was the worst experience of my life.

Followed by this morning, which was, well, *orgasmic*.

Not going to think about that.

Because I needed to focus.

Wyatt silently led us to a set of couches in the open reception area of the condo building. A dark-haired woman sat beside Garrett, her pretty face lit up in admiration as the lawyer chuckled. While I could see the physical appeal, my experience with the man granted me a very different opinion.

His sapphire eyes grinned up at us as we approached. "Ah, my client has arrived at last." He stood, smoothing a hand down his tie. "Miss Hanson, this is Mister Mershano."

The palm pressed against my back remained as Wyatt extended his opposite hand toward the now-standing brunette. "Wyatt, please. And this is my girlfriend, Miss Perry."

Girlfriend? Since when?

"Emily," the woman replied, shaking his hand and then holding out a palm for my own. I shook it on autopilot, my brain short-circuiting.

He didn't really mean that.

It was just… He meant… Okay, but…

"Miss Perry," Garrett said, a question in his voice. "You look a little mystified. Have you two met?"

I blinked. *What?* "Me and Wyatt?"

He arched a haughty eyebrow. "No, you and Miss Hanson."

I glanced at the woman, frowning. "Uh, no. Should we have?" Because I didn't recognize her. "Sorry, I didn't mean to be rude. Have I missed something?"

"Not that I know of." She sounded just as baffled. "I mean, you look a little familiar. Actually, you remind me of a former client." She smiled. "You could easily be sisters."

My gut churned.

"This is about Jean," Wyatt had said.

Oh no…

"I think we're getting ahead of ourselves," Garrett interjected smoothly, sitting down again. "The reason I've arranged this meeting is my client, Wyatt, is interested in a property in this building. One I believe you might be familiar with."

His blue eyes met mine as he said it, but it was the brunette who replied, "Which one?"

"Emily is a realtor," Wyatt whispered against my ear. He

slid his arm around my waist to grab my hip and pulled me down beside him on the couch across from Garrett.

"It's on the twelfth floor." Garrett's eyes were still on me, causing me to scowl.

Why does this feel like a test? I'd never been in this building before, and it was way too expensive for Jean to afford, even with whatever stipend Wyatt had sent her. We were in the heart of Buckhead. Property values here were five to six times as much as my house.

"Oh, I don't know of any available on that floor, but I'd be happy to look." She pulled a tablet out from her purse, but Garrett laid his hand over hers.

"That won't be necessary, darling. We know the condo number already." He uttered a number that had the realtor frowning.

"That's not available," she said. "Or, at least, I don't believe it's for sale." She pulled out her tablet and keyed in a few values while Garrett watched over her shoulder, and then she shook her head. "No, see, she's not selling it right now." Relief was evident in her voice. "But I can help by pulling up some other properties—"

"No, that's the one we want," Garrett interjected. "Perhaps you can put us in touch with the owner?"

"Uh, I mean, I can. But I doubt she's interested in selling."

Garrett's devilish grin was punctuated by a pair of dimples that had the realtor openly swooning. "You might be surprised."

"I can try to give her a call for you, if that's the property you're set on. However, there are others just like it in the building."

"We definitely prefer discussing that particular one," Garrett said, shifting to pull a portfolio from his briefcase. "In fact, I have all the details on it here. I just need you to confirm a few things for me."

Her brow pinched. "Uh, yeah. Okay. Like what?"

"Just some clarifications," Garrett murmured, pulling

out a file and glancing over it. "Such as this—that's the owner's name, correct?"

The realtor's eyes widened. "Yes, but where did you get that?"

"It's not important. I just needed confirmation. Oh, but I would like to know…" He bent to pull a photo from his bag, one I couldn't see because he showed us the back and the realtor the front. "Is this the Avery Perry you know?"

My lips parted as the realtor's gaze flung my way. "*That's* why you look familiar. You must be related to Avery."

My entire body went rigid. "What?"

She grabbed the photo and showed me a picture of Jean. "Avery. You look so much like her."

"Doesn't she?" Garrett's lips curled. "So that's who owns the condo upstairs, right?"

"I don't understand," I said, my voice a choked whisper.

"Yes. She's lovely. But I don't know if she's wanting to sell."

"As I said, Miss Hanson, you might be surprised." Garrett set the paperwork on the table, allowing me to see the deed to the condo showcasing my name. I snatched it off the table.

"This… this…" I couldn't finish, my eyes blurring as I read each damning line. "I didn't know." I finally looked at Wyatt, his expression unreadable. "I swear, I didn't know." But, of course, he wouldn't believe me. My name was all over this deed. And the papers beneath it only further nailed my coffin closed.

Financial documents.

All with *my* signatures.

And there was even a photocopy of my old license.

They were talking around me, Emily asking questions, but I couldn't hear any of them over the pounding in my head.

This can't be real.

But it was.

All of it.

Right there in black and white, it stated I owned the condo upstairs. I had signed for it. I had purchased it from an account I knew nothing about. "This… I didn't do this." The whisper sounded loud to my ears. I threw the papers down, my vision drifting out of focus from the tears threatening to fall. I voiced an apology, or tried to, and excused myself to get some fresh air.

Too much.

This was all too much.

Why would Jean do this to me? Steal *my* identity to live another life? "This can't be real," I breathed, talking to no one in particular. "She…" I shook my head, my feet carrying me into the parking lot, toward…

I didn't drive.

Fuck!

Not that I should leave in this state, but I couldn't stay here.

"She lied to me." I pinched the bridge of my nose, the headache forming overwhelming everything around me.

Jean led a completely secret life.

I should have known.

It's why she never stayed the night. She had a place of her own. This place. A place in my name.

My knees gave out beneath me, but a stern band around my abdomen caught me before I could fall. Wyatt was suddenly there, his chest providing a forbidden pillow for my face.

"You knew," I accused, my hands fisting against him. "You knew." And he hadn't told me. He'd fucked with me instead. Which, I supposed, he thought I deserved.

Because he thought I had played him. Just like Jean.

"I found out Friday night, yes," he admitted, his lips at my ear. "I'm sorry, Avery."

"You're *sorry?*" I wanted to laugh. To scream. To punch someone.

No. I wanted to punch *Jean.*

She had given me the most beautiful gift, and now her

159

actions would rip that gift from my arms.

"I didn't know," I told him. Not that I expected him to believe me. There was too much proof to the contrary. He had every right to hate me. To blame me. To assume I was cut from the same cloth as my sister. That was the purpose of all this, obviously. To give him final cause to take Jamie from my life in the cruelest way possible.

He cupped my face between his hands, pulling me away from his shirt, forcing me to look into his dark eyes.

Judgment, I realized. He wanted to deliver his final verdict. And I didn't have it in me to hate him for it. None of this was his fault. It all lay at my sister's feet.

How could someone be so selfish? She never cared about me or Jamie. She only thought of herself.

Cursing a dead woman felt wrong, but in this case, it was more than fucking warranted.

"Garrett is here to help," Wyatt said softly. "We're going to sort this out. Do you want to see the condo? Because we have a key."

"Wh-what?" He wanted to go upstairs? To see where Jean had lived? "Actually, yes." I did want to see it. To provide myself with some semblance of closure over all this insanity. All the lies. To see the world my sister had kept hidden away while leaving me to shoulder all her responsibilities. I wanted to know what life she chose over Jamie.

Wyatt swept the tears from beneath my eyes, his lips lightly touching mine.

A stroke of pity?

No, thank you.

I pushed him away, shaking my head. "Don't." Not after everything. This morning. The way I'd let him into my bed. "Don't do that." It would taint the brief affair between us, and I couldn't stand for that. These were my final memories, the ending of the worst month I'd ever endured. And I refused for it to culminate on a note of *pity*.

"Look, I didn't tell you because Garrett needed to see

for himself that this was all Jean," Wyatt said. "But I've not doubted you for a second. I knew this wasn't you, Avery. Your sister played us both. And frankly, I'm glad she's dead. She deserves to burn in hell for eternity for all of this."

Wait, what? That wasn't at all what I expected him to say. He thought I was mad that he didn't warn me about all this before walking inside? I mean, yeah, that would have been appreciated. But why would he feel obligated to tell me anything? He didn't owe me a damn thing. Apart from maybe some gratitude for raising his son. However, Jean was the culprit here.

She deceived me.

She lied to Wyatt.

She stole my identity.

She abandoned her son.

"Your sister was a sick and twisted bitch of a woman," a new voice said, joining us outside. I glanced around, realizing I'd not just walked into the parking lot but through it. Toward an adjoining park with swings.

Jamie would enjoy that, I thought numbly. "Why didn't she ever bring him here?" I wondered out loud, finally seeing the beauty of our location. Trees. A full playground. Walking paths. A richly elegant home, one Jamie would have adored. "Why did she hide all of this?"

"As I said, your sister was a bitch," Garrett replied dryly. "God rest her soul and all that fuckery." He waved a hand. "Regardless, Avery, I apologize for doubting you. For what it's worth, Wyatt never did. He adamantly told Kincaid that you were innocent, and I was the one who said otherwise. Which is why I intend to help eradicate you from this mess—free of charge. And Wyatt has agreed to let you keep the property and accounts as well."

"I… what?" I looked between them, flabbergasted by everything he'd just said. "Who is Kincaid? And what accounts? And why would I want to keep anything?" The only thing I cared about was Jamie. Always.

"Kincaid is the investigator we hired to look into Jean's

activities prior to her death," Garrett replied. "Specifically, her financial situation."

"I wanted to know where all of the money I'd sent for Jamie went," Wyatt added. "And, as I believe in honesty, I also wanted to know if I could trust you." His gaze bore into mine. "For the record, I already decided who you were before he delivered the report."

"Which is why he adamantly denied the allegations that you purchased the property in this building. But I don't rely on the instincts of a man driven by his cock. Hence today's meeting." Garrett certainly had a way with words. He shifted his attention to Wyatt. "Miss Hanson is gone, by the way. I have her information should we require her for any of the estate resolution."

"Yeah, it's clear that she had no idea," Wyatt replied. "Which was the other reason for today's meeting, Avery. We wanted to see if Emily knowingly committed fraud with Jean."

I hadn't even thought of that.

How many people did Jean deceive throughout the years?

"Miss Hanson didn't have any knowledge of it. Now I just have a lot of paperwork to file." Garrett checked his watch. "Right. Did you want to see the condo? Because I want to walk through it before I decide on how to proceed."

"I… Proceed?" My head was spinning. "I don't…" I swallowed, trying to formulate my thoughts, to focus.

"Do you want to see the condo?" Wyatt asked, his voice softer, his hand somehow finding my lower back again and offering a strength I didn't know I needed. "Or do you want me to take you home?"

"No." *To what?* "I… I want to see the condo." *Closure.*

"All right." Wyatt's arm slid around me, his touch warming my chilled skin. "Then we'll go upstairs and discuss more when we get there."

I nodded. "Yeah. Upstairs. Okay." The words sounded foreign to my ears. Like someone else was speaking for me.

How had this become my life?

What else had Jean kept from me?

I almost didn't want to know.

I just wanted to be done with it all. To move on. But something told me Jean would haunt me for years to come.

Jamie deserves better.

Wyatt brushed his lips against my temple, as if hearing my thoughts and confirming Jamie had a better option. His father. Someone who had been duped from the beginning, just like me. A man who could more than take care of his son and had proven himself to be tender and loving over the last few weeks.

Could I do it?

Could I give Jamie up to him? I wanted Jamie to experience the best in life.

Wyatt could give him the world.

A world away from Jean and the manipulations of her past.

A world of love and happiness and success.

A world without me.

Maybe Jamie didn't need me after all. Maybe all he needed was Wyatt.

My heart broke at the thought.

But I would always put Jamie's needs first. Even if it meant living a life without him.

21
WYATT

Avery hadn't said much since leaving Jean's condominium. The residence had been dusty but mostly clean, apart from the abundance of alcohol and controlled substances inside. It was very clearly *not* Avery's place, something Garrett noted several times while wandering through the two-bedroom condo.

He kept asking Avery what she wanted to do, but she seemed incapable of answering. I told him to give her a few days to process everything, to decide on next steps.

Now, she stood in the kitchen, cleaning up from dinner on autopilot. I offered to help twice, but she shrugged me off, telling me to play with Jamie.

But he didn't seem all that into our game of race cars. He kept looking toward Avery with a perplexed expression.

"Auntie A is acting we-ord," he confessed in that not-so-soft whisper of his.

"I know," I agreed. "I think she's tired."

He nodded. "Yeah, she was screaming this morning. I

think from a bad dream. That's why you were there, right?"

I bit my lip to keep from grinning. Now I understood why she'd wanted to be quiet. But his innocent mind had no idea what caused those noises. Thank God.

"Yeah, I was helping her feel better." Not a lie. I just chose not to elaborate on it.

"I have bad dreams sometimes. 'Bout Momma Jean. Her angels talk to me."

Well, that was a dark statement. "What do they say?"

Jamie shrugged. "I dunno. But my Auntie A cries lots. And I hate it."

"I don't like when she cries, either," I admitted. Last night, coupled with her reactions today, had left me more unnerved than ever before. She wasn't the first woman to break down in my presence, but she was the first one I wanted to console. That I had been the one to cause her tears only made it worse.

Well, perhaps not today.

I blamed Jean for Avery's emotions earlier, not myself.

Yes, I could have warned her. Maybe I should have. However, it had seemed more prudent for her to see it on her own, not be told about it. Somehow, that made it all the more believable.

Not to mention, Garrett required the test—one Avery passed with flying colors. The bastard actually felt bad about everything now, which I considered a win in and of itself.

"Let's make her happy," Jamie said as if it were the easiest thing in the world. "Another gift?"

I chuckled. "You're in for a world of hurt when you start dating, buddy."

"Dating?" His nose scrunched. "What's that?"

"When you decide to like girls."

"And kiss them?" Jamie sounded positively affronted by the notion. "Gross!"

"I'm going to enjoy replaying this conversation to you in about ten years." I ruffled his hair. "What kind of gift do you want to get her?"

Apparently, the necklace was the first gift he'd ever given Avery. I supposed that made sense with her always being the one to buy things. She didn't strike me as someone who indulged herself often. Which was why I didn't tell her where Jamie found that necklace or how much it was worth. She thought he'd picked up the *fleur-de-lis* key pendant in a tourist shop.

Good thing I discarded that trademark blue box first.

Or maybe she wouldn't have even recognized the brand.

Something told me Avery wasn't very familiar with famous jewelry chains.

"Pizza?" Jamie offered, his lips twisting to the side. "Pizza makes me happy."

That'd been his gift idea in New Orleans, too. I'd suggested a few more sustainable ideas, including a necklace or a bracelet. So, after my tux fitting, we'd wandered through a few stores and he'd selected the key. Now he wanted to give her food again.

"Pizza is for Fridays," I reminded him, grinning. "What else you got?"

"I think pizza should be allllll the time. And ice cream!" His eyes went wide. "We should get her ice cream!"

"Get who ice cream?" Avery asked, joining us in the living area.

"Youuuuuuuu!" Jamie stood and started dancing around. "Ice cream, Auntie A. Ice cream."

"He has a one-track mind when it comes to food," I commented, chuckling.

"Yes. He does." Her resulting smile didn't reach her eyes. "It's too late for ice cream, Jamie. It's bedtime."

I glanced at the clock, surprised to see it nearing seven thirty already. We'd eaten later than normal tonight, with having spent the afternoon at Jean's condo. Fortunately, Avery's babysitter, Katrina, was able to pick up Jamie for us from preschool. "Uh-oh, Auntie A is right, little man. Time to brush your teeth."

"Ughhhhhhh." Jamie threw his arms out to the sides.

"But I'm not tired at allllll."

"Then Wyatt can read to you until you fall asleep," Avery offered. "Maybe he'll do all the voices for you that you like." She gave another small smile. "I'm going upstairs, but I'll drop in to say good night soon, 'kay?"

Jamie frowned after her as she left. "But... I kinda wanted Auntie A to read to me tonight." He looked up at me with pleading eyes. "Can Auntie A read tonight?"

"Sure, little man. Why don't you go pick out a book and start getting ready while I talk to your Avery."

He nodded. "Yeah, 'kay. Don't make her cry." That last part was spoken as an order before he flounced away.

I shook my head. The last thing I wanted to do was hurt Avery. She'd been through enough. If anything, I wanted to take care of her—in the best ways.

This whole notion of wanting to make someone else happy—apart from myself—was a welcome experience. For the first time in my life, I felt needed. And not just that, but *wanted*. Like I finally had a family of my own.

That thought followed me all the way upstairs to Avery's room, where I knocked softly on her door.

"One minute," she called, her voice sounding off. And not in a good way.

"It's me," I said, cracking open her door. "Jamie wants you to read to him."

"What?" Avery cleared her throat. "Why?"

"I think the novelty of rebel friend Wyatt has worn off," I murmured, leaning against her door frame in the hallway. "And I think he missed you this weekend." *As did I*, I wanted to admit but didn't.

"Oh. Okay. I'll... I'll be over in a few minutes." There was that odd note in her tone again. It had me itching to push open the door to see her, but I didn't want to intrude.

"I'll help him with the routine, and he'll be waiting for you," I said, deciding we could talk afterward. There were a lot of topics we needed to discuss, including what to do about Jean's accounts and the condo. Avery seemed to be of the opinion that it wasn't her decision. I disagreed.

I pushed away from her door and met Jamie in the bathroom to help supervise his teeth-brushing skills. Then I helped him find suitable pajamas. He picked out a book and snuggled into his bed just as Avery walked in, her face freshly washed and her legs clad in a pair of sinful yoga pants. She also didn't appear to be wearing a bra with that tank top.

"You sure you want me to read to you?" she asked, her eyes on Jamie.

"Yep," he said, holding out a book—one I'd read four times last week. "This one."

"Okay, dude." She snuggled in beside him.

"Night, little man." I ruffled his hair. We hadn't really gotten to the kiss on the forehead bit. Mostly because I didn't know if he'd like it. Or how to really cross the boundary of telling him I was his father, not just a friend.

More things to discuss with Avery.

After I divested her of those clothes.

And licked every inch of her.

I smiled as I entered my room across the hall to change into a pair of sweatpants. I was on my way to the hall bathroom when I overheard Jamie unsuccessfully whispering, "Can you come with us next time?"

I leaned against the wall beside Jamie's open door to eavesdrop on her reply. It's not like I ever proclaimed to be a saint, and I sure as shit wasn't going to act like one now.

"Oh, I don't know, sweetie," Avery said softly. "It's up to Wyatt."

"But I want you to come," Jamie replied, his voice holding a pout I could visualize clearly. "You'd really like Sarah. She could be your friend."

"Hmm, maybe." Avery didn't sound so sure about that, causing me to frown. Because I actually agreed with the little man. Sarah and Avery would get along well. Actually, they'd be a force of nature together.

"Well, I don't want to go without you next time. 'Cause

I missed you too much."

"Yeah?" Avery laughed, but it was missing emotion. "Well, I missed you, too. More than anything in the world."

"Then you come with us next time." The words were spoken with finality.

"That's not up to me, little dude." Her response made me frown. "Wyatt makes the rules."

"How come?" he asked.

"Because he does."

"But how come?"

"Because he's in charge."

"But I thought you made the rules." A sound argument from Jamie.

Pretty sure she's in charge, too, little buddy, I thought at him.

"I used to, but things change."

"But why?" he demanded. "You're Auntie A. You make the rules."

Avery sighed. "For now, okay. And my rule tonight is you need to go to sleep."

"But you haven't read to me yet," he pointed out. "Rules are rules, Auntie A. Read, then sleep."

"You and your rules," she teased, but that note was in her voice again. "All right, dude. I'll read."

I pushed away from the wall, ignored the bathroom, and went downstairs to find my phone. I'd left it on the dining room table.

It felt strange dialing my older brother's number. I added it to the list of new experiences for the month because I'd never actually called him before. He usually phoned me.

"Wyatt," he said by way of greeting. "Is everything all right?"

I snorted. "Wow. I must really not talk to you often for you to think someone has to be dying for me to call you."

"Hold on." He said something in another language, which sounded like Japanese, then I heard a door swish open and closed. "What's going on?"

"Are you in the middle of a meeting?" I glanced at the

clock on the stove. "It's almost eight o'clock."

"Which is nearly nine in the morning in Japan."

Shit. "You're in Japan?"

"Yes, and I just walked out of a meeting. Now, tell me why you've called." The command in his voice grated on my nerves, but I also understood it. My older brother was all business, all the time. It made me feel foolish for calling him with my nonsense.

"I'm sorry. If I'd known you were in a meeting, I would have texted. This isn't important." That sentence seemed to define my life. I'd wasted so many years doing nothing while my big brother was off changing the world. And here I was, still not making much of a difference at all.

"*You* are important," Evan replied without missing a beat. "What's up?"

"I, uh, was just going to ask if I can bring Avery to the wedding. You know, with Jamie." I hadn't given it much thought, but the idea of being without both of them for two weeks didn't sit well with me.

"Of course." He didn't even hesitate. "We'd love to meet Avery, and you know we already adore Jamie. I'll let Sarah know."

"You're sure?" I pressed, not wanting to impose. "They might not be able to do the full two weeks. I haven't asked yet." Jamie would still be in preschool in May, and Avery had her job to consider.

"That's okay. Just let me know. And, Wyatt?"

"Yeah?"

"Thank you. We're looking forward to you being there."

"Uh, yeah, no problem." It sounded pathetic, but I didn't know what else to say. "Thanks for letting me bring them."

"They're family," he replied easily. "You all are welcome anywhere, anytime. But I need to get back to this meeting."

"I understand. And, uh, maybe we can chat again soon."

"I'd like that."

"Okay. Have fun in Japan."

He snorted. "I'm only here for the day. Flying back to Sarah tonight. Talk to you later."

I said a meager farewell, frowning. Maybe I should talk to him about helping more with Mershano Suites. A consideration for later. I had a woman to seduce. Then maybe I'd ask her opinion. We already had a dozen things to talk about; what was one more item for the list?

22
AVERY

I needed to check my work emails, to see what I'd missed from today, but I just didn't have the energy. Likely because I had slept all of three hours last night after being nearly destroyed by my emotions over the weekend. And also, the events of today.

Jean had a condo. A bachelorette pad where she lived, partied, drank, and didn't care about anyone other than herself. One she bought using *my* identity, which explained that one time I "lost" my driver's license three years ago. She'd borrowed it. And bought the place under my name. Paying cash so no one would bat an eye.

She also had a hefty account filled with funds Wyatt had sent for Jamie, all of which she'd been using to fuel her drug and alcohol habits.

While leaving me here, in this three-bedroom, mediocre home to raise her son.

I buried my head in my pillow and let out the scream that had been building inside me for hours. God, it felt good to let go.

So I did it again.

And again.

And again.

And lost track of time and space.

I hated Jean.

I hated what she'd done to me.

I wanted to murder her myself.

But I couldn't. Because she was already fucking dead! My parents would be so disappointed, not just in Jean but in me for cursing my sister in her grave. The bitch deserved it and worse. Yet, I couldn't do anything. Only scream. Vent. Cry. Hate.

The only good consequence of all of this was Jamie, and he was about to be taken away from me because of Jean.

One final selfish action, nailing my coffin closed to live with crimes I never committed.

"I hate you!" It came out as a muffled yell against the pillow, but I didn't care. I repeated the words, kicking, and didn't give a fuck at all that I was essentially throwing a tantrum.

I earned the right to let it out. No one could take that away from—

A warm palm met my shoulder, causing me to jerk upright. Wyatt stood beside the bed, shirtless, and wearing a concerned expression.

"Of course you're here," I said, collapsing back into the pillows and punching the mattress. It seemed he was just going to witness all my moments of weakness now. More fodder for him to use against me. Not that I stood a chance in a custody battle anyway.

No, I didn't even want to fight him anymore.

He'd proven to be too perfect with Jamie.

The ideal father I could never take away from the boy I considered to be my own son.

Wyatt slid onto the bed beside me, his arms offering a cocoon of heat I couldn't refuse. Because what did it matter? Why fight? He'd seen me at my worst already. Why not again? It wouldn't change anything between us, and I could use a fucking hug.

I had no one.

No friends.

No support.

No one to offer comfort.

And soon, I wouldn't have Jamie, either.

I shattered in Wyatt's embrace, no longer fighting the onslaught of emotions assaulting me from within. All the anger, the frustration, the heartache—I gave him everything. And for reasons I couldn't discern, he accepted it, his fingers combing through my hair while his other hand rubbed my back.

He said nothing. Just held me while I fell apart in the worst of ways and offered me the sympathy I craved. Not pity, no. Just support. Understanding. Because Jean had deceived him, too. He was perhaps the only person in this world who knew what that felt like, and how messed up was it that it brought us together?

But we're not together, I reminded myself. *This is temporary.* He'd be gone in a month. Maybe sooner. And why did that hurt me even more? It wasn't just about losing Jamie but about losing Wyatt now, too.

This was never supposed to be about feelings.

Or so I thought, anyway.

But it'd been an emotional train wreck from the beginning.

"We're going to figure this out," Wyatt whispered, his lips in my hair as he held me against his chest. "Garrett is going to have Jean's place cleaned up and staged for sale, but he won't move forward with marketing it until you've decided what you want to do with it. Just know that you don't need to worry about any of it. We're here to help, okay?"

"But why?" I asked, pulling back to study him, my face no doubt a mess of tears. "Why do you both keep asking me what I want to do with it? It's not my condo. I mean, yeah, it's in my name. But that's your money, Wyatt. Not mine. Nothing about any of this is my decision."

"Everything is your decision," he replied, cupping my cheek. "The condo, the money—it should have all been yours from the beginning, Avery. So it's almost bittersweet that Jean put it all in your name, as if she knew it'd one day be yours anyway."

"It's not mine," I snapped. "I don't want any of it. It's not my money. It doesn't *belong* to me. None of this does. The only thing I've ever wanted is Jamie, and he doesn't belong to me, either. He's yours. And I have no say over any of this. So you and Garrett figure it out. I'll sign whatever you need me to sign, but I don't want the condo or the accounts or anything. I just… I just want…" I trailed off on a sigh because what I wanted didn't matter. I could never have it. That much I understood now.

"You just want what?" he pressed, clearly not hearing my internal defeat. "Finish that statement, Avery."

"It doesn't matter."

"It matters to me."

"Why?"

"Because I want to know what you want. Tell me."

"It's an impossibility."

"Let me be the judge of that."

I laughed, but it lacked humor. Because yeah, he *was* the judge of that. At least, in a way.

"Jamie's yours. I can't have him. I understand and accept that, even though it kills me." I took a deep breath, my heart crumbling into ash between us.

"All I want is for Jamie to be happy," I continued, laying it all out there. "I want you both to be happy. And I can't be part of that with Jean hanging over all of us. I'll be the constant reminder of what she's done, and there will always be something. I'm convinced she's left me a graveyard of secrets to uncover, each one providing a new problem for me to solve. Apparently, that's to be my existence. And how pathetic is that?"

I wanted to cry all over again, but I had no more tears to shed. It was all I'd done for days after months of holding it all in.

Jean had finally broken me.

And Wyatt was my witness.

Fan-freaking-tastic.

I pressed my palm to his face, searching his eyes. "I know you have to take him from me. I know that's what's best for him. It kills me to acknowledge it, but I understand it. And I don't fault you for it. I'm not good enough for him, and I see that now."

His forehead creased, his eyes narrowing. "You don't think you're good enough for Jamie?" The words sounded angry, his flushed cheeks adding to the effect. "You've raised him for four years on your own, Avery. You've been his mother in every way that counts. And you're going to let your sister's bullshit make you feel inadequate? Now? After all these years?" He snorted. "I thought you were stronger than that."

I blinked, his words slapping me across the face. "Excuse me?"

"You know, maybe you're right. Maybe you're not good enough for him, if you're just going to give up after a bad few days. How utterly disappointing."

My jaw clenched, a different kind of heat pouring through my veins. "Are you fucking kidding me right now? I'm doing the right thing, and you want to make me feel guilty for it?"

"You're not doing the right thing. You're giving up. And that's unacceptable."

"I am not giving up," I argued. "I'm admitting that you'll be a better parent to him."

"Why, Avery? Why would I be a better parent to him?"

"Because you're his father! You don't have all this baggage. You have the means to take care of him. You... You..." I growled, losing my train of thought. "You're the better parent."

"Hmm, I see. So, money and a lack of baggage, oh, and paternity, qualify me to be a superior father. Fascinating. Because you know what I've witnessed?"

I rolled my eyes, annoyed by his poor summarization. But he continued before I could comment.

"I see a woman who has worked her ass off to afford her own home for a child she considered to be hers, not because she birthed him but because she loved him. She's taught him right and wrong. She's taught him how to be respectful. She's taught him how to make friends, how to act in public, how to communicate, and how to be a little person. He can get himself ready for bed. He can feed himself. He can make decisions. He's intelligent. He's not afraid to talk about feelings. He might have a bit of a pizza problem, but that's okay because he's fucking perfect in every way, and not because of what *I* have done for him. But what *you* have done for him."

His hand slid to the back of my neck, his gaze intense as he stared down at me.

"Avery, *you* are the reason he's thriving, the reason he's survived. And don't you ever let anyone tell you otherwise."

Okay, so I wasn't done crying. Because while he'd been speaking, tears had popped into my eyes. Not of sadness, but of something very, very different. "You see all that?" I whispered, my throat tight with emotion.

"Of course I fucking do. You're the reason my son is who he is, and I wouldn't change a damn thing about him. The baggage, as you call it, bears no weight on who you are to him and who he has become because of you. Jamie loves you, Avery. You're just as much the center of his world as he is yours, and I would never, in a million years, want to break that. Don't you see? All I want is to put Jean to rest for us all. It's not about compensating you for your time or trying to make up for the last four years. I just want to put her in the ground once and for all."

I… I didn't know what to say. He'd just flipped all my

logic on its head, pointing out facts that I knew deep down but had lost beneath the turmoil of our situation.

"And for the record, you're not the only one with baggage." His thumb traced the column of my neck, brushing my pulse and back up. "My childhood was not a dream, Avery. There's a reason I rebel against my father. He's a horrible person, someone I don't want in my son's life. Someone I don't want in your life, either."

Oh. Another statement I didn't expect. But this one was much easier to respond to. "What did he do?" I wondered out loud. Then I realized how intrusive that was. "Oh, you don't have to answer that."

"No, I don't. But I want to." His thumb continued to draw lines over my skin while he relaxed beside me.

At some point during his speech, he'd pushed me to my back to lean over me, as if needing the leverage to make me understand. But now, he seemed to want to be on an even level again.

I turned to face him, my head on a pillow while he cradled his own with his arm. The other hand remained against my nape, keeping us connected in an intimate way while his gaze found mine.

"What I'm about to tell you is one of the best-kept Mershano family secrets in history," he started, a warning in his voice.

"Okay." Did he want me to promise not to say anything? Because that sort of went unsaid between us.

He took a deep breath, then dropped the bomb on me. "Ellen Mershano isn't my birth mother."

My lips parted. "She's not?"

"No. Jonah had an affair with a twenty-year-old employee and paid her off to keep her quiet. I barely had a chance to know her, having only been allowed visitation rights in my early years, but it was enough to leave a lasting memory. It also made me the proverbial black sheep of the Mershano family, mostly because Jonah loves to remind Ellen that I'm not hers, like I'm a sort of trophy for his infidelity. In summary, he's a dick, and their marriage is not a fairy tale or anything close to it."

Wow. Wyatt constantly calling his parents by their first names suddenly made a lot more sense. "I... I don't know what to say," I admitted. Apparently, our theme for tonight revolved around leaving me speechless.

"Not much to say, really. But maybe it gives you a little insight into why I feel so strongly about Jamie staying with you. I was ripped from my mother's arms at the age of five and never saw her again. I would not wish that experience on anyone, let alone my own son."

"But I'm not..." I trailed off at the look in his eyes.

"You are his mother in every way that counts. And denying it not only belittles you but it belittles what exists between you and Jamie."

I swallowed. "You're right." The two words came out on a croak, my heart thudding hard in my chest. "It's just, well, hard. You don't know what it's like to consider someone yours but have society and everyone else constantly remind you that he's not. And when I tried to adopt him, to finally claim his as mine..."

"I arrived," he finished for me.

I nodded. "Yes. But I don't blame you, Wyatt. I get it. He's your son, too."

"Biologically, yes. However, I'd not earned the right for him to call me Dad yet."

"You will," I replied, certain of it. "He took to you faster than anyone else he's ever met. It takes time, but he'll be yours in all ways before you know it."

"While still remaining yours," he said, his grip on the back of my neck tightening. "I'm not going to take him from you, Avery. I know that's not as comforting as a legal document, that I could break my vow at any moment, but I need you to trust me not to. We still have a little over a month left of our current agreement, which may or may not be enough time for us to figure all this out. What matters is that we work together, all right? Stop doubting me. Stop doubting this. Stop doubting yourself."

I licked my lips, floored, yet again, by his words. "Are you staying here? With us? For the next month, I mean."

"That's my plan, unless you kick me out. Maybe even longer, if you'll allow it. Although, I have a two-week wedding to attend in May. Which reminds me—"

"A two-week wedding?" I interjected, my eyebrows flying upward. "Seriously?"

He chuckled. "That was my thought when I saw the invitation. Apparently, Sarah feels Evan needs a vacation from work. And I agree with her."

"Sarah," I repeated, recalling the name from Jamie. "Wait, Sarah is your, uh…?" I tried to recall my research from a few weeks ago but drew a blank on his sister's name. I just remembered he had a brother and a sister.

"Evan's fiancée," Wyatt replied helpfully. "She met Evan on *The Prince's Game*."

"The what?"

"A dating show." He arched a brow. "You didn't watch it, either? Oh, then you're the perfect date for this nonsense because I have no idea what actually happened. But apparently, Sarah's identical twin auditioned under Sarah's name as a practical joke. Which, I guess, ended well, because honestly, Evan and Sarah are perfect for each other."

"Her sister auditioned as a joke?" *Holy shit.* "That's horrible!"

"Well, I'd argue your sister is more of a bitch, but I'm biased."

"She must hate her sister."

"Not enough, in my opinion. Abby—Sarah's sister—is one of the bridesmaids."

"Shut up." After everything Jean had put me through, there was no way in hell I'd invite her to my future wedding, let alone into the wedding party. Well, my fictional future wedding. Because yeah, that was likely never happening.

"Yeah, so, do you want to go? I'm sure it'll be fun. And my sister, Mia, will be there. I haven't seen her in a few years, but I really want her to meet Jamie." His eyes crinkled at the sides as he smiled. "You'll love her. She's feisty as fuck, and she hates Garrett."

"She hates your lawyer? Sounds like my new best friend."

Wyatt chuckled. "Sarah hates him, too."

"I'm sensing a theme."

"He's an ass."

"Yes," I agreed. "He is."

Wyatt's lips curled. "So, is that a yes, then? You'll go?"

"I'll have to figure out work." My mouth twisted to the side. "I've used a lot of vacation time recently."

"I suspected as much and already told Evan you might not be able to go for the full two weeks."

"A week would be better," I admitted. "I'll look at my schedule tomorrow."

"Good." His palm slid to my shoulder, nudging me to my back and shifting to his elbow at my side. "Now, I have something important to discuss with you, Miss Perry. Assuming we're done with everything else?"

I swallowed. "Uh, yeah, I think so?" My brain short-circuited as his muscular thigh slid between my legs. "Wh-what do you want to talk about?"

"Well, Jamie mentioned your screams from this morning. He thought you had a nightmare."

Oh, crap... "That's why—"

"Shh." He pressed his finger to my mouth. "I understand now. So I have a proposition for you. I'm going to make you come again. What I need you to tell me is, do you prefer to scream around my cock or my tongue? Because I fully intend to come, too. Either down your beautiful throat or deep inside your hot, wet pussy. Which would you like more?"

23
WYATT

Avery's pupils flared with interest, but her lips remained parted on an "Oh" with no further sound escaping.

"Have I rendered you speechless, sweetheart?" I wondered aloud, tilting my head to the side. "Does that mean I get to choose? Because I already locked the door." There would be no interruptions this time. And Jamie was sound asleep anyway.

I warned Avery I wanted adult time later, and I considered myself a man of my word.

Her tongue slipped out to dampen her lower lip, giving me all sorts of ideas for her mouth. Hmm, for a later time. Because I wanted to feel her legs wrapped around my hips. To slide deep inside her and hear her moan my name while I kissed her.

I palmed her breast, loving her lack of a bra, and flicked her erect nipple with my thumb.

"I'm about to decide for us both," I warned, pinching her stiff peak. She arched into my hand on a needy whimper, her eyes taking on the glazed appeal of a woman thoroughly aroused. "I want to fuck you, Avery."

"Yes…" It came out on a hiss as I tweaked the hard tip.

"Good," I whispered, leaning down to kiss her neck. Her skin tasted clean and fresh, as if she had just come from a shower. It made me want to lick every inch of her, to claim and brand her as mine.

I traced her collarbone with my tongue and shifted my weight to my knees. Straddling one of her thighs, I sat up just enough to grab the hem of her tank top and lift it over her head to reveal her perfect tits. I hadn't worshipped them enough this morning, too eager to taste.

I rectified that oversight now, nipping and licking and memorizing her skin with my mouth while she writhed beneath me. "Mmm, I could do this for hours, Avery."

She threaded her fingers through my hair, her nails digging into my scalp. "I need more."

"I know." I did, too. But for now, I wanted to torment her in the best way. My thigh pressed into the apex between her legs, applying just enough friction to tease without letting her tumble over the edge. I tugged her nipple between my teeth, causing her to groan my name. "Careful, sweetheart. We don't want to wake the house."

She let out a frustrated sound that resembled a curse.

I chuckled against her supple breast. "So needy…"

Her grip in my hair tightened, her body bowing off the bed. I caught her hips, pushed her back down, and hooked my thumbs in her yoga pants.

Avery squirmed as I moved to pull the fabric down.

And I groaned at what I found. "No panties?" Fuck, that was hot. Almost as hot as the slick pussy waiting for my cock. "You're so wet, Avery. When was the last time someone fucked you?" I almost didn't want the answer, but I needed it. If it'd been too long, then I needed to prime her to take me.

"I…" She shivered as I bent to blow against her weeping sex.

"How long, Avery?" I asked again, my lips brushing her clit. "I need to know if you're ready for me." I slid a finger inside her tight channel while I spoke, finding the answer before she voiced it.

"A few years." She clutched the sheets beside her hips, her thighs quivering. "Can't… date…"

"Mmm, we're going to change that," I vowed, licking her swollen bud. My words referred to both her lack of dating and prolonged abstention from sex. I intended to fix both. We were just doing them out of order, but I never followed traditional rules. And it seemed Avery felt similarly.

I added another digit, slowly and gently expanding her.

Her legs tensed around me, her breathing coming in pants. Not from pain but from eagerness. So I slid a third finger into the mix while sucking her sensitive nub into my mouth. She vibrated beneath me, her orgasm edging closer by the second.

But I didn't want her to come yet.

No.

That, I wanted to feel around my shaft.

She growled as I moved, her blue-green irises flaring with a mix of ire and arousal that lit my blood on fire for her. "Hold that thought."

"You better be coming back," she said as I slid off the bed.

"Oh, we'll both be coming." I pulled a condom from my pocket before losing my sweatpants.

Her gorgeous eyes zeroed in on my package, the not-so-subtle parting of her lips giving my ego a thorough stroke. I never doubted my size or my looks—I knew I'd been blessed in both areas—but that didn't stop me from enjoying the appreciation in her expression now.

"You look like you need to touch me first." I handed her the condom before kneeling on the bed. "Explore at your leisure, Avery."

"You came in with a condom," she whispered, going up on one elbow.

"I did."

"So damn arrogant," she accused while lifting her opposite hand to wrap it around the base of my dick.

"You've wanted me to fuck you for weeks." My abs tightened as she intensified her grip, sending a shiver of want down my spine. "That's called being prepared, sweetheart. Nothing arrogant about it."

"Yeah, you're a regular Boy Scout," she teased, sitting up. "Lie down."

I arched an eyebrow. "Now who is being presumptuous?" It should be clear to her that I preferred to be in charge in the bedroom. However, the desire radiating from her had me complying. Anything to encourage her to keep touching me like that.

I fell to my back beside her and folded my arms behind my head. "Do your worst," I dared.

She smiled as she shifted to her knees, essentially trading positions with me. Her hold on my erection never wavered, leaving me eager and hard in her palm. She gave me a tentative stroke, then bent to lick the head.

"Fuck," I breathed, shocked to hell and back by that bold little move. She repeated the motion, then took me into her mouth and sucked me deep into the back of her throat.

It took physical restraint not to grab her head and keep her there. But I wanted to give her the semblance of control and allow her to explore to her heart's content before I fucked her into the mattress.

She set the condom to the side and cupped my balls, her other hand still wrapped around my base as her mouth worked me in hypnotic, wet strokes.

"If you've decided this is how you want to make me come, then I need you to straddle my face, Avery. Because I want to lick that sweet cunt of yours to completion."

Her responding groan reverberated against my shaft, making me impossibly harder in response. Fuck, I was going to come if she didn't stop.

My fingers itched to wrap themselves in her hair, either

to force myself deeper or to pull her off completely, I wasn't sure. Thankfully, she moved before I had to decide. The foil of the condom appeared, and she ripped it open with her teeth.

I arched a brow. "You might be the first woman in my existence to ever make a condom look sexy."

She ignored me and focused on covering me with the rubber, then moved to straddle me.

A woman who wanted to be on top.

Could she be any more perfect?

Her nimble fingers guided me into her entrance, stirring all sorts of sensations in my gut. Most of them hot and volatile, the need to take over causing perspiration to dance across my skin. But I let her lead, allowed her to take me slowly inside her until she was seated on top of me, her expression etched into one of yearning mingling with pain. She swallowed, her palms pressing into my chest, her eyes squeezed shut.

Then she moved just the slightest inch, and a breath escaped her luscious lips on a sigh. "More," she whispered. "I need more."

Me, too.

I flipped her to her back without breaking the contact between our legs and stared down into her heated gaze. "You ready to scream into my mouth, Avery?"

"Yes." She licked her lips. "Fuck me, Wyatt."

I didn't need to be told twice.

Her body readily received my thrusts, her walls tight around me, hugging me deep as if she never wanted me to leave.

And oh, how I longed to stay forever. Moving in and out of her, feeling her slick heat kissing me intimately. My only regret was the damn condom, but we would discuss that another time.

Her lips parted for my tongue, allowing me to fuck her mouth the way I took her body.

Punishing.

Rigorous.

Thorough.

It was quite literally the perfect fit. Tight, but not painful. And fuck, I was going to explode if she shifted her hips like that again.

She repeated the action as if hearing my thoughts, or maybe she just knew.

"Avery," I whispered against her mouth. "Fuck, Avery…"

"Harder," she begged. "Don't hold back."

Mmm, I wasn't, but I gave her what she craved, driving into her with a force that would shock most women. Avery merely moaned, accepting the pace and meeting me halfway, her body a work of art as it danced with mine.

Perfection.

I'd entered this bedroom with the idea of changing the course of history for her, yet she'd managed to mangle mine. Because no one had ever been this responsive, this addictive, in bed. And something told me there would never be another.

I kissed her with everything I owned, giving her my soul and shifting my hips at the angle I knew she needed. She shook beneath me, her orgasm mounting.

One more…

There…

She exploded, her scream delicious in my mouth and sending me right over the cliff with her. My orgasm shot down my spine with a force that caused me to growl her name. So fucking intense. Consuming. Blackening my vision, tightening my limbs, and tingling through every muscle.

But I never stopped kissing her, our tongues engaged in a slow, rhythmic song that didn't want to end. And so, it didn't. Even through our heavy breathing, the subtle spasms rocking us below, we didn't stop tasting each other.

A new experience, one I'd never thought to desire or want but, with Avery, was so perfect. As if vows were being whispered, a promise of a future we both desired and weren't ready to name. Of living in the moment without words, just feeling.

Her hands slid from my shoulders to my neck, holding me to her as her legs tightened around my waist, and a slower tempo began, my arousal still rock hard inside her.

This wasn't fucking.

This was... something else. Something with feeling. Something I craved without understanding what it meant.

And I gave in.

Reveled in it.

Adored her.

With my tongue. My body. My cock.

"Avery," I whispered, feeling her tightening around me again, her body lifting up off the bed on an eruption I felt to my very soul.

Her pleasure seemed to live within me, warming my heart in a way I didn't know it could be.

I didn't come with her, not this time, but it wasn't needed. Her euphoria pulled me into a different cloak of sensation that rivaled the most intense orgasms of my life. And I would happily live there forever—with her.

She kissed me with the laziness of a woman well sated, her pupils dilated with ecstasy as she gazed into my eyes. "I think you just destroyed me for any other man, Wyatt Mershano."

Pride unfurled in my chest, causing my lips to curl. "Good." I nuzzled her nose. "Because I intend to be the only one to ever hear you moan like that, Avery Perry."

And by that, I meant I'd be the only man to swallow her cries of passion. Hmm, damn, they'd been so hot. I refused to share them with anyone else.

"Yeah?" Her eyes twinkled.

"Yeah," I replied, smiling against her mouth. "And for what it's worth, I think you just destroyed me for any other woman, too." I licked her bottom lip before dipping inside to kiss her soundly, claiming her, marking her, redefining her as mine. "I want to do it again."

"We'll need more condoms," Avery whispered.

"I have a box in my room."

She lifted her hips into mine. "That's too far away. Use the box in my nightstand instead."

I shifted to stare down at her. "Now who is being cocky?"

Her mouth curled into a sassy little smirk. "A girl has to be prepared with Wyatt Mershano living in her house."

"Why, Miss Perry, I'm impressed." I reached over to open her drawer. Sure enough, there was an unopened box of condoms waiting to be used. "Oh, Avery. I might just have to fuck you again. Right now."

"I was hoping you might," she said, her gaze glittering with intent. "As you said, I've wanted you to take me for weeks."

"Are you implying that we need to make up for lost time?"

"Maybe." The coy look she gave me did not match the gush of heat against my dick.

"Mmm." I picked up the box of condoms and discarded the used one into the bin beside the bed. "I hope you weren't planning to catch up on sleep tonight, Avery."

Because she wasn't the only one who had fought these cravings for weeks. And now that we'd opened the door, every sordid, dirty thing I wanted to do to her was leaping forward with a vengeance.

"Sleep is overrated," she whispered.

"Yes." We'd be creating our own dreams tonight. *Wicked, wet, and fun.* "Open your mouth, Avery. I want to kiss you again before you take my cock."

"You say the most explicit things to me."

I smiled against her mouth. "Oh, sweetheart. We've only skimmed the surface. Now stop talking and part those beautiful lips for me. The only sounds I want to hear from you are ones of pleasure."

24

AVERY

"He's in a mood," Wyatt warned softly as he joined me in the kitchen. His warm lips brushed my cheek, sending a shiver across my skin. We'd grown closer over the last month—much, much closer. Including him practically moving into my room, something Jamie hadn't commented on aside from the one time he asked if he could join our sleepover party.

"Any idea what's caused it?" I asked, referring to his comment about Jamie.

"Gretchen mentioned the kids were supposed to draw a family portrait today." He reached around me to pluck a raw pepper from my cutting board. "Jamie drew one with four people and what I think might be a pizza."

I frowned as I turned on the burner. "Four people?"

"It looked like you, an angel, Jamie, and, I think, me." He winced a little, then stole another veggie slice.

I pointed a wooden spoon at him. "Keep doing that and I'll have to chop up another one."

He opened the fridge and grabbed another pepper, tossing it in the air and catching it deftly in his other hand. "Give me a knife, baby, and put me to work."

"Baby." I snorted. "The knife's right there."

Wyatt rinsed the pepper, then cut it up, leaving half for me and putting the other half on a plate. "I'm hungry," he said by way of explanation.

I shook my head. "I'm starting to understand where Jamie's impatience comes from."

"You say that like it's a bad thing." He pressed a red slice to my lips. "Open."

God, the man loved that word. And just hearing it had my thighs clenching. He may have meant to feed me a veggie, but usually, that command was tied to something much sexier. The knowing glint in his gaze as I complied said he knew exactly where my mind went, and he'd intended for that.

"I love when you're obedient, sweetheart," he whispered, nipping my neck. "I'll go see if I can figure out what's bothering our little man."

His words warmed me inside and out. *Our little man*. This wasn't the first time he had used that phrase.

We'd yet to really discuss the future, and the two-month agreement we struck was set to end next week. However, Wyatt hadn't said a word about what he wanted to do. To be fair, neither had I. It was much easier to just exist and take it one day at a time. But things did seem to be falling into place. *Finally*.

Garrett finalized the sale on Jean's condo last week and transferred the funds into an account under Jamie's name— per my demand.

I didn't want any of the money, something Wyatt only half-heartedly fought me on. All the assets Jean had hidden from me were transferred to Jamie. Of course, I had to play trustee of the account until his eighteenth birthday, which I only accepted because I had no intention of touching a dime of it.

I had my own job and my own home. But I couldn't deny that little nest egg would make affording college much easier for Jamie down the road. It would also set him up for a comfortable life beyond it.

A weight had lifted from my shoulders. I no longer had to worry about Jamie's future, only my own. And right now, I was content to live in the present.

I added the veggies to the saucepan, smiling as I thought about Wyatt playing with me in the kitchen. The man was a certified flirt. We hadn't discussed exclusivity, but it didn't seem to be needed. Not with him spending every night in bed with me. Anytime he did leave, it was with me or Jamie or both of us.

And he didn't seem to miss his old life, hadn't mentioned once wanting to visit any of his friends or family. The only plan we'd discussed was his intention to fly to Hawaii in ten days for his brother's wedding. Jamie and I would be joining him the week following, which Wyatt said would be for the actual ceremony.

"No." Jamie's sharp tone preceded his march into the kitchen, where he stopped with his hands on his hips. "Rebel friend is being annooooying. Tell him to stop."

"Yeah? What's he doing?" I asked, glancing over Jamie's shoulder to where Wyatt stood leaning against the kitchen island. He'd followed the little man with a smirk.

"He wants me to tell him 'bout my picture, and I don't wanna."

"Why not?" I wondered while adding the sauce to the sautéed beef and veggies. Spaghetti Bolognese was one of my favorites.

"'Cause I don't want to!" He stomped his foot for emphasis.

My eyebrows actually rose. "Don't you take that tone with me, young man." He knew better. I finished stirring the sauce, added a lid, and turned down the heat to let it simmer. "Why don't you tell me about your drawing?"

"I don't want to!" he snapped.

"You need to calm down," I snapped right back. "What's going on, dude? What happened today?"

"I don't want to talk about it!" he yelled, storming off in the direction of the living area.

"You weren't kidding," I muttered, looking at Wyatt.

"He's been acting like this since I picked him up."

"Yeah, well, it's about to stop." I followed Jamie to where he sat with folded arms in his chair. He'd turned up the television to a deafening level that I halted by clicking the *Power Off* button on the remote. "Talk to me, dude."

"No."

"Yes," I threw back at him. "Right now."

"No!" He glared at me with tears in his eyes.

Wyatt squatted down to meet him at eye level. "Jamie, man, you can't talk to your Auntie A like that."

"Why not? She's not my *mom*." He looked away. "I don't have a mom!"

My voice failed me, his words a knife through my heart. *She's not my mom.* I... I didn't know how to reply to that, didn't know what to say. He'd never said anything like that to me before.

"Who told you that?" Wyatt demanded, clearly not having the same issue as me.

"My friend at school," Jamie muttered. "He said Auntie A isn't my real mom 'cause I call her Auntie A."

Oh God...

My knees threatened to buckle beneath me, forcing me to grab the chair for support. I couldn't hide the horror on my features, the pure shock rippling through my veins. But Jamie missed it all, his focus on the fireplace beside the television.

Wyatt stared at his son, his intensity palpable. "What else did this *friend* say, Jamie?"

"That my picture isn't real 'cause it's not a fam-aly." He sniffled, breaking my heart. "That I don't have a real mom. 'Cause Momma Jean's an angel, so that's why Auntie A has me. And she's not my mom 'cause I don't call her that. And

I don't have a dad 'cause, well, I don't know why. But he said it's 'cause no one wants me."

"Well, this friend of yours sounds jealous to me," Wyatt replied.

"Gel-o-us?" Jamie repeated, his brow furrowing. "What's that?"

"It means he wants an Auntie A and a rebel friend, but he can't have one, so he's making you feel bad about it."

Jamie shook his head. "Nah. He has a mom and a dad. All my friends has 'em. 'Cept me." He looked down at his hands, twisting in his lap. "They kept askin' me 'bout Momma Jean. I told them she's an angel. They said it's 'cause my momma's dead. But... what's *dead* mean? That she's an angel? That I don't get a mom? 'Cause that's what they said. That I don't get one now. But I want one. So why don't I get one?"

I pressed the back of my hand to my mouth, willing the sob climbing up my throat to go away. But I couldn't stop the tears from forming in my eyes.

Wyatt reached out to grab my hand, but his focus remained on Jamie. "Just because Momma Jean is an angel doesn't mean you don't have a family. You have me, and you have your Auntie A."

"But that's not the same," Jamie said, his nose scrunching. "They said I don't has one 'cause I don't have a mom or dad, that my family isn't *real*."

Wyatt sighed. "Little man, you don't have to call someone *Mom* or *Dad* for them to be your family."

"But I want a mom and a dad!" Jamie shouted, losing his temper all over again. "I don't want an Auntie A or a rebel friend. I want a *real* family, jus' like everyone else!"

He jumped up and took off in the direction of the stairs, but Wyatt was faster. He snagged Jamie around the waist and pulled him into a hug.

I stood motionless, unable to speak or move. I'd never anticipated any of this—that children would be the ones to explain to Jamie that he no longer had a mother. Part of me had hoped I'd be his legal mother before that ever happened, that he could start calling me *Mom*.

"Jamie," Wyatt whispered, hugging his sobbing son. "You have a dad, little man."

"No," he cried, shaking his head back and forth rapidly. "I don't has one."

"Yes, you do." He pulled back to cup Jamie's cheeks. "I'm your dad."

My heart stopped. I suddenly felt like an imposter in the room, observing a moment never meant for my eyes. But I couldn't stop watching, couldn't take my attention away from Jamie's little face. His forehead wrinkled. "My dad?"

"Yeah, little man. That's why I'm here. I'm your dad."

"But you're… you're rebel friend."

"A rebel friend who is also your dad," Wyatt said, conviction underlining his tone. "It's why you have brown hair and brown eyes. Like mine."

Jamie blinked, his mouth forming an O. "Like yours?" he whispered loudly.

"Yep."

Jamie finally looked at me. "Does that mean you're my momma, too?"

I swayed, the world darkening around me. Because I realized in that second that I would never be able to say *yes*, that I would never be able to call him mine. That I would always be his Auntie A, not the one he could call *Mom* even though I loved him with every beat of my heart. "No, sweetheart," I managed to get out on a croak. "No, I'm just Auntie A."

But I wanted to be more.

I wanted to be his mom.

I'd *tried* to be his mom.

But the law refused me.

Wyatt tried to grab my hand again, but I stepped back. "I just need a moment," I mumbled, excusing myself to the other room. I didn't want to let Jamie see me break. I couldn't. I had to be strong. I had to pull myself together, force a smile, and pretend that everything was just fine. That I wasn't dying inside knowing that I could never have what I truly desired.

That the little boy I raised as my own would never truly be mine.

He had a father and a family. One that didn't include me. And never would.

I would forever be… Auntie A.

25
WYATT

"No, I'm just Auntie A."

Avery's words from that fateful night nearly two weeks ago played on repeat in my head while I watched the sun set over the Pacific Ocean from the balcony of my hotel suite. She'd put on one hell of a show after that, pretending to be fine and refusing to talk to me about it later that night.

Not that I knew what to say to her.

She was his aunt, not his mother.

Even though she acted as a mom in every definition of the word.

But I knew how the law worked—she couldn't adopt Jamie. Not with me around as his biological father.

And I refused to give that up, not after the way his eyes lit up at the reveal of just who I was to him. He'd already started calling me Daddy Wyatt, as if it were the most natural thing in his existence. And each time, I watched the light die in Avery's eyes because she knew he'd never have that bond with her.

I took a swig of my water, irritated as fuck that I couldn't help her fix this. The best I could do right now was to continue living with them, which allowed her to remain in Jamie's life. But we both knew it wasn't the same, not when I could just walk out with him at any moment.

"You look like shit," Garrett said, joining me on the balcony.

"Thanks." I glanced at him in his pristine suit and snorted. "It's, like, eighty fucking degrees out here."

He lifted a shoulder. "I live in Houston."

"Fair." I swirled the ice in my glass, refocusing on the waves crashing against the beach below. "It's weird not having Jamie here." *Avery, too.* It'd only been twenty-four hours, but I already missed them both.

"You know what's weird?" Garrett countered, collapsing into the chair beside me. "Seeing you all wrapped up in family life." His blue eyes slid sideways to meet mine. "I never thought I'd see the day when Wyatt Mershano wanted to play house, but here we are."

I smirked. "Don't knock it until you try it, G."

Because playing house with Avery certainly had its benefits—ones I explored every single night in her bed. Which I also missed right about now, but not as much as her beautiful smile and the way she murmured my name in the morning. We'd taken it easy in the sexual department after Jamie's profound announcement, but I still spent every night with her in my arms. It just felt right. Not because I had to be there but because I wanted to be there.

"So, when are you proposing?" Garrett asked, causing me to choke on my water.

"*What?*"

"You heard me." His lips curled. "I mean, it seems to be the thing to do these days with you Mershano men. And Hawaii's the perfect location."

"Dude, fuck off." Marriage? No. I'd never even considered it before; why would it appeal to me now?

"Seriously?" Garrett arched a haughty brow. "You're

practically married already, what with living at her house and all. She's proven she's not out for your money. You clearly love the woman. And it'd allow her to adopt Jamie. A winning scenario all around. Apart from the whole commitment for life bullshit." He feigned a dramatic shudder. "To each his own, but that fuckery is not for me."

My lips parted to tell him to fuck off again, but the words halted in my throat. *It'd allow her to adopt Jamie.*

I blinked.

Why hadn't I thought of that?

Oh, because I wasn't about to marry a woman just so she could adopt my son.

Except, I liked Avery. A lot. Would tying myself to her be that bad?

I shook my head, my mind blown by the prospect of even considering matrimony. If I still indulged in alcohol, I'd grab a drink, because *fuck.*

Was I even good enough to propose to her? I was a billionaire by inheritance, yes, but I barely knew how to be a boyfriend, let alone a husband.

I didn't have a job.

I had no future aspirations apart from raising Jamie.

So, did I want to be a stay-at-home dad? I frowned. Nothing wrong with that profession. However, it felt lacking in some way. Like I should be able to offer more somehow, not just financially but also in terms of being a role model for my son.

Like Evan, I thought for the millionth time in however many months. I still wanted to talk to him about, well, the future. I didn't want to manage a hotel or even a region, but I wondered if there were ways to help him without having to sit in an office all day.

"You've gone silent," Garrett mused. "Have I shocked you?"

"I forgot you were here," I admitted.

He snorted. "Dick."

"Pot, meet Kettle."

"Truth." He sighed, closing his eyes. "Your sister is due to arrive tomorrow."

"I know." I couldn't wait to see her.

"Evan has tasked me with picking her up from the airport. Said something about it being the best man's responsibility."

My brow furrowed. "I thought Will was his best man."

"And see, that's what I said, but your brother claims we're both his best men." He scoffed at that. "I think he's punishing me for something."

I chuckled. "Why's that?"

"Did you miss the part about having to retrieve your brat of a sister?" He sounded so irritated by the prospect. "How about you go find her instead?"

"Ah, I see. You came down here to try to pawn off your responsibility on me." I snorted. "Good luck with that, G."

"Come on. You owe me after all this shit in Georgia. I've been on my best behavior. I've helped. Now it's your turn."

I decided to fuck with him a bit. "Sorry. Can't. I hate the airport."

"You Mershanos are worthless," Garrett growled, scowling at the ocean. "Sometimes I wonder why we're friends."

I feigned shock. "You think we're friends?"

"I just suggested you propose to your girl—which I believe is a solution to your moping, by the way. And you repay me with that line? Yeah, fuck you."

My gaze narrowed. "I am not moping."

"Yes, you are," he argued. "You've been moping around since you got here. And it doesn't take a genius to figure out why. Propose to the girl. Get married. She adopts Jamie. You all live happily ever after and all that sappy shit. The end."

"Wow, no wonder you don't have a girlfriend," a feminine voice said from behind us.

Garrett grinned wickedly as he glanced at the gorgeous brunette. "I've just not found anyone as charming as you yet, my dear Sarah."

"I bet," she replied, folding her arms. "Did he come down here to ask you to pick up Mia?"

"Yep." I smiled widely at Garrett's resulting grimace. "But I agreed because I want to see my sister."

His eyes widened. "Really?"

I shrugged. "You know, for helping me with all that 'shit in Georgia.'"

"What is with you and Mia, anyway?" Sarah asked, causing Garrett's expression to shutter.

"Nothing." He stood. "She's just a brat."

"Uh-huh," Sarah replied, watching as he stalked off. "There's more to that story."

"Yep." I knew some of it but kept my mouth shut out of respect for my little sister. Once upon a time, Garrett broke her heart, and they'd not spoken much since. I pushed away from my chair to stretch my legs. "Hey, have you seen Evan?"

I didn't bother asking why she'd ventured downstairs. If she wanted something, she'd say it. Because if I'd learned anything about my future sister-in-law over the last few months, it was that she did not pull any punches.

"Yeah, he's upstairs on a conference call," she muttered. "Which is why I'm wandering."

"You should steal his phone," I suggested.

"I've tried that." Her gaze held a devious twinkle to it. "He always gets it back."

I looked her over with a smile. "I bet he does."

"Hasn't anyone told you it's rude to check out another man's woman?" a voice drawled from the foyer, causing me to squint into the interior of the suite. The lack of lighting made it difficult, but I was almost certain I knew the source.

"Says the man who checked me out blatantly on a game show for his cousin," Sarah returned, causing the male inside to chuckle.

"Minx," Will Mershano teased as he stepped onto the balcony.

They embraced each other in a quick hug before a series of squeals broke out between Sarah and the blonde woman who had entered beside him.

"Rachel," Will supplied, following my gaze.

"Your fiancée," I translated, aware of their engagement. As Garrett said, all the Mershano men appeared to be getting engaged. Maybe that was a sign I should follow suit. "How've you been?" I asked, shaking off the thoughts.

"Wonderful," he murmured, his gaze on the two women speaking in rapid female tongues that I couldn't understand. "You?"

How have I been? I wondered. "Happy," I said, meaning it.

Because of Jamie.

Because of Avery.

Because of the new family I'd found—a family I missed right now.

A family I may want to become permanent.

"Hmm. I need to talk to Evan." I didn't bother saying a goodbye to anyone. We'd be spending the next two weeks together pretty much nonstop. I could catch up with my cousin and his future wife then. Right now, I had more pressing things on my mind.

Like my own future.

"He's on the phone," Sarah called after me.

"I'll wait for him to hang up," I promised with a wave. "And I'll tell him to stop taking work calls during his wedding."

She muttered something in reply that I didn't hear, my feet already carrying me into the stairwell at the corner. Everyone else in this fucking hotel seemed to be allowed to barge into my room. Time to repay the favor to my big brother.

And then ask him for advice.

A lot of it.

26

AVERY

"Miss Perry, we'll begin our descent into Maui in about ten minutes." Wendy, the flight attendant, glanced at Jamie sleeping in the executive chair beside me and smiled. "He's going to be well rested when we land."

"I'm sure he'll be bouncing around all night," I admitted. After getting over his initial excitement during takeoff, he'd slept most of the flight. Which had been both good and bad.

Good because it gave me a chance to catch up on some reading.

Bad because it meant I didn't have any distractions when my mind decided to wander to Wyatt. Something that happened often considering he'd arranged both our transportation to the airport and our private jet to Hawaii. I thought we were flying commercial. How wrong I'd been.

It scared me how easily I could grow used to this treatment.

We weren't officially dating, but we weren't *not* dating, either. We were... undefined. Living together, sleeping together, raising a child together, calling each other every day while apart, and texting each other "I miss you" randomly, too.

It definitely felt like we were in a relationship. But I had no idea what to expect from him this week. What would his family think? Most of them would be meeting Jamie for the first time—including Ellen and Jonah Mershano. How would Jamie react to that? Would he be overwhelmed? Excited?

He was over the moon about having a dad. Would he feel the same way about grandparents? He never had them on Jean's and my side of the family. Our parents died before he was born.

How quickly his family had grown... replacing me.

I pushed that thought away, refusing to acknowledge it. I would always hold a place in his heart. I didn't need the title of *Mom* to achieve that. Even if it was all I ever wanted.

Stop, I told myself. *There's nothing that can be done.*

I had to live in the moment. Breathe. Focus on Jamie. Smile. And remain supportive.

The jet shifted, indicating we were descending, just as the flight attendant had warned. Jamie's chair was flat, like a bed. It made it easier for him to sleep, especially since the oversized cushion dwarfed his little body. I probably should have napped with him, but I would have wanted to move to the bedroom at the back. Instead, my brain had kept me awake. Too many scenarios running through my head, most of them starting with the moment we landed.

Wyatt said he would handle our pickup from the airport. By sending a chauffeur? By showing up himself? How would he act? How should I act?

Crap, I hated all of this. Why did life have to be so damn confusing?

Just act normal, I thought. *Right, but what is that, again?*

I busied myself by righting Jamie's chair, which amazingly didn't wake him. The kid could apparently sleep through a tornado. Something I'd learned over the last month… because Wyatt and I weren't always quiet.

My cheeks heated as a graphic image of Wyatt between my legs blossomed behind my eyes. We had sort of taken an intimacy break after Jamie's "mom" incident. Mostly because my emotions were all over the map. However, this past week without Wyatt made a few things clear to me.

First, sulking solved nothing.

Second, just because Jamie couldn't call me *Mom* didn't make me any less valuable in his life.

Third, I missed Wyatt.

Fourth, my vibrator did not compare to Wyatt's mouth.

And finally, I *liked* the life Wyatt and I had built over the last few months. Whatever it was, whatever it meant, really didn't matter. Because I enjoyed it. Jamie did, too. And maybe, well, maybe Wyatt did as well.

Jamie began to stir as the jet touched the ground, his eyes finally popping open to take in our surroundings. He blinked sleepy eyes, his brow puckering as if he forgot where we were, then widened when the window revealed we were at the airport.

"Woooooow," he marveled, causing my lips to curl. "Why's it dark?"

"Because we flew overnight." We'd left after dinner, then flew across the country, directly to Maui. That left my brain very confused about time zones. It was maybe eleven o'clock in the evening here? I checked my watch and did some quick math. Yeah, that seemed right.

The jet came to a standstill near the building but didn't connect to it. Instead, a set of stairs were rolled over to help us disembark.

"You ready, dude?" I asked.

"Yeah!" He tried to unbuckle himself. I leaned over to help just a little, and he practically sprung out of his seat. After unfastening myself, I went over to retrieve our bags from the closet and waited for the door to open beside him and Wendy.

"Thank you for everything," I told her.

She laughed. "I barely did a thing. You might be one of the easiest pairs of clients I've ever had."

It was true. I barely ate or drank anything on the flight. "I'm not used to... this."

Her resulting smile was kind. "Something tells me you're about to get used to it." She winked as the door opened to reveal an aircraft worker waiting to take the bags for me.

I wanted to argue, but Jamie had already taken off down the stairs. "Ah, sorry!" I said, chasing after him. "Jamie!"

"Daddy Wyatt!" he yelled, throwing his arms around the man standing beside a black car with tinted windows.

Oh. I hadn't seen him waiting for us near the bottom of the stairs, but Jamie apparently had. I slowed my pace, my heart galloping for an entirely different reason.

Because Wyatt looked amazing as ever in jeans and a fitted gray T-shirt. His hair was windswept as if he'd been driving with the windows down. He lifted Jamie into his arms with an affectionate expression. "'Sup, little man?"

"We flewwwww," Jamie said excitedly. "Like, super high!"

"Yeah?"

"Uh-huh. And it was super fast, too."

"Was it?" He glanced at me as I stopped before them. "He slept the whole time, didn't he?"

"Yep." Which was going to throw Jamie off completely for the time change, but he'd eventually adapt.

Wyatt chuckled. "He did that on our last flight, too." He set Jamie down. "Little man?"

"'Sup?" Jamie asked, sounding just like his father.

"I'm about to kiss your Auntie A, so if you don't want to watch, then look away."

"Ughhhhh..."

I barely had a moment to laugh before Wyatt's lips were on mine. His palm branded the back of my neck as his opposite arm wrapped possessively around my waist to yank me against him.

Yessss...

I'd missed this—the total abandon that came with Wyatt's kiss. He practically devoured me, not caring at all who saw us, his tongue almost desperate, as if he needed this more than air. Or maybe that was me. Because I couldn't stop him, let alone myself. I wove my arms around his neck, clinging to him, consuming him, worshipping him.

Perhaps even loving him.

But I refused to let that little thought interrupt the flow.

I needed more. I needed Wyatt. I needed—

Someone cleared a throat. "Seriously?" a feminine voice asked, causing me to frown and Wyatt to chuckle.

"You're the one who insisted on tagging along for the ride," he replied against my mouth. He kissed me again, softer this time, then pressed his lips to my ear. "I missed you, Avery."

"I missed you, too," I whispered as Jamie grabbed my jeans and gave them a tug. He'd moved behind me when the other woman started talking. I finally glanced over the hood of the car to the gorgeous brunette smiling widely at me. "Uh, hi." *I think?*

"Mia, stop scaring Avery and Jamie," Wyatt said without looking back at the woman.

"I've literally done nothing other than smile," she replied.

"Uh-huh." Wyatt pressed a final kiss to my temple before moving to my side. "Avery, this is my little sister, Mia. I'm sorry in advance for whatever she says to you."

His sister snorted. "He just doesn't like that I call him on his sh—uh…" She glanced down at the little boy hugging my leg. "*Stuff.*"

I smiled. "Then we should get along fabulously."

Wyatt just shook his head. "Come on, little man." He squatted to Jamie's level. "I want to introduce you to Mia."

"Why?" Jamie asked in his infamous whisper.

"Because I think you'll like her. She's my sister, which makes her your aunt."

Jamie tensed against my leg. "Aunt? Like Auntie A?"

"Sort of, yeah," Wyatt replied, suddenly sounding uneasy.

"But I don't want another Auntie A." The little arms around me squeezed tighter. "This my Auntie A."

His words warmed me, mostly because it was nice to know he didn't want to replace me.

"Oh, no one will ever compare to your Auntie A," Wyatt said, a smile in his voice. "She's too awesome. But Aunt Mia can be a friend."

"Friend?" Jamie repeated.

"Yeah, she'll play with you, too. You want to know how I know that?"

Jamie nodded against me.

"She used to play with me when I was younger. She stole all my toys, all the time." Mia made a derisive noise, but Wyatt ignored her, adding, "She's not very good at race cars. But maybe you can teach her."

"I love race cars," Jamie replied, his voice a little more confident now. "But…" He tugged on my pants again. "Did we bring my race cars?"

That hadn't been on my packing list. "Uh, no, I—"

"You're all set up at the hotel, little man." Wyatt ruffled his hair. "I hid them from Aunt Mia so she didn't steal them."

"Good, 'cause stealing is bad," Jamie proclaimed.

"That it is," Wyatt agreed, standing. His lips were warm against my ear as he murmured, "Mia has agreed to babysit tonight while you and I have a little adult time." He left my side before I could reply, my lips parting on silent words that jumbled in my thoughts.

That's a little presumptuous, isn't it?

Thank you.

Can we trust her with Jamie?

Adult time? Yes, please.

I shook my head to clear it and caught Mia's knowing expression. "Since Wyatt wants to jog down memory lane, I think you and I have a lot to catch up on," she said. "Oh, the stories I could tell you…"

"That implies I intend to leave you two alone together," Wyatt cut in, taking Jamie's hand. "Which is not happening." He looked down at his son. "Ready to meet Aunt Mia?"

"Okay, but only 'cause of race cars," Jamie said, his other hand still on my leg. "'Cause I already has an Auntie A."

"And no one will ever replace her. I promise," Wyatt said, winking back at me. "She's too awesome, remember?"

"Auntie A is sooo awwweee-some." Jamie nodded as if pleased with the statement. "And she plays with race cars, too."

"Sir, where would you like Miss Perry's luggage?" The airline attendant asked gruffly.

"In the trunk, please," Wyatt replied, sliding his hand into his pocket and popping open the compartment with, I assumed, a key fob. *Sleek, sexy, black. Yeah, this must be his rental car for the week.* And the car seat in the back proved it.

After Jamie's tentative introduction to Mia, Wyatt buckled him in and grabbed me before I slid into the backseat beside him. "Aunt Mia can entertain Jamie while you entertain me up front." He kissed me soundly, eliciting a not-so-pleasant sound from Jamie.

"Right? Wyatt is so gross," Mia said, slipping past me.

"He does that allllll the time," Jamie replied. "It's so *yuck.*"

A statement I did not agree with, especially as Wyatt pulled me even closer, his mouth curving against mine. The back door closed, silencing whatever response Mia had for Jamie.

"I'm going to do a hell of a lot more than kiss you tonight, Miss Perry," he whispered.

"That sounds like a threat." And a good one at that.

"It is." He tugged my bottom lip into his mouth and gave it a nibble. "I intend to demonstrate how much I've missed you—with my tongue—and allow you to return the favor with your mouth."

"Oh? Is that how it's going to go down?"

"It's certainly how you're going to go down," he replied, his chuckle deep and sexy. He started to pull away, then paused, a smolder darkening his gaze as he studied my lips. "By the way, our suite is huge, which means you won't have to worry about your screams waking up Jamie tonight. And I look forward to taking full advantage of that, Miss Perry."

And there went my panties.

Soaked through.

This man, with his devious intentions and filthy mouth, had ruined me for anyone and everyone else.

And I accepted that.

Just as I accepted his place in Jamie's life.

This was my world now, and I welcomed it with open arms. Because it was the only way to truly live.

27
WYATT

My plan to spread Avery out naked on the king-sized bed in the other room went to hell in a handbasket the second I opened the door to my suite.

"Seriously, do you all enjoy finding ways to infiltrate my personal space?" I demanded as we entered the living area. Evan, Garrett, Will, Rachel, and Sarah were all playing some sort of card game on the coffee table.

None of them bothered to reply to me, too enamored with Jamie—who had ducked behind Avery's legs. She looked just as unnerved as him, causing me to curse internally at the idiots on the couches. As if this wasn't nerve-racking enough, they had to bombard them, too. And directly after their flight. *Jackasses.*

Evan stood first, his eyes kind. "Hey, Jamie. Remember me?"

"No," Jamie said immediately, clinging harder to Avery.

"I'm Evan. This is Sarah. You met us in New Orleans."

"Or-linz," Jamie repeated, sounding confused.

"That's where you got my necklace," Avery reminded him, touching the key hanging from her neck. "The last time you went on the plane. Remember?"

"Ohhhh!" Jamie smiled. "I like flying!"

"I know." Avery put her hand on his head, combing her fingers through his hair. "And you like Sarah, too. You told me all about your new friend when you got back."

"Sarah." Jamie scrunched his nose up at her. "New friend?"

"Yep. You said I would like her."

"I did?"

She smiled. "Yes, you did."

"Then she can be a new friend," he decided. "Like Mia. And play race cars."

"Exactly," Avery replied. "Assuming she wants to play race cars."

"Oh, I'll play whatever the little man wants." Sarah joined Evan, her grin reaching her eyes. "I'm Sarah, by the way."

I sighed. "I wasn't planning to play the introduction game tonight, but as you all have left us no choice… This is Avery and Jamie." I pressed a palm to Avery's back and pointed to the corner by the open balcony door. "You already know the jackhole lawyer over there. Beside him is my cousin, Will. And that's his fiancée, Rachel. Lastly, my brother, Evan, and my future sister-in-law, Sarah."

Avery gave a little wave. "Hi."

"We're excited that you could make it," Sarah said. "And I can't wait to see Jamie in his little-man tuxedo."

Ah, yeah, I hadn't told Avery about that yet. As was evidenced by the look of panic she flashed me. "I already ordered it," I told her. "He can try it on, and if it doesn't fit, there's a tailor on standby."

"Oh." She frowned. "Right."

I kissed her cheek, sensing her unease in the tension of her spine. "It's going to be fun. You'll see." The words were a breath against her ear. "Trust me." When I stood up straight, it was to see everyone in the room giving me a knowing look. Yeah, this welcoming party was done. "Seriously, I need you all to leave."

"Except me," Mia piped up from behind us. "Because I promised to watch Jamie."

"How appropriate," Garrett drawled, his blue eyes simmering with disdain as he looked at Mia.

"And what is that supposed to mean?" she demanded.

I looked up at the ceiling, already over this act. They'd been at each other's throats since Mia landed last week. I understood that she once harbored a crush for the man, but for fuck's sake, they both needed to get over the past.

"Just seems appropriate that the child among us would want to watch the one closest to her age," he replied.

"I'm twenty-seven," she snapped. "Not seventeen."

His eyes danced over her summer dress. "Could have fooled me."

Her audible gasp had Evan stepping in. "Right, we were just leaving." He glowered back at Garrett. "Right?"

"Sure. The scenery at the bar is far more enlightening." The pointed comment had Mia growling as he sauntered past her. If Garrett kept this up, she'd be feeding him his balls by the end of the week.

"You know what?" she said, turning on her heel. "I think I'll join you at the bar, Garrett. If anything, just to prove I can order my own fucking drink."

Avery cringed while Jamie's mouth fell open. "Bad word!" he accused. "Bad, bad word!"

Mia clenched her jaw and looked down at him. "You're right. I'm sorry." She met my gaze. "Rain check on babysitting?"

I nodded. Because yeah, the mood was effectively killed, thanks to the impromptu party in the room.

She gave me a thankful look and stalked after Garrett, no doubt with a litany of curses waiting to be unleashed on the idiotic jackass.

"I'm not following that show downstairs," Evan said, his

arm around Sarah.

"Neither am I," Will agreed. "Let them argue it out. It'll give us all a mental break."

Rachel and Sarah shared a knowing look, their years of friendship clear in that single exchange. Then they looked at Avery. "We're having a spa day tomorrow in the hotel, if you want to join," Sarah offered. "You know, and be around normal people. Do girly things."

"And talk about the Mershano men," Rachel added. "Offer tips. Tell you how to negotiate. The usual."

Will and Evan snorted at the same time, their expressions amused.

"Darlin', the only thing you'll be negotiating—"

Rachel pressed a finger to Will's lips. "Shh. I'm having a conversation."

He grinned down at her with his eyes. Then nipped the tip of her finger. "Make it quick."

"See what I mean?" she asked, rolling her eyes. "Demand after demand after demand."

Avery started to grin. "I might know something about that."

"Which is why you need to join us tomorrow," Sarah said, her welcoming personality pleasing me greatly.

Avery hadn't admitted it, but I knew she was worried about meeting everyone. What she didn't know—because I hadn't really known until last week—was that Rachel and Sarah were both workaholics. Just like Avery. And none of them came from money, making this world foreign to them all. It provided the perfect ground for them all to interact and get along.

"Is that okay with you?" she asked, glancing at me.

"Jamie can hang out with me," I replied, picking him up. "We can go swimming."

"Swimming?!" he repeated, clearly excited.

"Yep. In the ocean."

His eyes resembled the size of dinner plates. "Like, with fish?"

"He's never been to the ocean," Avery informed quietly, grimacing. "I haven't had a lot of time with work, and, well, everything."

I leaned over to kiss her temple. "Then he'll experience his first ocean this week. Starting with tomorrow, right, little man?" I winked at her and started walking toward the bedroom, leaving Avery to bond with the girls behind us.

"Swimming with the fish!" he cheered.

"I'll have to get you some pool floaties, dude," I decided out loud. "And maybe we'll go out on a boat."

"Woooow," he marveled. "I like boats."

"Then you're going to love Hawaii." I set him down beside the play area I'd put together for him in his room. "What do you think?" There was a racetrack, cars, and a bunch of Lego sets.

"Yes!" He did a little jig and immediately plopped down to play. "Let's goooooo."

"Isn't it way past your bedtime, little man?"

"Nah. I'm not tired."

"You always say that."

"But I mean it!"

Right. Because he slept on the plane. "What about Auntie A? Did she sleep on the plane?"

"No, she didn't," she replied behind me, leaning against the door frame. "And she could really use a shower and a nap."

My lips curled. "If only I could join you in that endeavor." That'd been part of my plan. There was a giant Jacuzzi tub in our room. Alas, it appeared I would be staying up with Jamie for a bit. "How about you go shower and relax, and I'll play some cars for a bit. Until he's ready to sleep." Which might not be for a few hours yet. Time change with him was going to be fun.

"Your bags should already be in our room," I added, pointing across the living area to the hallway beyond. "We're the last room at the end."

Her brow crinkled. "How many people are staying

215

here?"

"Just the three of us."

"So what are the other rooms?"

"One is empty. The other is a study. And also another bathroom." Mershano Suites didn't skimp on the upper floors. Hell, the entire hotel was posh and oversized. That was part of the Mershano grandeur.

"Maybe we should put Jamie in the other room? So he's not so far?"

I smiled and pointed to the monitor I purchased because I knew she'd feel that way. "There's a matching one in the master suite. And there's security on this floor. He won't go anywhere."

"What about the balcony?" she asked, eyeing the sliding glass door along the side of his room.

"It's bolted in a place he can't reach. I'll also be locking up the ones in the living area before going to bed and setting an alarm. Trust me, he'll be fine."

She smiled. "You're a good dad, Wyatt." She sounded tired, but I caught the hint of emotion beneath the words. It was the first time she'd ever said that to me, and the proclamation caught me off guard in the best way.

I'm a good dad.

She thinks I'm worthy.

And she doesn't even know what I have planned yet…

"You two are being we-ord again," Jamie mumbled.

"I'm about to kiss your Auntie A again, too," I warned, pulling her to me and pressing my lips to hers. I kept the embrace soft and far too short due to our audience. "Thank you," I whispered.

"I meant it," she replied, her palm on my chest. "You're good with him."

"So are you." I kissed her once more before releasing her. "I'll be in bed soon-ish."

Now her look was one of humor. "Somehow, I doubt that. But see if you can exhaust him."

"I have ideas," I admitted.

She smirked. "Well, good luck." I smacked her ass as she turned, eliciting a squeal from her. "Hey!"

"That's for being sassy," I told her, a myriad of wicked thoughts clouding my mind. "Be naked." I mouthed the words at her, causing her to flush a pretty pink.

"Maybe," she mouthed back before jumping out of my reach and practically skipping toward our room.

Jamie sat on the floor, lost in his new toys and not paying us any mind. Aside from calling us weird, of course. Something he mentioned often. Which was why I wanted to have a little chat with him.

I waited until Avery disappeared from view before kneeling at his side. "So what did you think of Aunt Mia?"

He shrugged. "She's okay."

"Just okay?"

"We didn't get to play," he explained. "But she's nice to me. So I like her okay."

"But not as much as your Auntie A?"

"Nah. Auntie A is my Auntie A. I loves my Auntie A." He spoke while zooming one of his new cars along the track, the words completely innocent and profound at the same time.

I'd been thinking about how I wanted to approach this for weeks, without even realizing the importance of what I needed to say. Ever since Jamie claimed not to have a mom, I'd been thinking about how that just wasn't true. One didn't need to possess the label to already be doing the job.

And *that* was what required explanation.

When I conceptualized all of this, it'd been under the guise of wanting to make Avery feel better. However, now I realized it went so much deeper than that.

"Do you know why you feel different about your Auntie A?"

"'Cause she's mine," he answered simply.

"But Mia is your aunt, too."

His lips twisted. "Yeah, but she's not Auntie A."

"And why is that?" I pushed.

"I dunno. 'Cause no one is Auntie A 'cept Auntie A."

"And she's very special to you, right?"

He nodded. "Yeah."

"Do you want to know why?" I asked, folding my arms around my knees as I shifted to a seated position beside him.

"'Kay." He finally looked at me, his car in one hand. "Why?"

"Because she's always been there for you. She's taught you everything. She takes care of you. That makes her really special." I tilted my head. "You know Momma Jean?" He nodded. "Well, she was supposed to be your mom, but she didn't do a good job. So Auntie A took over and did it for her. Which means, she's like your mom."

His forehead creased. "But Auntie A is Auntie A, not a mom."

"That's because 'Mom' isn't her name. She's always been Auntie A. But I think she's more like your mom because she acts like one and she loves you more than anything in this world."

"But I don't call her Mom."

"Why not?"

"Because she's Auntie A."

"What if you could call her Mom?"

His nose scrunched as he considered. "But… like… Momma Jean?"

"You could call her Momma Avery, or Momma A."

He shook his head. "I don't know. I don't think she'd like it."

"Why not?"

"'Cause whenever we talk about Momma Jean, Auntie A gets sad."

"Do you know why? Because Momma Jean did some bad things that upset your Auntie A. So when we talk about Momma Jean, it makes her sad. But your Auntie A loves you, Jamie. And I think she'd like it if you called her Momma A."

His dark eyes—so intelligent for a child his age—

widened a little. "You think I can?"

"I do. But only if you want to, little man."

"And it wouldn't make her sad?"

"I think it would make her very happy, little man. Because she's already your mom. She loves you, takes care of you, sings to you, reads to you, plays with you, feeds you. That's what moms do, right?"

He seemed to really think about that before nodding. "Yeah."

"Do you like that idea?" I prompted.

"Yeah."

"Then can I ask you something else?" This was going to be the tricky part. I'd rehearsed this in my head a thousand times over the last few days, but I doubted it would come out right.

"Yep." He swapped cars but kept most of his focus on me.

"How would you feel if I came to live with you and Avery forever?"

"And, um, never leave and stuff?"

"Exactly like that," I replied, smiling.

"I thought you already did that?"

"Not officially."

"What's officially?" he asked, tilting his head.

"It means I haven't moved all my stuff in yet, and that I could still leave."

He frowned. "I don't want you to leave."

"I don't want to leave, either. That's why I want to live with you and Avery forever."

"Okay," he agreed. "I like that."

"So you don't mind if I ask your Avery if I can live with you both forever?"

"Nah, it's good. She needs a friend. You can be her friend."

"I want to be more than her friend, Jamie," I admitted. "I want to be her husband."

"Does that mean, like, the wedding stuff?"

"Exactly like the wedding stuff," I said, laughing a little at the disinterested expression on his face. "But it would mean keeping your Avery forever."

"So you'll, like, move into her room and stuff?"

"Yes." Which I'd technically already done, but Jamie didn't seem to understand that yet.

"And sleep together?"

"Yes." *Every damn night.*

"And kiss?" He sounded so disgruntled by that last part.

"Probably a lot, yes."

He gagged a little. "So gross. Girls are gross."

I really needed to start recording him saying that, just so I could replay it in ten years. "You think Avery is gross?"

"No, but kissing is so ughhhh."

I laughed a little, amused. "Well, I am going to kiss your Avery a lot."

More gagging noises. "Okay, but you better not make her cry."

"I'll do my best," I vowed.

"And you have to buy her lots of pizza."

"I can do that."

"And gifts!" He seemed to really favor that idea, something I probably should never have introduced him to. The poor kid would be broke when he started dating. Well, maybe not broke. But he'd be spending a hell of a lot of money.

That said… "I plan to give Avery a lot of gifts."

"Okay." He beamed at me. "Can we play race cars now?"

I chuckled. "Yeah, little man. We can play now." Since he seemed to agree with my intentions. "But don't say anything to Avery, okay?" I wanted the proposal to be a surprise.

"'Bout what?" he asked, already lost in the track.

I ruffled his hair. "Never mind." Even if he did say something, she'd assume he misunderstood me. "I get the blue car."

"Why?"

"Because it's my favorite color, and I'm your dad, so we play by my rules."

"Rules, rules, rules," he sing-songed.

I arched a brow at him. "Are we playing or not?"

"Yessss." He bounced around. "Play!"

Avery was right.

It was going to be a long night.

28
AVERY

Jamie rocked a tux better than everyone in the room. Except maybe his dad, who had lost his jacket hours ago and rolled his sleeves to the elbows.

Mmm. Wyatt Mershano made everything he wore—or didn't wear—look good. His sinful gaze rose to mine as if sensing my thoughts, his resulting smile causing my heart to speed up.

We had yet to experience any adult time this week, despite my going to bed naked each night. I kept falling asleep before Wyatt joined me, only to find myself in his arms the next morning. Then Jamie would arrive before I could follow through on anything.

The kid loved Hawaii. He wanted to swim all day, every day. And his father was all too happy to indulge him.

It painted a beautiful picture, watching them in the waves together. Just as it did now as they danced across the ballroom floor. They were two peas in a pod, and there was no doubt as to their relation.

Jamie and Wyatt had captured the hearts of everyone in this room. Even Ellen Mershano smiled at them, something that didn't seem to happen often. I'd barely spoken a word to either of his parents, not that they'd really tried to talk to me or Jamie. The disdain between Wyatt and his father was palpable. It seemed Evan felt similarly.

Whatever their history, Wyatt wasn't letting it bother him as he lifted Jamie off the floor and tossed him over his shoulder. I smiled at his resulting giggles while also feeling a little jealous that Wyatt couldn't do that to me and carry me off upstairs. Especially with the way his muscular forearms tensed.

I need an orgasm, I decided. *Or twelve.* It'd been weeks, and clearly, I was addicted to Wyatt Mershano. Something I wholeheartedly blamed him for doing to me.

"Jamie says he's tired," Wyatt said, approaching me.

"I did not!" he yelled from above, squirming. "I only yawned!"

"It's way past your bedtime, little dude," I said, noting the near-midnight hour. Not that Jamie had really experienced a bedtime this week. Letting him sleep on the jet had obviously been a huge mistake that I would not be repeating in the future. However, Wyatt had done everything in his power to tucker the little guy out, which, unfortunately, left him tired as well.

"Ughhh," Jamie groaned, slumping over his dad's shoulder.

"Let's get him upstairs." Wyatt gestured toward the doors with his chin.

I stood, happy to follow his lead. With a wave to the bride and groom, as well as the rest of the bridal party, we ventured out of the ballroom and toward the hotel elevators. The wedding technically wasn't done, with us still having five days in Hawaii with the family, but the main ceremony had taken place today.

"They make a beautiful couple," I said as we entered the elevator.

Wyatt shifted Jamie's weight so he could pull out his card and swipe it to send us to the appropriate floor. "Yeah, I suppose Evan chose well." He smiled. "My parents are thrilled."

I snorted. "I noticed." At least Sarah's parents, and her identical twin sister, appeared to be supportive. Jonah and Ellen just seemed bored. No, actually, *miserable* was the better term. "I like Rachel and Will, too. And Mia."

"Not Garrett?"

"Does anyone like him?" I wondered aloud, only partly joking.

"He's not that bad when you get to know him," Wyatt replied, his lips curling. "Actually, he's pretty loyal. We give him a lot of crap, but…"

"He's family," I finished for him.

"Yeah. He is."

A *ding* announced our arrival, and the doors opened to reveal the foyer of our gigantic suite. I glanced at Jamie to see his eyes were closed, which explained his quiet behavior on the way up. "He's definitely tired."

"I know," Wyatt murmured. "I'll tuck him in, then maybe we can have some champagne on the balcony?" It was spoken as a suggestion more than a command.

"I'd like that," I admitted.

"Good, because I already ordered some. It'll be up in about five minutes." He winked and took Jamie toward his room.

Rather than change, I decided to wander outside and admire the midnight waves crashing against the shores below.

Hawaii wasn't a destination at the top of my bucket list, mostly because it was too common. I always chose the locations true adventurists thought of, like Iguazu Falls or Victoria Falls. Not that I'd been to any of those places. They were just on my dream list for some day.

I could see myself wanting to come back here—if anything, just to hear Jamie's excitement over the ocean again.

"He's out cold," Wyatt said, joining me with a chuckle. "I saw through all that bravado about being wide awake."

"You've worked hard to exhaust him," I replied, turning to lean back against the balcony railing. "Are you tired, too?"

"Actually, no. I feel pretty wired."

The elevator let off a *ding*, interrupting my ability to reply, and a robust man in a suit arrived to drop off a pair of flutes, a bottle of champagne, and a bowl of strawberries. He popped the cork and served the drinks before leaving.

Wyatt lifted the crystal glasses, holding one out for me.

"Are you trying to seduce me, Mister Mershano?" I teased, accepting the drink. "Because your chances of getting me naked are pretty high already."

"Are they?" he asked, his lips curling. "I'm tempted to dare you to prove it right here, right now."

I raised a brow. "You might be surprised by my response."

Intrigue danced in his smoldering eyes. "Which would be?"

"My asking you to hold my drink so I can comply." I started to hand it to him, but he pushed it back toward me.

"A toast first," he said, his expression taking on an oddly serious note that didn't seem to fit the teasing of the moment. "Well, maybe not so much a toast as a proposal to our future."

I frowned. "All right." I couldn't tell if that was ominous or positive.

He leaned his elbow on the railing beside me, the warmth of his body blanketing my own. "I spent our week apart thinking about us, about Jamie, about our current living situation. And I have a few things to say on the subject."

And he wanted to do this while drinking alcohol?

Yeah, that couldn't be good.

But he'd been so, well, *close* the last few days. Like he

couldn't stop touching me or being near me. That directly conflicted with the idea that he would want a break or to take Jamie from me, didn't it?

Actions speak louder than words.

He chuckled, his free hand lifting to cup my cheek. "I've learned to read you over the last few months, and I can tell your mind just went to the wrong place. This isn't about me taking Jamie. We've been over that a few times, so don't go there. You're his mom, sweetheart. He might not call you by the title, but we both know you've earned it. Which is what I want to talk to you about. And other things. Future things."

He set his flute on the railing and stepped into me, both his palms cradling my face now. "I need to start this over, okay? Because I had this whole speech planned, and I've already fucked it up."

I bit my lip to keep from smiling. "I didn't say anything," I managed to say, the humor in my voice coming through without my permission.

"Your eyes did," he countered. "Stop. I'm messing up again."

"I didn't do anything."

"You're still talking."

"Because you're in my face."

"Avery."

"Wyatt."

"I like being in your face."

"I know. I like it, too. But I'd rather you kiss me." I thought about the words. "Actually, no. I want you to fuck me. It's been, like, a month, and I'm dying. And here you are, wanting to drink champagne when I'd much rather take off my dress, lie in that lounge chair right there, and force you to give me orgasms all night."

He laughed, the sound far too amused for my liking, particularly after everything that had just spewed from my mouth. And without the assistance of alcohol, no less. *Crap.*

"Oh, no, don't you hide from me." He kept my face

secured between his hands when I tried to glance away. "I will give you as many orgasms as you'd like, Miss Perry. Once we're done talking."

"Maybe I don't want them now." He slid his thigh between mine, causing the slit up the side of my dress to shift and reveal an indecent amount of my leg. One hand fell to my hip, the other sliding to the back of my neck.

"Don't lie to me, Avery," he whispered, brushing his mouth over mine.

I never dropped the flute, my body quivering beneath this unexpected sensual assault. "Wyatt..." I swallowed. "Whatever you want to say, say it. Because I'm... You've..."

Damn it!

I couldn't figure out how to properly respond. Not with his lips trailing across my cheek to my neck like that. I arched into him on a moan as he bit my thundering pulse, my body strung tight from days—*weeks*—of foreplay without follow-through.

Which had mostly been my fault after the "mom incident."

But... "*Wyatt*..."

His lips traced my collarbone, to the V-neck of my dress and down. He kissed my stomach through the material and went to his knee, his hands on my hips, his gaze devilish.

"Do I have your attention now?" he asked, arousal deepening his voice.

"You always have my attention," I admitted. "Since the first time I saw you."

"The feeling is mutual, Avery." His palms shifted to my upper thighs, holding me before him. "I've never been traditional or into formalities or the type to conform to society's rules. You know that, right?"

I grinned. "That's glaringly obvious, yes."

"Good." His thumb drew downward and then upward just enough to begin pulling my dress up an inch. He repeated the motion, sending a shiver of anticipation through me.

I like where this is going, I wanted to say. But I refrained out of fear that he might stop.

"I like you, Avery. A lot. Actually, you know what? Fuck that. I've fallen in love with you over the last few months, and I'm not afraid to admit that."

"What?" I couldn't have heard that right. It... "You've fallen...?" No. No, he didn't mean that. He—

"I love the way you've raised Jamie," he said, sending a shudder across my skin.

Oh, that's what he meant.

"I love how hard you work," he continued, his eyes glimmering in the moonlight. "I love how you won't put up with any of my crap. I love that you aren't afraid to break in front of me, how you let me hold you when you need it, and how you process things afterward. You're proud. You're beautiful. You're intelligent. You're damn near perfect in my mind, and Jamie couldn't have a better mother in his life. You're strong. You make me want to kneel and worship you for hours, days, weeks. Whatever it takes just to hear you moan my name again and again."

My dress began to shift upward again with the words, his gaze taking on a devious twinkle that had my thighs clenching.

"Why are you saying all this?" I asked, the words sounding far breathier than I intended.

"Because I want you to say yes to a future with me," he replied, the fabric of my dress reaching my knees. "And I'm going to lick this beautiful pussy until dawn when you do."

Oh God... "Wyatt—"

"I'm not done, Avery," he cut in, my gown skimming the bottom of my thighs. "See, I had a chat with Jamie about this already, and we decided that I should stay. Forever. But to do that, I need you to agree to a few terms."

This can't be happening... But the wicked glint in his irises said otherwise. "Wh-what terms?"

"Marriage," he said, the word heavy between us. "I want

you to be mine in every way, Avery. In every way. Until death do us part and whatever else is required. But what matters to me is that we would be together, as husband and wife, and raise Jamie as our own. Because that's my second stipulation, Avery. You're already his mom, so you should understand why I want you to adopt him, too. To share him equally, wholeheartedly, forever."

I couldn't breathe, his words hitting me in the chest one after the other. The glass clacked against the railing as I fumbled to set it down, my knees feeling weak. "You... This..." Yeah, that came out right. What did I want to say?

My skirt reached the middle of my thighs, causing him to grin up at me. "Are you going to say yes to me, Avery? Because I can smell your desire, sweetheart, and it's making my mouth water."

"You're not playing fair," I whispered, my limbs tense from need and my heart racing in my chest from his words. "This... Are you... Is this a proposal?" Because it was the most unconventional one in the history of the world.

His lips skimmed my inner thigh on a kiss that seared my skin. "Is it considered a proposal when the man knows his woman is going to say yes?"

"So damn arrogant," I breathed, grabbing the railing behind me and nearly knocking the champagne flutes off the edge in the process. "*Wyatt.*" His head had disappeared beneath my dress.

"Are you going to shout your approval for me, Avery?" His tongue traced a path upward to my drenched thong. "Will you be mine forever?"

"Oh God..."

"No, sweetheart. *Wyatt.*" His teeth unerringly found my clit through the fabric covering my mound, eliciting a shudder of wanton *need* from deep within.

"You can't propose from beneath my dress."

"Did you miss the part about my opinions on society's expectations?" The words vibrated my center, heightening the burning sensation growing in my lower belly. "I can propose however I want, and right now, I want to propose to this delicious cunt with my tongue." My thong disappeared with a rip, my silk gown barely shifting an inch before Wyatt caught it and heaved the fabric over my hips. "Say yes, Avery."

He didn't give me a chance to think, his mouth closing over my sensitive nub with a finality that had me seeing stars. I nearly fell from the onslaught of rapture flooding my body. My fingers wove into his hair, holding him against me, my other hand gripping the railing for dear life as he ravaged me with his tongue.

"Wyatt…"

"Mmm, I love how you say my name," he murmured, nipping and licking. "But that's not the word I want."

He actually expected me to accept his proposal? With his head between my legs?

Oh, hell, of course he did.

This was Wyatt Mershano.

A rebel to the very end.

And he wanted to marry me. Wanted me to adopt Jamie. Wanted to be with us forever. How could I possibly say no to that? Because I knew it wasn't Wyatt acting out of pity or anything of the sort. No, he only did things he wanted to do. As was evidenced by his completely indecent proposal method. I'd never be able to tell this story to anyone. It would always remain our own intimate little secret.

The day Wyatt asked me to marry him by demanding I say yes while stroking my clit with his wicked, dirty tongue.

"Stop thinking," he urged. "Marry me, Avery."

"Convince me," I countered, deciding on a whim to play him at his own game.

He pulled back to stare up at me, his lips glistening with my arousal. "Oh, sweetheart. That's a dangerous proposition."

"Does that mean you're not up to the task? Because I need a husband who can keep up, Mister Mershano."

Wyatt stood and grabbed my hips. "Fuck the

champagne." He lifted me into his arms and carried me through the still-open balcony doors, all the way to the bedroom, and tossed me onto the mattress. "I'm going to lock up in the other room. I expect you to be naked when I get back, my darling future wife."

I narrowed my gaze at his back as he sauntered toward the door. "I haven't said yes yet."

"You're about to say it over and over, sweetheart," he called back to me.

My lips curled. *Yes. Yes, I am.*

29
WYATT

Avery lay naked and ready for me in the bed when I returned, her legs spread in invitation. I shut the door with my foot, my hand on my tie, deftly unfastening the knot.

"Have you given more thought to my proposal?" I asked, teasing her now. Because we both knew she was going to say yes.

"Still not convinced." The heat in her eyes telegraphed the lie, but I let it hang between us.

"Mmm." I started unbuttoning my shirt while she watched. "So, you require some convincing."

"I definitely do."

"My last name and financial situation are not enough?"

She shook her head. "I'm not interested in that."

"Just my cock, then?"

Avery lifted a shoulder. "Your mouth interests me as well."

"Being married for my body and skill in the bedroom," I mused, my shirt falling to the floor. "And here I listed all your traits, calling you strong, hardworking, a good mother. But all you see in me are looks and sex. I'm hurt, Avery. Truly."

She didn't appear apologetic at all. "Listing your traits would be a waste of time. You already know you're amazing."

"Maybe my ego could use a little stroke." I touched my belt while I said it. "Maybe I want you to say why you'd want to marry me."

Her pupils dilated, her tongue dampening her lower lip. "You never say what I expect and constantly keep me guessing."

"Is that a compliment or a complaint?" I wondered, dropping my belt on the ground and unfastening the top button of my pants.

"A compliment. Every moment with you is exciting, even when I'm frustrated. You're easy to be myself around. You've awoken things inside me I didn't know existed. You…" She trailed off, her gaze dropped to my zipper as I slowly drew it down.

"Go on," I encouraged, enjoying this game.

"You make me happy," she whispered, her mouth quirking up. "That sounds stupid out loud, but it's true. You're a great dad. And partner. And lover…"

The last word was uttered as I dropped my pants, revealing that I wore nothing beneath. I kicked the fabric away with my socks and shoes. Then I pulled my undershirt over my head, leaving me just as naked as Avery.

"Since we're engaged now, we don't need condoms, right?" I asked, kneeling on the bed. We'd already done the whole history talk, and I knew she took birth control. However, for historical reasons, we continued to use condoms every time we fucked. I wanted that to change tonight.

"I haven't said yes," she reminded me, her expression deviously playful.

"Your agreement at this point is just a formality, but if

you prefer I wear a condom, then—"

She grabbed my wrist when I started to stand again. "No condom."

"Then you agree to be my wife?" I countered.

"Fuck me and we'll talk about it more."

I narrowed my gaze. "Some would call that bribing."

"I prefer 'negotiating.'"

"My new sister-in-law has been talking to you."

"Maybe."

I pushed Avery onto her back, crawling over her to cage her beneath me. "You realize I never back down from a challenge, right?"

"You are a rebel," she taunted.

"I am." I settled my hips between hers, my cock hard against her damp flesh. "A rebel who is going to fuck some sense into you, future wife."

"All I hear are words and—" She bit off a sharp moan as I slid into her on a single thrust, her back arching up off the bed with the force of my entry.

I cocked a brow. "You were saying?" I penetrated her deep again before she could reply, causing her walls to clench down on my shaft. "*Fuck…*"

No more condoms.

Ever.

Because the feel of her slick heat drenching my dick had to be one of the most amazing experiences of my lifetime. I wanted to revel in it forever, to live between her thighs and never surface. Oh, and to feel her tongue against mine while she groaned in pleasure. Yes…

I bent to take her mouth, my hands framing her face as I balanced on my elbows over her. She pushed her hips up into mine, accepting me even deeper and taunting me into a sensual dance—one I intended to command. Her nails scraped over my back, down to my ass, to encourage my pace.

But I wanted to go slower.

And so, I did.

Rotating my pelvis against hers at just the right angle to excite her clit.

"Wyatt," she said on a delicious moan that would forever live in my memories. "I'm so close… I need… *Please…*"

"Still not hearing the word I want," I whispered, drawing my cock out slowly to the head before slamming back into her. Just enough to push her upward without allowing her to fall over the edge. "Give it to me, Avery, and I'll let you come." I repeated the action, eliciting a growl from her chest that vibrated mine.

"You already *know*," she panted, her nails turning into punishing claws against my shoulder blades.

I smiled against her mouth. "A man needs words." I licked her bottom lip before dipping inside to taste her thoroughly. She trembled beneath me, her nearing orgasm palpable and oh-so sweet. "Tell me, Avery. Please. Tell me you'll marry me." All teasing aside, I needed to hear the words.

"Yes," she hissed, her fingers threading through my hair while her arm clamped down around me. "Yes, Wyatt. I'll marry you."

Her words unlocked something inside of me, a fiery emotion that spread and was unleashed with my tongue against hers. A vow. A claiming. An irrevocable bond wrapped up in one.

I love you, I was telling her. *To my very soul.*

And she answered me in kind, only she spoke the words out loud. "I love you."

I kissed her, the pace between us shifting from teasing to a thorough declaration of passion unlike any I'd ever experienced. Not hard. Not punishing. Not rough. But destructive all the same. As if every barrier between us had shattered, and our bodies were mating in a manner that defied thought.

"I love you, Avery," I whispered, the proclamation so, so right. And brand new. I'd never said those words to anyone. But she deserved them, owned them, returned them.

"I love you, too."

Time melted around us, our marriage essentially complete without the audience or the ceremonial bullshit.

This was our declaration.

Our promise.

To forever.

And I accepted it, accepted her, accepted *this*.

Avery came on a scream, her channel clamping down around me and forcing me to follow her on a bellow of my own.

Oblivion descended, pulling us both under into a series of violent spasms and heated kisses. Her addictive taste held me captive, her legs around my waist welcoming me home.

My Avery, I thought, whispering the proclamation with my tongue. *You're my Avery*.

She held me for what could have been minutes or hours, the raw emotions flowing openly between us, the future paved and accepted.

But there was one thing I had yet to tell her.

An item that left me feeling a little uneasy and excited.

I waited until she was settled into my side, her head resting on my shoulder, her long legs intertwined with mine. "Avery?"

"Mmm?" she murmured.

"I… I've been doing a lot of thinking about you and Jamie and our future together." That part was probably obvious. "And one thing I want to do is start working. To be a better role model for Jamie."

She tilted her face back to see me. "What do you want to do?"

"Well, technically, part of Mershano Suites is mine—has always been mine—but I never accepted it because of my issues with Jonah. So Evan's been running it all alone. And I sort of don't want him to shoulder that burden anymore." The conversation with him had not been an easy one, and I may have begrudgingly apologized a handful of times along the way, but the end result was worth it.

"What does that mean?" she asked, her tone curious. "For us, I mean."

"Well, it depends on what we decide to do. Nothing is set in stone yet. Evan knows I wanted to talk to you first, to see what you were comfortable with me doing, and go from there. It would likely require moving, and he knows you have a job in Atlanta. Jamie also has school. Although, I suppose if we were going to move him, now would be the time, before he starts kindergarten."

She nodded. "Technically, I can do my job remotely. Or find a new position. I enjoy what I do, but I'm not tied to it."

Yes, I'd gathered that over the last few months. She excelled in her career, but it was clearly not her passion. It seemed she'd never had time to discover it, responsibility overtaking her before she had a chance. Perhaps I could give her some of that back… and more.

"You mentioned not being tied to Atlanta, too," I said, recalling our discussion about dream jobs and locations.

"I'm not. I've just never had an opportunity to move or, really, to do anything other than what I'm doing."

"So, you're open to me providing you with that opportunity? And you would be okay with me going to work with Evan?" He wanted me to come on as his vice president, to essentially work at his side on everything. I preferred something a little less stressful, like being in the legal department, but we were still negotiating.

"I'm okay with figuring this out together," she said softly. "And I think Jamie will approve, too."

The thought warmed me. "I want to be someone he can look up to."

She smiled, her palm cupping my cheek. "Wyatt. You're already someone he can look up to. Don't you realize that? You don't have to be successful in a career to be a role model for your son. It's *you* he sees. The caring man who explains things, plays with him, and introduces him to new lessons every day. That's who he adores—his rebel friend Wyatt."

I smirked. "I'm Daddy Wyatt now."

"You are," she agreed, eyes shining. "And he loves you."

"He loves you, too," I said, tucking her hair behind her ear. "Which is why you need to become Mommy Avery."

Her cheeks flushed. "I don't know how he'll feel about that."

"Then we'll ask him." I already knew he'd be thrilled. Jamie wanted a mom. What he didn't realize was that he already had one, just not in name. Yet. "You're his Auntie A in name alone, but we both know you're the mother of his heart. That boy loves you like you're his own, just as you love him." I tilted her chin higher and bent my head to kiss her. "And I love you, too, Avery mine."

She smiled. "Avery mine?"

"Yes." I nuzzled her nose. "And soon to be Avery Mershano."

"What if I prefer Avery Perry?" she asked, a taunting note in her tone.

I grinned. "Am I going to need to convince you otherwise?"

Her lips twitched. "Perhaps."

"Another challenge," I said softly, meeting her tempting gaze. "I'll have you yelling your acceptance by dawn, Avery Mershano."

She glanced at the clock and raised a brow. "Then I suggest you get started."

"The things I do for love," I sighed, beginning my path downward while holding her gaze. "Prepare yourself, sweetheart. I'm about to do wicked things to you."

"Best proposal ever," she breathed, her eyes falling closed.

"Mmm," I agreed, smiling. *And she said yes.*

Agreeing to be my future wife. The mother of my child. The love of my life.

My Avery Mershano.

EPILOGUE
AVERY

Six Months Later

I pulled the pizza from the oven and set it on the rack to cool. I'd opted for homemade, needing to calm the nerves curling inside my stomach.

Tonight, we were going to tell Jamie the big news.

Wyatt stood in the doorway, a phone to his ear. "Seriously? It's been, like, a year since I last heard from you, and the first thing you want from me is a favor?"

He chuckled at whatever the deep voice on the other line said in return.

"Leipzig? Why the fu—?" He glanced over his shoulder at where Jamie sat in the living area. "Actually, never mind. I don't want to know. But it's not *my* hotel. My brother owns the empire. I'm just a VP."

He paused, smirking.

"You know I can."

He snorted at whatever the guy said back to him.

"Fine, but you owe me. Actually, how about a weekend

in Monaco? You can babysit while I take my new wife out." He winked at me while he spoke, making me wonder who the heck he was talking to on the phone. "Then consider it done, K." He hung up with a chuckle and immediately dialed a new number. "Killian needs a hotel room," he explained before switching to a greeting in German.

His brother had put him in charge of the Mershano Suites European region, and so far, he seemed to be enjoying it. As a result, the three of us were moving to Switzerland at the end of the month. I wasn't sure what I would be doing career-wise yet since my company couldn't allow me to work overseas.

The adventurous part of me enjoyed the idea of a fresh start with Wyatt and Jamie, while the practical side of me couldn't believe I'd agreed to this leap of faith.

Then again, I couldn't believe any of this had become my life. Yet, here I was—Mrs. Avery Mershano—standing in the kitchen, preparing dinner for my husband and *son*.

Wyatt hung up and sent a text off with a shake of his head. "I swear Killian is secretly CIA or something more sinister. He's one of the most cryptic people I've ever met."

I arched a brow. "He seemed pretty normal at our wedding." Killian had spent most of the occasion drinking with Powell—another one of Wyatt's old college buddies. Both men were fun and not at all what I would have expected from Wyatt's party-style background.

He slid his phone into his pocket. "Well, he needed the room under an alias."

"And you didn't ask why?"

He scoffed at that. "Yeah, I learned a long time ago never to ask him questions. He just evades them." He stepped closer, his palm lifting to cup my cheek. "Speaking of avoidance, are you ready yet?"

I wiped my hands against my jeans, biting my lip. "Yes. No. I don't know."

"Like ripping a Band-Aid off," he murmured, leaning in to brush his lips over mine. "He's going to be thrilled."

"I hope you're right."

"I am." All confidence and swagger, as always. He kissed me again, this time a little harder, lingering. "Mmm, come on. Let's tell him now, then celebrate with pizza as a family before our adult time."

"Wine and a movie?" I sighed dramatically. "It's like you read my mind."

"Sure. We can make a movie, sweetheart. I'll enjoy watching it later."

"Wait, that's not—"

He cut me off with a searing kiss, his hand dropping down to capture mine. He tugged me forward. "Stop stalling, Avery."

I wanted to argue, but we'd both hear the lie if I tried. So I nodded and allowed him to pull me into the living area, where Jamie lounged on his chair with a game in his lap.

"Hey, little man," Wyatt said, ruffling his hair. "Avery and I want to talk to you about something."

Jamie set the remote aside and lifted his chin, a move Wyatt had taught him. "'Sup?"

"It's important," Wyatt continued, crouching down before him. "So I'm going to try to explain some of it, okay?" This was what we had rehearsed, mostly because I didn't know how to approach this without bawling my eyes out.

"'Kay. But I'm almost five," Jamie reminded him. "So I know lots."

"Oh, I know. You're a genius," Wyatt agreed. "Which is why I think you'll understand this."

Jamie nodded. "Yep."

Like father, like son, I thought, smiling.

I took the couch while Wyatt remained in his squatting position, his gaze on his son. "Okay, so we've talked about this a few times, that your Auntie A is like a mom. Remember?"

"Uh-huh. 'Cause she takes care of me and stuff."

"Exactly. But you've never called her *Mom* because that's

not her name, right?"

His lips twisted. "Yeah. She's Auntie A."

"What if she wanted to change her name to *Mom*? Would you like that?"

He tilted his head. "That can happen?"

"Uh-huh," Wyatt glanced at me. "It can, right, Avery?"

I clasped my hands tightly in my lap, trying to stop my arms from shaking. "You remember our last trip on the plane? How we went to the beach and I wore the white dress?"

"Yeah!" Jamie bounced a little. "And the ocean with the fish! We're going again?"

"Maybe, but you know how I changed my name to Avery Mershano? To be Wyatt's wife?"

His nose scrunched. "Yeah. You kissed lots." Then his eyes went huge. "Oh! So we're going to do something at the beach and you change your name again?"

Wyatt chuckled. "Not quite, little man. Avery can only marry one man—me."

"Oh." Jamie deflated.

"But by changing my name and becoming a Mershano, it means I can be your mom now," I explained. "Because we have the same last name. You're Jamie Mershano and I'm Avery Mershano."

His lips parted, his eyebrows shooting up. "Really?"

"Yep." I smiled, hoping this next part went okay. "In fact, I signed some papers this morning that finalized it. I'm officially your mom, Jamie." Tears gathered in my eyes, the admission meaning more to me than I could ever express. I'd managed to keep it together while completing the forms, but now, it suddenly felt all the more real.

Nine months ago, my world shattered. The possibility of this happening disappeared.

And now, I had everything I ever wanted, right before me.

Sometimes life twisted fate for the best, and I had the man across from me to thank for it.

As if sensing my thoughts, Wyatt reached out to grab my hand, giving it a squeeze. "She's officially your Momma Avery now."

Jamie glanced between us, his brow furrowing. "Like, forever?"

We both nodded.

"So I have a Daddy Wyatt *and* a Momma Avery?" he asked.

My vision blurred at those words coming from him for the first time. Even if it was phrased as a question, just hearing the nickname from his lips was worth all the heartache I'd gone through to reach this point.

"Yes, Jamie," Wyatt replied when I couldn't. "You have a daddy and a mommy."

"Forever?" he repeated, the word ending on a squeak.

I waited with bated breath, not sure how he'd react, his face telegraphing a myriad of emotions.

"Yes!" he cheered, leaping from his chair to my lap and throwing his arms around my neck. "You're mine now?"

"I've always been yours," I said, hugging him back. "You know that."

"But you're my momma now? Forever and ever and ever and ever?"

"And ever," I agreed, meeting Wyatt's warm gaze over Jamie's shoulder. He hadn't released my hand, knowing I needed his strength.

Jamie squeezed me so tightly it almost hurt. "I love you, Momma A," he whispered.

"I love you, too, Jamie," I whispered back, my voice catching on his name.

Momma A.

He called me Momma A.

Wyatt joined our hug, kissing me on the forehead and holding us both. "I love you, too, *Momma A*," he said softly in my ear. "Thank you for being the perfect mom to him."

I opened my mouth to reply, when Jamie piped up, "Is the pizza done yet? 'Cause I'm hungry."

He slid out from our embrace, causing Wyatt to chuckle. "That kid has a one-track mind."

"He's your son," I managed to say, smiling.

"No, he's *our* son," he corrected me, his lips brushing mine. "Now, let's go feed him so I can properly enjoy dessert later." He stood and held out a hand.

I accepted it with a shake of my head. "You never hold back, do you?"

"What would be the fun in that?" he asked, smiling. "I'll always be a rebel, Avery."

"My rebel."

"Indeed." He slid his arm around my shoulders. "You wouldn't have it any other way."

He was right; I wouldn't.

This was my world now.

My home.

My family.

The End

THE DEVIL'S DENIAL
A MERSHANO EMPIRE NOVEL

I did a bad thing.
I was young and stupid.

I thought I loved him, but he corrected that falsehood after our one and only night together.

I promised never to acknowledge him again… Until my brother's wedding left me no choice. Now I'm stuck walking down the aisle with Garrett Wilkinson and pretending he means nothing to me. Too bad the man is still as sexy and arrogant as I remember.

But he taught me how to guard my heart, and I have no intention of giving in to him again. Even if it is just for one night.

This time it's my turn to deny the devil.

SCARLET MARK
A CAVALIERI DELLA MORTE STAND-ALONE NOVEL

Deceit requires punishment.
But what happens when the mark is innocent?

Killian "Dagger" Bedivere

My latest assignment has evolved into a game of deciphering whom to trust—the renowned politician who hired the *Cavalieri Della Morte*, or the runaway bride?

She's gorgeous, conniving, and everything I crave in a woman.

She's also my target.

Rule number one: Never fall for the mark.

Rule number two: Fuck rule number one.

Amara "Scarlet" Rose

I never wanted this world, but the decision wasn't mine to make. I always belonged to *him*. Now there's a new player on the board—one hell-bent on destroying all my plans.

He's lethal, handsome, and everything I should fear.

Rule number one: Don't trust anyone.

Rule number two: Do everything you can to survive, even if it means breaking rule number one.

And rule number three: When in doubt, kill.

ABOUT THE AUTHOR

USA Today Bestselling Author Lexi C. Foss loves to play in dark worlds, especially the ones that bite. She lives in Atlanta, Georgia, with her husband and their furry children. When not writing, she's busy crossing items off her travel bucket list or chasing eclipses around the globe. She's quirky, consumes way too much coffee, and loves to swim.

Where To Find Lexi:
www.LexiCFoss.com

ALSO BY LEXI C. FOSS

Blood Alliance Series:
Chastely Bitten
Royally Bitten

Dark Provenance Series:
Heiress of Bael
Daughter of Death
Son of Chaos

Immortal Curse Series
Blood Laws
Forbidden Bonds
Blood Heart
Elder Bonds
Blood Bonds
Angel Bonds

Mershano Empire Series
The Prince's Game
The Charmer's Gambit
The Rebel's Redemption

Other Stand-Alone Books
Scarlet Mark

Printed in Poland
by Amazon Fulfillment
Poland Sp. z o.o., Wrocław

53632395R00155